CASSIE EDWARDS

THE *SAVAGE* SERIES

Winner of the *Romantic Times* Lifetime Achievement Award for Best Indian Series!

"Cassie Edwards writes action-packed, sexy reads! Romance fans will be more than satisfied!"
—*Romantic Times*

LOVE AND SACRIFICE

"My life as a dancer is exciting for me," Kathia murmured. "I'm not certain if I could live without it. I have been a dancer for so long, it is a part of me."

"Then you would find it hard to give it up for any reason?" Bright Arrow asked guardedly, wishing to hear her say that she would give it up to marry him!

"I have never considered giving it up," Kathia murmured. "I . . . I . . . have never had any reason to."

"Then a man's love could not change your mind about such a thing?" Bright Arrow dared to ask. Before she could respond, he blurted out another question that seemed to come out of the blue. "Have you ever been in love?"

Kathia felt the abruptness of the question, and was caught off guard. How could she confess to him that she had not loved until she met him?

Other books by Cassie Edwards:

TOUCH THE WILD WIND
ROSES AFTER RAIN
WHEN PASSION CALLS
EDEN'S PROMISE
ISLAND RAPTURE
SECRETS OF MY HEART

The *Savage* Series:

SAVAGE TRUST
SAVAGE HERO
SAVAGE DESTINY
SAVAGE LOVE
SAVAGE MOON
SAVAGE HONOR
SAVAGE THUNDER
SAVAGE DEVOTION
SAVAGE GRACE
SAVAGE FIRES
SAVAGE JOY
SAVAGE WONDER
SAVAGE HEAT
SAVAGE DANCE
SAVAGE TEARS
SAVAGE LONGINGS
SAVAGE DREAM
SAVAGE BLISS
SAVAGE WHISPERS
SAVAGE SHADOWS
SAVAGE SPLENDOR
SAVAGE EDEN
SAVAGE SURRENDER
SAVAGE PASSIONS
SAVAGE SECRETS
SAVAGE PRIDE
SAVAGE SPIRIT
SAVAGE EMBERS
SAVAGE ILLUSION
SAVAGE SUNRISE
SAVAGE MISTS
SAVAGE PROMISE
SAVAGE PERSUASION

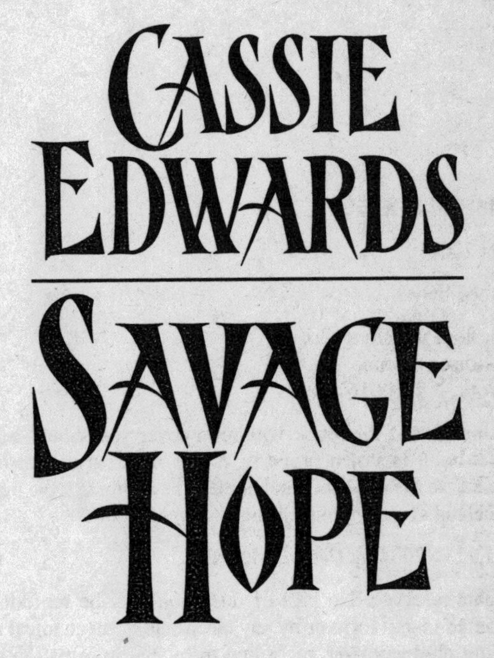

LEISURE BOOKS  NEW YORK CITY

A LEISURE BOOK®

August 2004

Published by

Dorchester Publishing Co., Inc.
200 Madison Avenue
New York, NY 10016

ISBN 0-8439-5054-4

Printed in the United States of America.

Visit us on the web at www.dorchesterpub.com.

With much love I dedicate Savage Hope *to my big brother Fred Cline, who was known as "Flashbulb Freddy" during his high school days at HTHS (Harrisburg Township High School in Harrisburg, Illinois) in the 1950s, when he was the high school photographer. He still loves to work with cameras today!*

Love,
Little "sis" Cassie

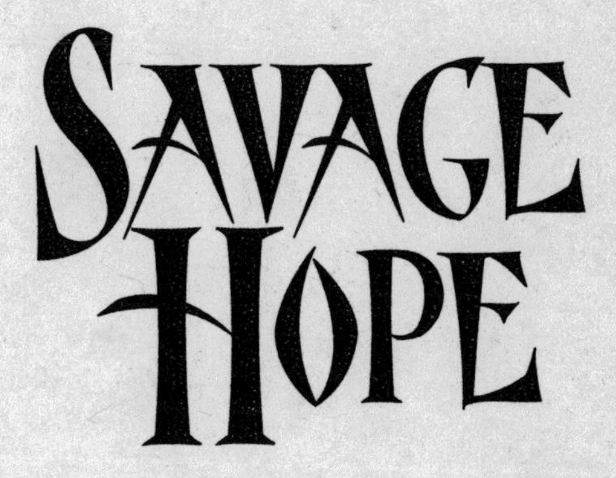
SAVAGE
HOPE

Who is this man of copper skin
and such a handsome face?
Who rides his spirited steed with such skill
and with such grace?
Who is this man with coal black hair,
hanging long and free?
Who stands just as tall and sturdy
as the mightiest oak tree?
Who is this man with eyes
the color of the blackest coal?
Who can look so deep inside of you,
into your very soul?
Who is this man who is the leader
of his own kind?
Who has to be constantly alert
with his body and his mind?
Who is this man who hunts with
a bow and many arrows?
Whose arrows fly so fast and accurate,
like many darting little sparrows.
Who is this man who invades my dreams
every time I sleep,
Who has fully captured my heart
and holds it, oh, so deep?
Would you like to know this man
that I am speaking of?
He is the bravest of all Indians,
the man I love.

—Darcie Wright,
a devoted fan

Chapter One

Imagination shows me all your charms,
The plenteous silken hair and waxen arms.
—Lady Mary Wortley Montagu

Ozette, Washington, 1880

Bright Arrow, chief of the Thunderbird clan of his Makah people, rode on horseback today, his long, jet-black hair blowing in the breeze behind him.

As he looked proudly around him, he saw everything that was dear and near to his heart. The forested mountains and hills in combination with a rugged, irregular coastline made his homeland beautiful and breathtaking.

The spectacular rocky headlands of the Makah

coastline could be seen from many vantage points.

Dressed in fringed buckskins, his copper-skinned face shining in the warm afternoon sun, Bright Arrow rode straight and tall on his ash-colored roan horse. He found himself lost in thought, reflecting on the way winter had brought the spirits closer to him and his people than at any other time within the cycle of the year.

Ah-ha, yes, it was the main season for ceremonies.

But at every season the Makah celebrated the spiritual in their daily lives. Life was a whole. No activity was separate from that wholeness, therefore, every act contributed to spiritual well-being.

But there was one thing that neither he nor his people could ever forget. Illness or an unsuccessful hunt, or a poor salmon run or berry harvest, came when harmony was temporarily broken.

Bright Arrow hoped that things would remain as they were at this time. His people were calm and filled with contentment; nothing disturbed their peaceful lives.

Ah-ha, yes, it was spring. It was an exciting time, for his warriors especially. The migrating California gray whale would soon arrive in the waters close by Makah land. The hunt this year was expected to be good . . . to be huge, for nothing yet this spring, or even last winter, had broken the harmony of their lives.

Nothing!

He gazed far to his right, where he could see the brilliant blue of the ocean. Soon he would be riding his powerful hunting *can-im*, his canoe.

Soon he would be . . .

Suddenly his eyes were drawn to a flurry of movement on an ice-covered pond. He saw a sight that made him draw rein and stop.

His gaze was fixed upon a beautiful woman at the other, far side of the pond. The *toke-tie* seemed to be dancing on the ice as she spun, turned, and then glided forward, only to spin again.

She wore a fur hat and coat and gloves and strange things on her feet that seemed to be helping her move so gracefully over the ice.

He had never seen such a sight as this: the woman skimmed mysteriously over the ice, as though she might take wing at any moment. She was enchantingly beautiful.

His heart skipped a beat when she looked his way, allowing him to see even more of her face.

Her skin was white. The ends of her hair, which hung free around the edge of her hat, were a beautiful golden color. Her cheeks were flushed from the cold. Her lips were red and perfectly shaped.

When she saw him, she didn't seem afraid of him, despite the fact that he was a stranger, an Indian. Instead she smiled, a smile that melted Bright Arrow's heart.

And then his eyes were drawn to something . . .

someone . . . else. It was a man who had stepped into sight behind the woman, on the edge of the pond. He held a strange contraption in his hands. He was pointing it now at the woman!

Bright Arrow's eyes moved quickly to the woman.

She wasn't aware yet that someone stood behind her, threatening her with a strange object pointed right at her head.

Bright Arrow was sure that it was some sort of weapon that he had not yet been introduced to. He knew that white people were always inventing new ways to kill one another.

Was this woman some sort of a threat to this man? Was that why he had come up from behind her so quietly, the contraption in his hand now up close to his face, as though he must place it there before firing it?

Bright Arrow had been about to warn the woman that the ice might not be strong enough to hold her weight for long, since the recent rains and occasional warm temperatures of early spring had thinned the ice on most of the ponds and rivers.

But instead he quickly dismounted and ran toward the woman to warn her about the man and the danger he posed to her.

He saw the alarm in the woman's eyes when she spotted Bright Arrow running toward her. She must think that he, an Indian, was about to attack her.

He didn't take the time to explain that she was wrong.

The man could kill her at any moment.

He rushed onward to the man and grabbed the contraption from his hands, then slammed it to the ground and stamped on it with his moccasined foot.

All was silent except for the crunch of metal.

The woman looked at him in disbelief; the white man's eyes filled with a sudden rage.

"How dare you!" the man growled out as he raised a fist and swung it up in an effort to hit Bright Arrow.

But Bright Arrow was the quicker of the two. He grabbed the man by a wrist and twisted it behind his back.

"Who are you? Why would you do that?" the woman asked as she glided closer to Bright Arrow on her strange footgear. They were part shoe, yet the glint of steel on each reflected up into Bright Arrow's midnight black eyes. "Please release him."

"I thought he was *me-sah-chie*, bad, a threat to you," Bright Arrow said, releasing the man's wrist. "I thought I was protecting you from harm."

He fought against being mesmerized by her sky-blue eyes and the loveliness of her face, and especially her voice, which was soft even when she seemed to be scolding him. Her voice was like a song, so soft, sweet, and lyrical!

And there was no actual accusation in her voice. Only questioning.

She could have been furious over what he had done. There could have been so much distrust that she would have fled from him.

But there was trust in her eyes and voice even as she questioned his motives.

He knew from this very moment that he would never forget this woman. She seemed to be all sweetness and pureness.

"From harm?" she said, raising her golden eyebrows. "Why would you think that I needed protection?"

"The man held a strange contraption," Bright Arrow said thickly. "He was pointing it at you."

He gestured toward the man, and then the mangled object that still lay on the ice. "I thought that he was about to hurt you with it," he said tightly.

"You were wrong," the woman murmured. "He was taking my photograph with his *camera*."

Not wanting to show that he knew nothing of cameras, or photographs, and beginning to feel foolish, Bright Arrow gazed at the woman for another moment, then turned and ran to his horse.

He mounted his steed in one leap and rode away.

He could feel both the man and the woman watching him until he finally found privacy in the thickness of the forest.

But although he could no longer see her, nor she him, Bright Arrow could not forget those brief moments with the alluring woman.

He wished that he had questioned her and discovered her name, for he had never seen her before and now doubted that he would ever again. She was more than likely visiting the man with the camera.

Perhaps she was even this man's wife.

Knowing that he should concentrate on anything *but* the woman, a mere stranger who had momentarily entered his life, Bright Arrow tried hard to think of other things, but for the moment found it impossible.

He knew that he must see this beautiful woman again, at least from afar.

Chapter Two

All the night, I waking sigh your name,
The tender sound does every nerve inflame.
—Lady Mary Wortley Montagu

The waves crashed against the rocky shore, making a sound like distant thunder. The moon's glow was challenged by the great, powerful beams of the lighthouse that rose tall and sleek above the ocean, casting its moving lights far out to sea, and along the rugged terrain beside it.

Kathia Parrish stepped lightly down the corridor of the lighthouse living quarters, candlelight from the wall sconces showing the way toward her father's bedroom.

Dressed in a lovely, long orchid velveteen skirt

and a white ruffled blouse, her hair hanging down her back in golden waves, Kathia tiptoed up to the door that led into her father's bedroom and stopped. She leaned her ear close, to see if she could hear any movement in the room beyond.

Disappointment filled her very soul when she heard nothing. Her father was still in bed, unable to leave it since he had come down with a strange sort of ailment several weeks before.

Normally living alone in Port Angeles, some distance from Ozette, Kathia had dropped everything and come to care for her widowed father.

Kathia's brother, Fred, a photographer, had also moved in with their father at the lighthouse. He had not come, however, for his father's welfare, but to complete a project of his own. He had even established a darkroom at the back of the house.

Needing to check on her father before retiring for the night, Kathia carefully opened the door, where soft light from a kerosene lamp beside her father's bed shone on him. He still slept; indeed, he was asleep now more than he was awake.

Slightly lifting the hem of her skirt, Kathia tiptoed into the room and stood over her father's bed. Her eyes filled with tears as she gazed at him. He looked so much older now than he had the last time she'd seen him. He had lost so much weight of late, and his hair, always coal black and thick, had turned gray and thin.

His face was gaunt.

His lips were dry as he snored slightly, then tossed over to his side away from Kathia, making it impossible for her to see his face any longer.

"Papa, Papa," she whispered as she bent low and rearranged the patchwork quilt that lay just beneath his armpits.

He wore a cotton nightshirt that gaped at his neck because of his leanness.

His neck was longer now, it seemed, and much, much too thin.

Thinking it best to sit vigil at his side for a while instead of retiring to the privacy of her own room, Kathia sat down on a plush, overstuffed chair beside the bed and watched for any sign that he was awakening. She had been told by Mariah, her father's live-in housekeeper, that he had slept a good portion of the day. He had hardly taken any nourishment. All he seemed to want to do was sleep.

Of late, her father had not even asked about the lighthouse and how it was faring under the control of another man. While her father was too ill to perform his lighthouse duties, a substitute keeper had taken over.

His name was Dusty Harper. He lived in a back room of the house.

Even the thought of that man made Kathia shiver, for none of the family liked him. He seemed cold, except for when he was around Kathia. She had been the victim of his flirtatious remarks, so much so that she had finally taken it upon herself to put him in his place.

He had become angry and vindictive because of her attitude toward him, yet with no one else to take over her father's duties, Kathia and her brother had no choice but to tolerate the man. It was imperative for the lights to be lit every night in order to warn boats away from the rocky shore.

Actually, Kathia had come to believe that Dusty's true reason for having accepted the job at the lighthouse was mainly because of her.

She had won much fame as a ballerina, and he had seen her dance. He seemed obsessed with her.

Being a lighthouse keeper by trade, one who was temporarily unemployed, Dusty had jumped at the chance to take over Kathia's father's duties. Kathia had tried to get someone else, but to no avail.

Sighing deeply, and realizing that her father was more than likely asleep for the night, Kathia rose from the chair, bent low, and brushed a soft kiss across his brow, then left the room and went to the parlor, where Fred was trying to put his smashed camera back together again.

Her brother grumbled beneath his breath before he suddenly threw the broken camera across the room. Kathia gasped at his show of angry frustration.

"I see that you can't fix it," Kathia said softly.

She moved into the room and sat down on the

sofa with him before a leaping fire in the huge stone fireplace. Books lined the walls on the far side of the room. Elsewhere tables flanked various chairs, where kerosene lamps glowed and flickered on the ceiling and walls.

A handmade braided rug lay in the center of the floor, a rug made by Kathia's mother's hands. Signs of her beloved mother were everywhere in the house, her embroidered and knitted items cherished.

A huge oil painting of her mother hung over the mantel of the fireplace, her sweet smile always there to remind Kathia of the love she had given everyone, especially her family.

"No, I can't fix it," Fred said tightly. He glared at the camera that now lay in several pieces on the oak floor. "Thank God I have another one, or all of my plans would be ruined, like the camera that savage broke today."

"Fred, you're wrong to call the warrior a savage," Kathia said softly as she ran her hands across the softness of her skirt. "You heard what he said. He thought I was in trouble. He thought you were going to harm me. He is a gentleman, Fred, not a savage."

"Yes, Sis, I know," Fred said, stretching out his long, lean legs and resting his feet on a footstool. "Sometimes I find it hard to concentrate on what I'm doing. My mind drifts to Magdalena and how I miss her. And then there's Father . . ."

"That's still no excuse."

He gazed into the dancing flames of the fire, his brown eyes narrowing. "I know that I have to stop thinking of them as savages if I'm going to have a chance to photograph the Makah."

He ran his fingers through his thick coal black hair as he looked at his sister.

"The main reason why I didn't continue lashing out at the Indian is because I came here for the express purpose of taking photos of the Makah. The Indians could be an interesting study. There is something exotic about them and the way they live. They seem so primitive a people compared to us whites."

"And might that not just be because of how the white people have taken advantage of them?" Kathia softly demanded. "It is disgraceful how land has been stolen from the Indians of this nation. I am certain the Makah have had to fight for all they have."

She felt a blush rush to her cheeks when she again thought of the handsome Indian who had come to her rescue today. This man who hunted whales instead of bison was tall, muscled, and lithe, and ah, how uniquely sculpted was his face!

And when he had gazed directly into her eyes, she had become mesmerized by his gaze, which seemed to be looking into her very soul.

She had known then that she felt something for him.

It was a sweet sort of feeling inside her heart, one she had never felt before. His mere presence had conjured a lovely warmth in the pit of her stomach.

This was the first time she had ever been so intrigued by a man, and not because he was an Indian, but because he *was* a man . . . a *gentle*man.

Fred stared at his sister. He was getting more irritated by the moment as he realized that she had grown thoughtfully quiet and at the same time was blushing. He saw how she stared into the flames of the fire and smiled as though whatever, or whomever, she was thinking about, was extremely pleasant.

He knew that she was thinking about the Indian warrior.

"Sis, come back down to earth," Fred said, interrupting her thoughts.

She fluttered her lashes and blushed an even deeper shade of red when she turned her eyes quickly to him.

"Kathia, I've never seen you react like this to any other man," Fred said. He raised an eyebrow. "Why now? Why an Indian? Lord, Sis, don't you see the danger in that? He is Indian. You are . . ."

"Yes, I am white," Kathia said, interrupting him. "Fred, stop it. Don't try to tell me what to do, or think. I am my own person now. You know that I don't need your brothering any longer. I am independent. I like it that way."

"Yeah, probably too independent for your own good," Fred said, grabbing a cigar from the inside pocket of his tan suit jacket. He lit it and sat back, smoking it for a moment.

"Fred, you said how you miss Magdalena," Kathia murmured. "I'm sure you do. I do, too. We've been best friends for so long. But our lives have taken us in different directions. I just enjoy being with her when there is time for us to have short visits."

"Yes, I miss her. I miss her terribly," Fred said, nodding. "But like you, I'm used to it. You know how long her ballet tours separate us even when I am back home in Seattle."

"Yes, I know," Kathia said, her own touring taking her away from her home in Port Angeles so often.

"Sis, I have big plans for the photos that I take of the Makah," Fred said. He took the cigar from his mouth. "I plan to get the photographs published in a book. I could make big bucks for photos of people who are rarely seen by the civilized world."

"Fred, you shouldn't take advantage of the Makah," Kathia said. "They are a private people, causing no one any harm. Why can't you leave them be?"

She gazed at her handsome brother in his tan wool suit. Most times, his being so handsome worked to his advantage. People took an instant liking to him, for in his eyes one saw a genuine kindness.

Lately, however, that kindness was absent when

he talked of Indians. He had no true cause to dislike them. It was just that certain friends of his always spoke negatively of Indians.

She had hoped that during his stay at the lighthouse he would get to know what the Makah were really like. Their father had made friends with them long ago when he had first come to this lighthouse. The Makah used his light to guide their large whaling canoes safely to shore on stormy nights. They had never made difficulties for her father.

Even today, when she had seen the Makah warrior watching her skate, she had not felt threatened by him.

"Take advantage of them?" Fred said, his eyebrows arching. "Sis, I won't be taking advantage of anyone. I will be helping them. I plan to pay each person who poses for me twenty-five cents."

"Fred, the Makah don't need your money," Kathia said, sighing heavily. "They are a rich people, thriving on their fishing business." She laughed. "And twenty-five cents? That small price will surely insult them."

"There you go again," Fred said, himself sighing heavily. "You are only speaking on their behalf because you became infatuated with that Indian warrior. I could tell by the way you looked at him that you found him fascinating."

"Yes, I did," Kathia said, slowly nodding. Her eyes twinkled as she again envisioned the warrior. "I'll admit I thought him very handsome, muscular and gallant. Yes, Fred, I am infatuated. What woman wouldn't be?"

"Women who have more sense than you, it seems," Fred replied. "Sis, you had best heed my warnings against having such feelings for a red man. It could jeopardize your career as a ballerina. If word spreads in the white community that you are infatuated with Indians, especially one of their warriors, you might be shunned. People might stop coming to your performances. Sis, go back to Port Angeles tomorrow. I am here. I can keep an eye on Father. Mariah is here. When Father hired her to see to the house and kitchen duties after Mother died, he hired a jewel of a woman."

"I know Mariah is dependable, but I need to know, firsthand that Father is all right," Kathia murmured. "And since you are so adamant about taking photographs of the Makah, I know you wouldn't want the full responsibility of seeing to our father's needs."

"But what of your own needs, Sis?" Fred continued to argue. "Your career, Sis. You have your career."

"Fred, you're wasting your breath by trying to tell me what to do," Kathia said, rising from the chair. She stood over her brother and gazed intently down at him. "I won't return to my home. Not for a while, anyhow. Not until our father's health improves."

She looked over her shoulder toward the door

that led out into the corridor, then at her brother again. "And I want to be here to keep an eye on that man who has moved into our lives so quickly, who has taken over our father's precious lights," she said, her voice drawn. "If he was so skilled at working at a lighthouse, why wasn't he already employed elsewhere? And . . . he has made too many advances toward me. Now that I have put him in his place, he holds a grudge against me. He might do something to get back at me. He might even sabotage the lights. I just feel too uneasy about him. I can't shake the foreboding I have."

"But, Sis, don't you see?" Fred said, rushing from the sofa. He tossed the half-smoked cigar into the flames of the fire, then gently touched her face with a hand. "Sis, Dusty is another reason you should leave and go back to your own home. I agree that the man can't be trusted in any respect. Yet there isn't anyone else who *can* come now to work the lights. I've checked on it. Dusty is the only one in the area who is available."

He stepped away from her and went to look outside at the moonlit surroundings.

Then he turned and gazed at Kathia. "Sis, you are scheduled to perform soon," he said. "Are you going to back out of that commitment? Both you and Magdalena love to perform. I know how you adore hearing the applause after your ballet performances."

Kathia went over to Fred and took his hands in

hers. "Yes, big brother, I love to perform and, yes, I do enjoy the applause, but at the moment Father is my main concern," she murmured. "Please quit worrying about me and my career. Will you?"

"How can I not worry when I know that your ballet performances are threatened by this long stay at the lighthouse?" he said thickly. "You *do* have a scheduled performance soon in Port Angeles. Surely you won't disappoint your fans, will you? You do still plan to perform, don't you?"

"Like I said, while Father is so ill, I will not leave his side. I just *can't*," Kathia said, slipping her hands from her brother's. She turned and stared out at the lovely moonlit night. "Father no longer has a wife for him to depend on, but he does have a daughter."

She spun around and gazed into her brother's eyes. "I will stand by him until I know he is well enough to climb the stairs to care for his precious lights again," she said flatly. "That's that, Fred. You might as well get used to it."

Fred gazed back at her with a frustrated anger in his eyes, then turned and stamped from the room.

Not liking to disappoint her brother so much, Kathia almost went to him, then decided against it.

She instead went to the window again, but this time she found herself looking in the direction of the Indian village.

Yes, she *was* infatuated, so much so that she couldn't get the warrior's face out of her mind's eye.

He was the other reason she couldn't leave for Port Angeles just yet. She did hope to see him again . . . to know him.

Trying to turn her mind from the warrior, she thought about her brother and Magdalena. She smiled at how even the mention of Magdalena always brought a spark to her brother's eyes.

Her brother had become smitten with Magdalena when she was a mere child of twelve, practicing ballet with Kathia.

After they both became known as ballerinas, they had found such fun touring together. Kathia missed those days.

Again the Indian came to mind. She wondered how he would react to her being a ballerina. Would he ever see her perform? Oh, he must! She wanted him to share her passion for the ballet.

"Maybe one day . . ." she whispered to herself.

Chapter Three

By starlight,
And by candlelight and dreamlight—
She comes to me.
—Herbert Trench

The sounds outside the longhouse were the wash of the surf, the seagull's chorus, a sea lion's bark, the sighing of hemlocks, spruce, and cedar. The fire burned low yet warm in the fireplace of Bright Arrow's mother's longhouse.

As his mother, Whispering Wind, sewed a calico dress by hand from a new bolt of cloth that Bright Arrow had brought to her from Port Angeles, he found it hard to focus on anything but what had happened a short while ago . . . his meeting with the white woman.

He made himself think of other things, for he knew that he must. He thought of how his mother and most other Makah women got up early every morning, sometimes before breakfast, to sit and weave. All of these women wanted to make their baskets beautiful. They took such pride in their work.

He had never seen his mother discontented.

He thought of how he would soon hear the cry of killer whales as the hunting season came upon them. His home, Ozette, with its long beaches on the Pacific Ocean, was the most important Makah sea mammal hunting village.

There was no site better for launching the spring hunts.

And the Ozette River boasted the best streams for hunting salmon.

Ah-ha, yes, Bright Arrow was of the Thunderbird clan, and his heart pounded even now at the thought of soon boarding his huge whaling *can-im*.

Only he was allowed to cast the first harpoon of the season, for he was *tyee*, chief, of his clan.

And then all of his warriors would share in the thrill of the hunt with their own harpoons.

Although it was good to know that the hunt was near again, for the whale meat was necessary to the survival of his people, there was always a sadness linked to taking the life of something as grand and beautiful as the whale.

Because of his feelings, he made certain that neither he nor his men took more from the sea than what was absolutely needed.

And when they *did* take a great whale, they always thanked the whale's spirit for giving its life for the welfare of the Makah. Children would grow up into adults because of the successful hunts.

All of this was on Bright Arrow's mind, but then again the woman came into his thoughts, even where the images of his canoe, harpoon, and the *eh-koi-i*, the great whales, had just been.

The woman.

Would he ever see her again?

Should he even want to?

And what of the white man with the strange contraption called a *camera?*

He had seen neither the man nor the woman until today and wondered where they made their residence and, especially, what the man was to the woman.

They both seemed protective of each other.

"My son, there is something in your eyes and attitude that is distant today," Whispering Wind said. She rested her sewing on her lap. She gazed intently at him. "Are you thinking about your first whale hunt of the season? Spring is here. It should not be long now before all of the whaling *can-ims* will be back at sea."

"I am always eager for the first hunt of a new season," Bright Arrow said, leaning back more comfortably in an overstuffed chair.

He was in his mother's home, a traditional longhouse made of split cedar planks placed horizontally and lashed to upright poles with lengths of twisted cedar withes.

The roof was nearly flat, supported by huge beams, placed atop posts set in the ground.

His mother's home was of only two rooms, whereas his own was of five.

Bolts of cloth and sewing apparatus were on shelves along her walls. The floors were covered with handwoven rugs made by her own deft fingers. Benches hung on a wall opposite the entrance to the lodge, an entrance that was, like the hearts of the Makah people, facing the sea.

His mother not only had a huge stone fireplace in her home, she also had a potbellied cooking stove that Bright Arrow had brought from Seattle.

She was proud of everything her son had given her, especially her cookstove, for it helped fill her lonely hours as she prepared food that she shared with Bright Arrow, and others who were less fortunate than she and her chieftain son.

But no matter how busy she kept, she could not get past the pain of having lost her husband during a hunt at sea three moons ago. Still, she had her son. She and Bright Arrow were close, each always looking out for the welfare of the other.

Today Whispering Wind wore a bright calico skirt and a white blouse, with silver earrings on which were engraved her name.

She was on the heavy side, with a round face, and fleshy arms that were always hidden beneath the sleeves of her fine blouses and dresses.

Her hair was wiry, coarse, and gray, and was worn in a tight bun atop her head.

Her eyes were a faded gray color, yet seemed to be able to look into the very heart of everyone she met.

"My son, again you have grown quiet," Whispering Wind said, sighing. "Did something happen today that you would wish to share with me?"

"Something did happen today," Bright Arrow said, nodding. He met his mother's questioning gaze. "There was a man with a strange apparatus. I thought the apparatus might be *me-sah-chie*."

"Evil?" Whispering Wind gasped.

Then she said, "Son, I sense there is still more that you have not told me. What about this man? What sort of apparatus did he have? *Kah-ta*, why? And why did you think it evil?"

"Mother, there was also a *woman*," Bright Arrow finally confessed, not certain he wanted to speak of the mysterious beauty. He knew it would be best to forget her, yet he also knew that was impossible.

"A woman?" Whispering Wind said, leaning forward. "A woman from our village, or of another clan?"

"She is not from our village, nor is she of another clan," Bright Arrow said, sensing that he had spoken too guardedly. His mother's eyebrows had shot up at his hesitation.

"Then what woman are you talking about?" Whispering Wind said. "If she is not from our village, or of another clan, that could only mean that she is . . ."

When she paused, as though she was reluctant to actually say what she surmised, Bright Arrow finished for her.

"She was white," he blurted out. "Mother, she seemed filled with special spirits. She did not walk on ice, but instead seemed to fly. She wore strange shoes with sharp edges that she balanced upon."

"First you speak of a man, who had an apparatus that you thought might be *me-sah-chie*, and now you speak of a woman who seemed filled with special spirits," Whispering Wind said softly. "It seems to me that you should avoid them both. We need no one around here with something that is evil, nor do we need a woman who is filled with spirits, who wears something besides shoes when she is on ice. Avoid her, my son. Avoid the man. Do not go near them again. They could cause disharmony now, when it is the worst time for it. The whale hunt is near. Do nothing to cause our people harm."

"I do not see how either the man or woman can cause us harm," Bright Arrow said thickly. "Especially the woman. After I spoke with her, and saw the truth about her, I realized she was someone who was pure at heart. Then I discovered that what the man carried was something called a 'camera.' The woman did not seem alarmed by it, so I decided it was not dangerous."

"Why did you go near either of them in the first place?" Whispering Wind asked, resuming her sewing.

"It was because the woman was on the ice," Bright Arrow said. "I started to warn her about the dangers of the ice, that it wasn't strong due to the recent rains and warmer spring temperatures. But I did not get the chance to tell her. I was distracted by the man and his so-called camera."

"That is twice that you have spoken of this thing called a 'camera,'" Whispering Wind said, again resting her sewing on her lap as she questioned Bright Arrow with her eyes. "What is it?"

"I truly have no idea," Bright Arrow said solemnly.

"It is best, my son, not to concern yourself over the white man's contraption any longer, or the white woman," Whispering Wind said tightly. "You have many other things that are more important to consider."

She paused, began sewing again, then stopped once more. "Anyhow, son, why should you have troubled yourself with the white woman at all?" she said softly. "Wouldn't the white man have saved her from the ice had she fallen into the pond? Perhaps he was even her husband. *He* should protect her, not a powerful Makah *tyee*."

"I felt I had to warn the woman, because it seemed that the man, whoever he was, was more interested in his contraption than the safety of the woman," Bright Arrow said tightly.

"*Ah-ha*," Whispering Wind said, smiling softly at him. "I am proud of you for doing the right thing."

Bright Arrow smiled back, then glanced quickly upward when he heard rain falling on the roof. He leaped to his feet, went to the door and, opening it, looked outside. "The rain will melt the already weakened ice," he whispered to himself.

He hoped that the white woman realized the ice would be weakened by the rain.

The rain slowed to a mist, but Bright Arrow knew that it, too, was weakening the ice.

He knew that he shouldn't be so concerned about a stranger, but he could not help himself. This woman was not just any stranger.

She was entrancing! She was unforgettable!

But . . . was she a married woman?

Was the man with the camera . . . her husband?

Chapter Four

When they have looked upon their images,
Would none had ever loved but you and I?
—William Butler Yeats

Night had fallen like a dark shroud across Makah land. Kathia was always concerned about whether or not Dusty was treating her father's precious lighthouse equipment carefully enough.

Carrying a kerosene lantern to fight off the eerie darkness in the narrow space, Kathia was going up the spiral staircase to the top of the lighthouse, where the beams were even now illuminating the ocean's waves.

She was going to check on Dusty tonight, as she had done more than once since she had arrived at the lighthouse.

She hated to be alone with the man, fearing he might again try to take advantage of the situation, but she had to put her father first, her own concerns second. She just hoped that she had rebuked Dusty enough now so that he knew better than to try anything with her again.

Kathia knew that the lighthouse's beams weren't truly needed all that much right now. There was little sea traffic close to shore at this time of year, but there would be more soon.

Her father had told her that spring temperatures stirred seafaring activities, especially among the Makah, who would soon be out in their whaling vessels again, hunting the large sea creatures.

But even when sea traffic was light, her father's lights were lit every night of the year, and she wanted to make certain that Dusty did nothing to damage the equipment, either from carelessness or spite.

As she continued to climb the narrow, winding staircase, the trapped mildewy smell stung her nose. She hadn't been around the lighthouse enough to get used to the smell, or the claustrophobia she felt in the tight, dark space.

When her father had taken up the position of lighthouse keeper, she had continued to make her residence in Port Angeles, where her parents had originally lived. It was there she first attended and finished school, and now performed as a ballet dancer.

She had only been to her father's lighthouse for short visits. Traveling by boat along the Strait of Juan de Fuca was the only way to get between Port Angeles and Ozette, and Kathia hated the water. Ever since her mother had perished during a sudden storm at sea, she had feared the ocean.

Now she planned to stay at the lighthouse until her father was back on his feet and could tend to his beams again. It was good to have the family together again, with her brother, who usually lived in Seattle, temporarily making his home at the lighthouse, as well.

Finally, breathing a sigh of relief, she reached the top of the lighthouse. She was glad that the heavy metal trapdoor was open so that she could go on up into the small room where her father's beloved equipment awaited his return.

As she climbed up, she saw Dusty Harper sitting in her father's chair as he peered out to sea, his eyes following the slow beams that reached far out over the water.

She flinched when he jumped with alarm at her sudden appearance, then shivered when the alarm on his ruddy face was replaced by a flirtatious grin that made his thin, narrow red mustache twitch above his thick lips.

"Well, pretty lady, what brings you here?" Dusty asked as he rose from the chair and took a slow step toward her. "Did you come up to see me?"

The usual terrible taste she got in her mouth when she was in this man's presence was noticeable again, a bitterness that was almost the same as what one experienced after vomiting. She hated the way he scrutinized her with beady eyes that seemed to look through her clothes, mentally undressing her.

She now regretted with every fiber of her being having put herself in this position again, yet she had come for a purpose and would not retreat down the dank, dark stairs until she knew that her father's lights were being well tended.

"I'm here for my father," Kathia said tightly. She set the kerosene lamp on her father's oak desk. "He can't check on things for himself, so I am doing it for him. I want to make certain his equipment is being taken care of."

"You just can't trust me, can you?" Dusty said, his voice tight with sudden anger.

He turned his back to her and went to place his hands on the delicate mechanism that controlled the heavy iron lanterns suspended by chains.

"I don't believe you've given me much cause *to* trust you all that much," Kathia said, even more tightly.

As gusts of wind suddenly knifed around the lighthouse windows, the lamps flickered, but the wicks, fueled by kerosene, continued to send their faithful beams out to sea.

"Don't fret, pretty lady," Dusty said, still keeping his hands steady on the controls. "I'm keeping your father's lights clean. I understand how the powerful lens of the lamps are the pride of a lighthouse keeper. If I had this lighthouse, I'd . . ."

"It's *not* yours," Kathia quickly said, interrupting him and trying to burst his dreams of grandeur. "My father will be well soon. He'll be here guarding and caring for his beams, not you."

Dusty turned quickly and walked to Kathia; he towered over her with his six-foot-four height. She stiffened as he glared down at her. "This ain't your father's lighthouse, either," he growled out. "He is only its keeper. And right now he ain't even that. I am. *I* am."

Hearing his insolence, seeing it in his eyes, Kathia glared at him, then turned and started to leave, but just as she reached out to get her lantern, a hand was suddenly on her wrist, stopping her.

Dusty turned her to face him, then yanked her body against his and brought his lips down hard on hers.

Loathing his kiss, and hating him for taking advantage of the situation, Kathia yanked her lips from his and struggled to get free.

"Don't fight what we feel for one another," Dusty said thickly as he held her tightly in his grip. His eyes searched hers. "Kathia, I fell in love with you the moment I saw you that first time on stage. I can't help lusting after such a body as yours. Damn, Kathia, it's so delicate . . . so pretty. . . ."

There was a sudden rush of feet.

Then Fred was there, yanking Kathia away from Dusty.

He pulled her into his embrace and held her as he glared at Dusty.

"Listen well, you stupid man, when I tell you that if you ever attempt anything like that again, by God, you'll find yourself *in* the sea, not only *looking* at it from this tower," he warned.

Dusty glowered. He doubled his hands into tight fists at his sides. He took a step closer to Fred and Kathia.

"You'll regret what you just did," he snarled. He looked at Kathia, and then Fred. "Both of you. Do you hear? You'll regret doing this to Dusty Harper."

Fred glared at Dusty a moment longer; then, after Kathia grabbed the lantern, he went with her down the steep, narrow steps, and they both hurried into the parlor.

Kathia was breathing hard, and not from the quick descent of the stairs.

She was still experiencing the horrors of the kiss, the repugnance of Dusty's embrace. Her hand trembled as she set the lantern on a table, then turned to her brother.

"Thank you," she murmured, then flung herself into his arms. "Thank you, big brother."

"Kathia, Kathia," Fred murmured as he stroked her back. "This is only one time. There will surely be more. What if I wasn't there to help stop this man's lunacy? He could've . . ."

Kathia pulled away from Fred. She looked into his dark eyes. "No," she said, swallowing hard. "It wouldn't have gotten that far. I'd have grabbed something. I would have protected myself."

"But you hadn't yet when I came upon what was happening," Fred said. He raked his long, lean fingers through his dark hair. "Sis, it's time for you to come to your senses and return to Port Angeles. Mariah is here. She can see to father's needs. When she isn't, I can. Please return to Port Angeles tomorrow. Don't you see, Sis? In one day I've seen you threatened not by one man, but by two."

"If you are referring to the Indian as one of them, you are wrong," Kathia said, sighing hard. Then she walked to the window, drew back the sheer white curtain, and gazed in the direction of the Makah village.

She had never been there. But she knew where it was.

Surely the Indian had been from that village. Surely he was Makah.

All she knew was that he was more handsome and intriguing than any other man she had ever seen.

She wanted to see him again so badly. She wanted to thank him.

"Fred, do you know who that Indian was?" she asked guardedly, afraid he would snap back at her and tell her that she shouldn't even want to know.

Yet deep down inside herself, where her desires were formed, she did want to know! And if Fred didn't tell her, she would find out in her own way.

She was an independent person. She had learned long ago to look after herself. Living alone in Port Angeles as she did, she had to know how to take care of herself.

"If you must know, he is a Makah chief," Fred said. "His name is Bright Arrow."

She turned on her heel and gazed at her brother. Her heart pounded at the thought that the man who had showed an interest in her was a chief.

Then her eyebrows rose. "How would you know that?" she asked, searching his eyes.

"Yesterday I went to the Indian village," Fred said. He sat down on the broad velvet sofa before the blazing fire. He pulled a cigar from his inside coat pocket and lit it.

He inhaled, exhaled, then looked at Kathia as she sat down beside him on the sofa. "Bright Arrow was just going into council," he said. "He didn't see me. I asked around as to who he was. That is how I know, and because Bright Arrow was in the council house, he didn't recognize me when he saw me at the pond with my camera. He had not met me yet, as some others have."

"How were you received at the village?" Kathia asked, surprised that when she and Fred were talking about his going to the Makah village earlier, he had not told her that he had already been there.

"Well enough . . ." Fred said, then looked over at Kathia. "Sis, you've got to return to Port Angeles. I insist."

"And just how many times, of late, have I done as you insisted?" Kathia said, laughing softly. "Big brother, you know that I am my own person. I do as I wish, and I wish to remain here to look after Father. I *do* intend to stay until he is well. Say nothing more about it, Fred. Please let it go. All right?"

Fred took another deep drag from his cigar as he stared into Kathia's stubborn blue eyes, then sighed heavily, rose from the sofa, and left the room.

Kathia smiled to herself at her brother's protectiveness. She loved him so much for his brotherly feelings.

She again went to the window and stared in the direction of the Indian village. She was even more interested in the Indian, now that she knew who he was.

He was a chief! A *handsome*, kind, and powerful chief.

Yes, she would see him again.

Somehow.

She would find a way so that it wouldn't be obvious that she had feelings for him. This was the first time she had let her guard down and allowed herself to have feelings for any man, for until the moment she looked into his midnight dark eyes, her career had taken center stage in her life.

"And then, too, there is Father," she whispered.

She had put everything in her life on hold to care for him. After all, if it were not for him and her mother, she never would have become a ballerina. They were the ones who introduced her to the ballet when they took her to see her first performance when she was only four years old.

They had encouraged her to take ballet lessons. No parents could have been as proud as they on the day when Kathia had had her first dance recital.

Tears fell from her eyes as she recalled how her father had gazed up at her as she pirouetted on the stage, so tiny, yet so talented.

"Papa, you *will* see me on the stage again," she whispered, for she would not give up her hope that he would recover.

Then she wondered what the handsome young chief would think about her performance on the stage. He had already seen her skating and seemed to admire her grace and skill.

Perhaps in time Bright Arrow would get to see her perform on the stage as the acclaimed ballerina she was.

"I can dream, can't I?" she said just beneath her

breath. A strange sort of thrill coursed through her veins at the thought of his being in an audience, gazing up at her, admiring, even caring for her!

But she reminded herself that he was a powerful chief. He had no time for things like ballet performances. It was just chance that he had come along when she was skating.

She would probably never see him again.

"Unless . . ."

She smiled almost wickedly, for she knew that she *would* meet him. She would see to it!

Chapter Five

Love is such a mystery,
I cannot find it out;
For when I think I'm best resolved,
I then am most in doubt.
—Sir John Suckling

The rains had stopped almost as quickly as they had arrived, leaving a beautiful day this morning for Bright Arrow to seek out his private place of prayer.

Bright Arrow rode onward, his heart ready for many hours of prayer today.

Weeks went into the special preparations for *eh-koi-i*, whale hunting. To get ready for the hunt, whalers went off by themselves in the lush forest to pray.

Each man had his own place, where he had his own private ritual to seek his individual power.

Because whaling was such a big part of the Makah's livelihood, the whalers devoted their whole lives to spiritual readiness for the hunt.

Just as Bright Arrow was going to his own private place for his prayers, so were many of his warriors on their way to the forest also. On his first trek into the woods this year, he had done as he was taught by his chieftain father. Bright Arrow had been instructed that when he was in the woods that first day of praying, he should take water at every creek, then blow it out and start praying while spraying mist from his mouth.

Now that he had concluded that ritual, he focused on praying for a good whale harvest this year.

As seagulls cried behind him while gathering along the shore close to his people's homes at Ozette, Bright Arrow rode onward. The forest was lush with pines, ferns, and mosses.

He inhaled and enjoyed the pleasant aroma of pine and spruce, and even spring flowers that were just blooming today on the forest floor since the rain yesterday.

In fringed buckskins and knee-high moccasins, his long, jet-black hair fluttering down his back in the morning breeze, his face lifted to the sun as it filtered down through breaks in the trees overhead, Bright Arrow squared his shoulders proudly.

He was excited that the gray whale would soon be arriving in the waters just off the shore of his people's homeland. He would feel the splash and taste of the sea against his lips.

He would . . .

Suddenly his thoughts were interrupted when he heard someone singing a soft, sweet song from somewhere close by.

He looked around himself, suddenly aware of where his travel this morning had taken him. Unconsciously, he had not gone in the direction of his secret praying place after all, but instead . . . toward the pond!

The place where he had seen the lovely woman yesterday.

He drew a tight rein and listened to her beautiful voice. The song she was singing was sweet. Her voice was so soft.

His heart pounded within his chest, for surely the woman singing *was* the one he had become briefly acquainted with yesterday.

Surely she was on the ice again!

That thought made his heart skip a beat, then pound furiously within his chest. He was anxious to see her again, yet fearful for her safety. Yesterday's rains had weakened the already thin ice, and if she was on the pond again, wearing the strange shoes, she was in danger!

He sank his heels into the flanks of his roan and

rode onward at a hard gallop, drawing rein when he came alongside the pond. There, gliding slowly across the ice, was the golden-haired beauty.

For a moment everything was forgotten as he was again enraptured by her.

He seemed to feel her voice deep within himself. He was transfixed by her beautiful face as she turned in his direction. His heart did a strange sort of flip-flop when he saw her notice him there.

As had happened the day before, she showed no fear at his presence. She smiled at him and waved!

Then there was an ominous sound that broke through the special moment. Bright Arrow's face drained of color when he heard a cracking noise that resembled the low rumbling of thunder.

He saw how the woman stopped, her face frozen in surprise and fear as she watched a split in the ice hurrying toward her.

Shaken out of his own frozen state, desperate to reach her in time, and knowing that he had to move quickly or the woman would die, Bright Arrow dismounted and began running along the embankment.

His eyes wild, he watched the crack reach her.

Her scream split the air as she fell downward, downward into the water.

Just as Bright Arrow reached the place where she had fallen, her head went beneath the water.

A quick panic filled Bright Arrow, for he realized that his weight was too great for him to go on the ice and save her. He would only join her in the frigid water. Just that quickly his people would no longer have a *tyee*.

Frantically he tried to figure out how he could get her; how he could save her!

He would never forget the look in her eyes just as she fell into the pond, for she was looking at him, her eyes silently begging for help.

Knowing that he must do anything possible to save the woman, even if the attempt brought danger to himself, he stretched out on his belly on the ice. He slid on his stomach across a part of the ice that was still solid.

He died a slow death inside when the woman's head bobbed to the surface, eyes wide and wild. She took deep gulps of air, then went under again.

Moving quickly, Bright Arrow managed to grab her hands just before they sank below the surface.

Bright Arrow rejoiced when she grabbed back, her fingers clinging to his.

Breathing hard, praying to himself that the ice on which he lay would hold him long enough for him to pull the woman to safety, Bright Arrow gripped her hands tightly and started pulling while she clung desperately to him.

Suddenly her face appeared above the water, purple, wet, her expression one of stark fear as she choked and gagged on the water that she had swallowed.

Chapter Six

To think a soul so near divine,
Within a form so angel fair,
United to a heart like thine,
Has gladdened once our humble sphere.
—Anne Brontë

Breathing hard and struggling, Bright Arrow kept pulling on Kathia as she clung desperately to him.

She was shivering, feeling the iciness of the cold clean through her, into her bones.

Her wet clothes were heavy. She had lost her hat in the water. Her skates were pulling at her. But finally, she was free!

Bright Arrow had dragged her to dry land. But

Kathia couldn't stop trembling. She was shaking so hard, her teeth were chattering together, making strange clicking sounds.

Watching Bright Arrow run toward his horse, Kathia sat up. She would be forever grateful to him. If he had not come when he had, she would even now be at the bottom of the lake.

Still shaking uncontrollably and consumed by cold, she hugged herself hard. She was so glad when Bright Arrow brought a blanket from a bag on his horse and wrapped it around her shoulders.

She was still too cold to speak . . . to thank him. But she did manage a weak smile on lips that were tight with coldness.

Seeing just how cold the woman still was, he thought of another way to help her, yet . . . would she allow it?

He decided to chance it.

He grabbed the blanket from around her shoulders, pressed his warm body against hers, then pulled the covering around both of them.

Kathia was stunned by his kindness. She understood that he thought to lend his body heat to hers and did not fear what might, under any other circumstance, seem to be an intimate, bold act.

She was just so thankful that he'd come along at the right time. He *had* saved her life.

"Thank you," she finally managed to say in a soft whisper. "Thank you so much."

"I must get you to your home, where you can take off your wet clothes and be near a warm fire," Bright Arrow said, wondering about the panic that entered her eyes as she looked quickly up at him.

Kathia didn't know what to do. She realized that it was imperative to get out of these wet clothes, and as soon as possible, and to get somewhere warm.

But her father's health was so fragile. If he was awake when she arrived home in such a condition and he saw her like this, it might startle him into a heart attack.

No. She couldn't risk that. But that meant she had only one other choice. . . .

"Could you please take me to your home instead of mine?" she asked. She was glad that at least she was warm enough now from his body heat to be able to speak. "Could you please take me there until I am more presentable? I don't want to frighten . . . or worry . . . my father."

"Who is your father?" Bright Arrow asked. He was glad that finally he might know whom this woman belonged to, and where.

And why wasn't she mentioning her husband?

He had assumed that the man with her yesterday was her husband, yet he had hoped not. He wanted her to be free so that he might manage to see her now and then.

He wanted to test the feelings he felt for her, to see if they were right, or only infatuation with a woman who was so beautiful just looking at her made his heart almost stand still inside his chest.

"My father is Melvin Parrish," Kathia murmured. "He's the lighthouse keeper. He's quite ill. But no one knows why. Not even the doctor has been able to diagnose it. But I must be certain not to do anything to aggravate whatever his illness may be."

"I know your father quite well," Bright Arrow said, pleased to learn that this woman was related to such a fine man as Melvin Parrish. "We have met and talked many times. I have gone to thank him more than once for saving my warriors when they became lost in fog or storms in their canoes while out at sea. Your father's beams have led them safely to shore many times."

He didn't say any more about her father's kindness, for he saw the urgency in getting her to his village and warmed by his fire.

But one day he *would* tell her about one particular great act of kindness by her father, her *ahte*. It was well remembered by all Makah.

He was glad to have found a way to repay the man's kindness by saving his daughter.

Then he realized what she'd said about her father being ill. That news saddened him.

But now was not the time to discuss it any further, to ask how serious his illness was. The longer she was in her cold, wet clothes, the more she risked coming down with pneumonia.

He took the blanket from around them, wrapped her alone in it, then whisked her up into his arms. He carried her to his horse and placed her on it.

Then he stared at the skates.

Kathia saw the puzzlement in his eyes. But this was not the time to explain what they were, or even to remove them.

She was so cold. All she could think about was removing all of the wet things on her and getting warm beside a fire.

Bright Arrow made certain the blanket was wrapped snugly around Kathia, and when he saw that it was, he mounted the horse behind her.

When she turned to him and nestled close, again seeking warmth from his body, Bright Arrow was lost in a feeling of wonder. This woman made him realize what he had missed by not having given his heart to a woman.

Now that he had seen her, and had held her against his body, he knew that he had finally found someone that he could love . . . the only one he would ever want.

Yet there was one question he had not yet asked. Was . . . she . . . married?

Was that man with the contraption called a camera her husband?

If so, why hadn't he come with her today to protect her? Surely he had seen the trouble that she could get in by being alone.

He must have known that she shouldn't have been on that dangerous ice today, yet he hadn't stopped her from going, nor had he gone with her to help should the ice break.

Ah-ha, Bright Arrow realized at this very moment just how much he could care for this woman.

Or did he already?

He had not given any woman a second glance since the death of the girl he had planned to marry, but who had died tragically only hours before they were to become man and wife.

He suddenly realized that he didn't even know this woman's name!

"Your name," he said thickly. "You have not said."

"Kathia," she murmured as she gazed up into his dark eyes.

"That is a beautiful name," Bright Arrow said, lost in the blue pools of her eyes. "And what is your . . . your . . . husband's name?"

"There is no husband," Kathia said, keenly aware of his reaction to the news that she wasn't married.

There was relief in his eyes, and then . . . there was his smile. It brought warmth into Kathia's very soul, so that for the moment she was not even aware of being wet and cold.

His eyes, his smile, had warmed her through and through. She knew now that she was definitely lost, heart and soul, to this handsome Makah chief.

Then she paled.

"Your wife's name is . . . ?" she dared to ask.

"There is no wife," Bright Arrow said, seeing that his answer made her smile softly into his eyes.

Ah, but this moment was one that he would never forget, the moment when they both understood their feelings for one another, and that they were free to pursue them.

"I will have you at my house soon and by my lodge fire," Bright Arrow assured her.

Kathia nodded and snuggled even closer to him. Strangely, she felt as though she had belonged there forever!

Chapter Seven

Yes, thou art gone! and never more
Thy sunny smile shall gladden me.
—Anne Brontë

Dusty Harper was dumbfounded as he stood at the high lighthouse windows, peering from them. He could hardly believe what he had seen.

Yet Kathia *had* fallen through the ice. And an Indian had saved her!

Dusty had just started to climb down the stairs for his usual day's sleep when he had seen Kathia skating.

He had delayed going to his room so that he could watch her.

He could not help being entranced by her beauty

even though he now knew just how much she detested him.

Of late, he had thought that he had changed her feelings about him, but last night's encounter had convinced him of the impossibility of her ever caring for him. Yet today, as he watched her skating, as he had watched her so often while she performed on the stage as a ballerina, he could not let go of his incessant longing for her.

Although she was a spitfire who seemed to despise the very ground he walked on, he was as smitten as that first day he had seen her perform. Ah, what a vision of beauty she had been as she pirouetted across the stage.

He would never get over wanting her in his arms.

He would never get over wanting to taste the sweetness of her lips over and over again!

Moments ago, when she had fallen through the ice, he had felt utterly helpless because he knew that even though he might try, he could not reach her in time to save her from drowning in that ice-covered pond.

He had then been filled with jealousy when he saw Bright Arrow ride up on his horse and go to her rescue, moments later succeeding at pulling her from the water.

He watched even now, even more stunned, as Bright Arrow rode away with her on his horse, and not in the direction of the lighthouse, but instead toward Bright Arrow's village.

Kathia had seemed perfectly willing to go with him. Dusty had even seen her clinging to him as though she had known and trusted him forever!

What truly confused him was why she hadn't insisted on being taken to her own home. Could Bright Arrow be taking advantage of her weakened state? When they arrived at the Makah village, would Bright Arrow force himself upon her?

How could the Indian not be as entranced with Kathia as Dusty was? Would Bright Arrow, aided by Kathia's weakened state, succeed where Dusty had failed? Would he get to taste more than her lips? Would he seduce her over and over again while she was too weak to fight him off?

The thought infuriated Dusty so much, he slammed a fist against the glass of the window, wincing when he felt a sharp pain in his hand and realized that if he had hit the glass any harder, it would have shattered into a million pieces. Just as his heart was now broken over the realization that he would never have the woman he desired, another man might take from her what Dusty had only been able to dream about.

Rubbing his sore hand, he stood there for a moment longer, until Bright Arrow rode out of sight with Kathia into the thickness of the forest.

Dusty was torn. Should he go and tell Kathia's father or brother about what had happened?

But no. Her father was too ill to go to her rescue, and Dusty despised Fred so much, he wouldn't give him the satisfaction of going to save his sister from an unknown fate at the hands of the Makah chief.

"I will rescue her myself," he whispered.

Somehow he had to find a plan to win her over. Wouldn't a daring rescue be the best way?

If he played his cards right, he might still get everything he wanted.

He smiled wickedly as he hurried down the spiral staircase. Only he knew to what extent he would go to make all his dreams come true. In time, he was bound to succeed.

Day by day, his plan was coming closer to fruition. But for now, all he could think about was Kathia and where she was, and with whom.

He hurried to his private quarters, pulled on his leather coat, yanked on a toboggan hat and gloves, and left the house in a flurry.

He ran to the stable and saddled a dark mare, then mounted it and rode away from the lighthouse in the same direction in which he had seen Kathia traveling with Bright Arrow.

He smiled at the thought of being able to take her from the savage. Once he had her all to himself while she was too weak to fight him off, once he made love to her, she would belong to him forever.

She would never want any man to know that her virginity was gone, for that was the pride of all women, to be able to prove they had saved themselves for the man they loved on their wedding night.

When she married Dusty, realizing that no other man would ever want her, he would be proud to see that her virginity had been stolen away, for it would have been taken by him!

He rode hard toward the thickness of the forest, his crazed laughter following on the gentle breeze of morning.

Chapter Eight

Come to me in the silence of the night;
Come in the speaking silence of a dream;
Come with soft rounded cheeks and eyes as
  bright,
As sunlight on a stream.
—Christina Rossetti

Still trembling from the cold, and also with a little apprehension about where she was being taken, Kathia leaned somewhat away from Bright Arrow. She looked slowly around her as he rode into his village. She saw how the houses that were made of cedar were arranged in rows close to the beach, grouped together along the shoreline.

The beautiful yet cold morning had brought

many people from their homes. Children were running and playing. The elderly were sitting beside a huge outdoor fire, smoking long-stemmed pipes and talking. Women were doing chores that took them from their homes.

Several warriors were down at the shore, working on their huge, beautifully carved canoes.

Kathia had admired the canoes from afar, from her father's lighthouse windows, during prior hunting seasons.

She knew that soon those canoes would be out at sea, battling the waves and weather, as the hunt began again. She knew that whales were their prime catch.

"This is my home," Bright Arrow said, drawing rein before a huge longhouse.

Kathia saw that this longhouse was much larger than any other in the village. She surmised that Bright Arrow's was largest because he was the chief.

Kathia soon became aware that many of the Makah had stopped what they were doing to gather around. Obviously they were curious to see who she was, and why she was with their chief.

Her attention was drawn from them when Bright Arrow dismounted, then reached up and gently took her from the saddle.

She blushed when she heard gasps rippling from person to person as Bright Arrow carried her into his longhouse.

She soon realized the true size of this lodge. From where she was now, in what she guessed must be the living room, with its huge stone fireplace at one end, she could see through a door that led down a long corridor, along which appeared to be perhaps four different rooms that she surmised were bedrooms.

She even glimpsed more than one fireplace. Each room seemed to have one of its own for the long, cold nights of winter.

She now looked slowly around this outer room and saw right away that this was a whaler's house. Harpoons hung from one wall, as well as other fishing gear. She saw bows and arrows hanging from another wall, which meant that Bright Arrow hunted more than whales.

Her gaze fell upon beautiful wood carvings, and supplies for carving. Along the walls were fine benches, the wood carved with designs of whales and inlaid with shell.

She then saw something else that caught her attention. She gazed in wonder at deer antlers that had been carved into the shape of a harpoon and fitted with sharpened mussel shells.

Kathia's thoughts were interrupted when Bright Arrow placed her on her feet, still in her water-soaked skates, in front of a roaring fire. Just then an elderly woman came into the longhouse unannounced and stood gaping at her.

Kathia shivered and clung to the blanket as she

looked slowly from the woman back to Bright Arrow. "Thank you for what you are doing for me," she murmured. "You . . . are . . . so kind."

"You are still too cold," Bright Arrow said, aware of the purplish hue of her lips, and how she still shivered beneath the blanket. He glanced down at the skates, then up at her. "And I am afraid that being so cold will make you sick. I am going for my uncle, who is our people's shaman. He will see to your welfare."

Before leaving, he knelt down on one knee before Kathia, and while his mother watched in what seemed to be utter horror, Bright Arrow removed the skates from Kathia's feet and laid them aside, close to the fire, to dry.

He then rose to his feet and turned to his mother, who still stood aside, not saying anything. The look in her eyes, however, was easy to read.

Ah-ha, a mother *would* question why her son brought a strange lady to his home, especially one who was not only white-skinned but wet from head to toe.

Bright Arrow sensed her questions, but he didn't want to take a lot of time to explain any of this just yet. The shaman's presence was more important at this time than words.

"Mother, this is Kathia Parrish," Bright Arrow said hurriedly. "Kathia, this is my mother. She is called Whispering Wind."

He turned to his mother again. "Mother, will you stay with Kathia while I go for Uncle White Moon?" he asked, his eyes asking hers for understanding. "I rescued her from the pond. She fell into the icy water. Don't you agree that Uncle White Moon is needed?"

Whispering Wind paused for a moment, gazed more intently into her son's eyes, then glanced over at Kathia with a look of wonder. "*Ah-ha*, my son, go for my *kah-po*, your uncle," Whispering Wind said as she took a step closer to Kathia. "I shall care for the woman until he arrives if this is what you wish of me."

"*Mah-sie*, thank you, Mother," Bright Arrow said. He bent and placed a soft kiss on her fleshy cheek.

Whispering Wind gave her son another questioning look, then stepped aside as he hurried past her and out of the longhouse.

Kathia clutched the blanket around herself even though it wasn't giving her any warmth now. It was as wet as her dress.

She was uncomfortable in this older woman's presence. She seemed disapproving of Kathia's presence there, a mother who was looking out for her son's welfare as far as women were concerned.

And Kathia was not just any woman. She was white.

Surely Bright Arrow didn't make a habit of bringing white women into his village, much less his lodge.

Kathia's feelings of discomfort were increased by the prospect of a healer, coming to look her over. She was wary because she did not know what an Indian healer might do, or how he might choose to do it.

Yet she was in no position to question anything. Bright Arrow had saved her life. She would never forget that, or his sweet kindness to her.

"My son is *kloshe*, which in Makah language means 'good,'" Whispering Wind said as she stood stiffly away from Kathia. "My chieftain son offers protection to all those who are in need of it—his people—even needy, worthy strangers. Today he proved his goodness again, as he does every day. I hope you understand, though, that he brought you here out of sheer kindness, nothing more."

"I . . . I . . . understand," Kathia murmured. "And I feel so blessed that he came when he did." She lowered her eyes and swallowed hard. "Had he not, I . . . I . . ."

"You do not need to say it, nor relive those terrible moments," Whispering Wind said, feeling some sympathy for this young woman who had touched Bright Arrow's heart.

Whispering Wind could tell by the way he had held Kathia and looked at her that she was special, even though they had just met.

But those feelings could not lead anywhere. Once this woman's health was seen to, she would leave the village and the Makah's lives.

She had her place in the world.

And so did Bright Arrow.

His place was with his people, not with a woman whose skin and ideals differed so much from the Makah's.

Nevertheless, being the kind woman Whispering Wind was, she could not just stand there while this tiny thing shivered and quaked beneath a blanket that was now just as wet as her clothes beneath it.

"I will get you a dry blanket," Whispering Wind offered as she hurried from the room and into one of Bright Arrow's three bedrooms.

She took a folded blanket from the foot of one of the beds, then brought it hurriedly back to Kathia. "Give me the wet blanket," she softly urged. "Then wrap this dry one around your shoulders in its place."

Kathia smiled weakly at Whispering Wind, so badly wanting to feel accepted by her, at least in some small way. But Kathia still saw resentment in the older woman's dark eyes.

She wished that Bright Arrow would return, even if he brought someone quite foreign to Kathia with him. Though she and Bright Arrow were new acquaintances, they seemed destined to be much more.

She only hoped that she wasn't wrong to allow herself to envision a relationship with this handsome chief that would continue beyond today.

She wanted time alone with him. She wanted to

talk with him. She even wanted him to hold her in his arms again.

She could envision, could even feel, his lips against hers. This was a rarity for her. Never before had her imagination worked overtime where a man was concerned.

Until now, her career was her life. She had never made time for a man.

She had concluded long ago that men would only get in the way of her dream of being a performer . . . of being a ballerina!

Now she wanted time away from her career to be able to know Bright Arrow better.

Kathia pulled the blanket from around her shoulders. She handed it toward Whispering Wind.

She saw how Whispering Wind hesitated to take the blanket; her eyes were on Kathia, raking slowly over her.

Kathia blushed, for she knew that the wet dress clung to her body as though it were a second skin. Was the woman seeing the difference between Kathia's tiny body and her own plump form? Would that make her resent Kathia even more?

But all Whispering Wind said was, "You must get out of that dress." Already she was ushering Kathia from the living room, into the corridor, then into a bedroom where another fire burned high and steady in the grate.

"This is one of my son's bedrooms that is used only when neighboring clans and family friends come to stay overnight," Whispering Wind murmured. "Feel free to remove all of your wet clothes. Wrap yourself in the blanket. I will leave only long enough to get one of my robes from my house, which sits next to my son's. Drape your wet clothes over the back of that chair next to the fireplace."

Whispering Wind turned to leave, then swung around and smiled at Kathia. "You will have all the privacy that you need here," she murmured. "I will return quickly with the robe. My brother will arrive shortly to see to your health."

"You are both so kind," Kathia said. She was truly touched by the way Bright Arrow and his mother seemed concerned about her welfare.

But she realized that each had his or her own reasons for helping Kathia. Bright Arrow wanted to help her because he cared. Whispering Wind hoped that with dry clothes, Kathia could leave soon and return to her own world.

Little did Whispering Wind know that Kathia could never turn her back on Bright Arrow and forget him.

Although the attraction had happened so quickly, Bright Arrow would be a part of her heart forever. Even now she counted the moments until she could see him again.

She would not let his mother discourage her from returning to the village to be with Bright Arrow again.

Still feeling anxious about the shaman, Kathia hoped that Whispering Wind would arrive with the robe before Bright Arrow and his uncle returned.

Kathia was still shivering so much, she could hardly remove her coat or dress but finally got them off. She dropped them to the floor and wrapped herself in the dry blanket again.

Still alone, she backed herself up to the fireplace. She was so glad when the warmth of the fire and the blanket seemed to melt the coldness embedded within her.

As she waited, she again looked around at the richness of the furnishings. In this room there was a bed, the headboard made of cedar and inlaid with the shells of what she knew were opercula, the stout "doors" with which red turban snails closed their shells.

Even around the door she saw the same sort of designs made from the same kind of shells.

It all seemed to be an indication of wealth.

"Here is the robe I have brought for you," Whispering Wind said as she entered the room again. She handed the robe to Kathia. "I shall leave the room while you slip into it. My son and brother are in the outer room waiting for you."

Anxious to see Bright Arrow again, yet still apprehensive about the healer, Kathia smiled at Whispering Wind as she took the robe. She thanked her softly, but was glad when she was alone again.

She hurried into the robe, sighing as she savored against her skin the warmth of whatever fur it was made from.

Finally she felt warm again, through and through, as though she might survive the plunge in the cold, dark pond after all.

Remembering that Whispering Wind had said Bright Arrow and his uncle White Moon were waiting for her, Kathia got the courage to go into the living room.

When Bright Arrow saw her, he came to her and gently placed an arm around her waist, then slowly ushered her over to where White Moon stood.

Kathia avoided looking at Bright Arrow's mother, for she knew that the elderly woman would be angry at her son's attentiveness to a woman Whispering Wind disapproved of.

Instead of thinking further about Whispering Wind, Kathia focused on the healer. He was a hunched-over, elderly man with a knot on his back at the upper part of his spine.

His thin, old body twisted strangely as he moved or walked. Slowly he checked Kathia over, touching her here and there, looking closely at her as he leaned his face almost against her.

He wore a heavy robe made of what appeared to be some sort of grass that was woven together.

Even though it was cold outside, he was barefoot.

His gray hair was wiry and worn long and loose, so long it almost touched the floor.

"I do not see anything about you that causes alarm," White Moon finally said as he stood away from Kathia, his old eyes peering into hers. "I have brought you something for your inward chill. It is a warm berry mixture."

He nodded at Bright Arrow. "It is in the jug that I brought with me from my house," he said, nodding toward the jug that sat on the floor just inside the door. "Get it for me, nephew, then hand the jug to the woman. She can drink directly from it, instead of a cup."

Kathia's insides grew tight with sudden apprehension again, just as she had felt when she first arrived in the village. She could imagine all sorts of things that might be in something a healer would concoct.

But she had no choice but to drink it or she would insult the old man.

She smiled awkwardly at Bright Arrow as he handed her the jug.

"I will get a cup if that would make drinking the *la-mes-tin* easier for you," Bright Arrow said, aware of the apprehension in Kathia's eyes.

"*La-mes-tin?*" Kathia said, her voice wary. "What does that mean?"

"In my language the word means medicine," Bright Arrow said, his eyes searching hers.

"Medicine?" Kathia repeated. She swallowed hard.

She wanted to ask what was in the medicine. At first she had thought it was only a mixture of berry juice.

But now?

If Bright Arrow called it medicine, and it had been made by the healer, surely it was more than just an innocent berry drink.

"It is something that will help, not harm you," Bright Arrow said as he reached over and gently touched her on the cheek. "Drink. You will soon feel warmed, through and through."

"Warmed . . . by . . . the medicine?" Kathia asked guardedly, still hesitating to drink it.

"By what is in it," Bright Arrow said, growing uneasy over her hesitation. His uncle was old and his feelings were hurt easily. His prescriptions were rarely questioned, but any doubt seemed twice as injurious to his feelings as when he was young. Then he'd seemed to have a shield between himself and disbelievers of his craft.

Bright Arrow placed his other hand on the bottom of the jug and eased it up closer to Kathia's lips, relieved when she finally drank from it and did not show any signs of finding the drink repugnant.

Glad that the drink was only slightly medicinal in taste, and otherwise sweet and reminiscent of strawberries, Kathia handed the jug back to Bright Arrow. "It was quite good," she said as she smiled at the shaman.

She saw how her compliment lit up his old eyes, and how his thin lips quivered into a smile.

"It was sweet and good and already I feel better for having taken it," she declared. "My insides *are* warm. It is good not to be so cold. Thank you, White Moon."

She turned to Whispering Wind. "And thank you," she murmured. "You have all been so very, very kind."

She smiled up at Bright Arrow. "Especially you," she said. She felt a blush rush to her cheeks. Her compliment seemed to reach clean into his soul, for his smile was suddenly radiant.

"We will leave now," Whispering Wind said, already walking toward the door with White Moon. She stopped long enough to look again at Kathia. "You will be leaving soon, as well?"

Kathia understood that was a roundabout way of telling her that she should.

"Yes, soon," she murmured.

She saw a keen relief in the older woman's eyes and noted her smile as she turned and walked from the house with the shaman.

"I will get something for you that will help remove the taste. I know you did not enjoy it all that much," Bright Arrow said, smiling almost mischievously at Kathia. "But *mah-sie*, which in my language means thank you, for pretending you did. You made an old man's heart very happy."

He nodded toward the rocking chairs that sat beside the fire. "Sit and I will join you soon," he said, then left the room.

Kathia sat down on the thick, comfortable cushion on the rocking chair. As she slowly rocked, she went over all that had happened. It was strange how quickly one's world could change as hers had changed. For her, it had happened in just two days.

It was all because of Bright Arrow. She had never met a man quite like him before.

His kindness and sweetness made her insides quiver, and this time not because of coldness. Instead, a sensual sort of feeling made her tremble all over.

She felt as though, if she allowed herself the pleasure of such feelings, she would fall in love. Maybe she already had!

She sniffed and became aware of the aroma of coffee brewing in the house. She was surprised that the Makah drank coffee.

She was curious about almost everything having to do with the Makah, and especially Bright Arrow.

"Here is something that will taste good and will warm any part of you that is still cold," Bright Arrow said as he handed a wooden cup of coffee to Kathia, then sat down on the rocker beside her, sipping from his own cup.

"Can you stay long enough to talk awhile?" Bright Arrow asked, smiling into Kathia's eyes.

Kathia started to say yes without hesitation, then stopped. Her smile waned when she heard Whispering Wind come into the lodge again.

Kathia stiffened, for surely Whispering Wind had returned as a reminder that it was time for her to leave.

Kathia wasn't sure how to let this mother know that she wasn't quite ready to go just yet, and that she hoped to return often to visit Bright Arrow.

Kathia wasn't sure if she wanted to turn and look at Whispering Wind. She was not ready to face her just yet.

She stiffened as she finally did turn in the chair, and her eyes widened when she saw what Whispering Wind had carried into the longhouse.

Chapter Nine

My light thou art—without thy glorious sight
My eyes are darken'd with eternal night.
My love, thou art my way,
My life, my light.
—John Wilmot, Earl of Rochester

"Son, here is something for the woman," Whispering Wind said, approaching and handing a tray to Bright Arrow. "As you can see, these are my special berry cakes. It will be good to give nourishment to the woman to help her recover. These will give her strength."

Kathia was stunned by the generosity of the woman, whereas only moments before she had been sure Bright Arrow's mother's resented her.

That was why Kathia had been stunned almost speechless when she saw that Whispering Wind had brought food into the lodge.

"Her name is Kathia," Bright Arrow said gently, then smiled warmly at his mother. "*Mah-sie*, Mother. Your gift is appreciated."

"The nourishment was advised by your uncle," Whispering Wind corrected, only giving Kathia a quick glance, then focusing again on her son. "It was he who thought the woman . . . I mean . . . Kathia . . . would need to regain the strength she lost while fighting for her life in the water."

Kathia was disappointed that the food was not really a gift from Bright Arrow's mother. It seemed Whispering Wind would be pleased, after all, if Kathia disappeared as soon as possible.

"My uncle was right to suggest you bring nourishment for Kathia," Bright Arrow said, then took the tray to Kathia. "These are berry cakes. My mother made them. They are her specialty." He chuckled as he glanced over his shoulder at his mother, who still stood just inside the door. "They are also my favorite."

Kathia saw the look of pride in Whispering Wind's eyes over the compliment paid her cooking by her son.

That gave Kathia an idea.

Were *she* to pay such a high compliment, surely Whispering Wind would be pleased, and she might even begin to like Kathia, if just a little.

"*Mah-sie* for bringing these," Kathia murmured, delicately plucking a cake from the tray. She had purposely used the Makah word in order to please Whispering Wind.

She saw a look of surprise at her use of the Indian word leap into Whispering Wind's eyes, and a proud look that came into Bright Arrow's.

All then became quiet in the longhouse as both Whispering Wind and Bright Arrow waited for Kathia to eat the cake, both sets of eyes on her.

Kathia looked awkwardly from Whispering Wind back to Bright Arrow. She was a little apprehensive about biting into the cake.

Oh, Lord, what if she actually hated the taste? Could she hide her feelings and pay the compliment that she knew the elderly woman was waiting for?

Hurriedly she bit into the cake, her eyes widening in wonder when she tasted its pure sweetness. She enjoyed the flavor so much, she took another quick bite.

Whispering Wind was so pleased, she let out a heavy sigh.

Bright Arrow, who seemed equally relieved, placed the tray on a table, then took one of the cakes himself and began eating it.

After swallowing the last bite of her cake, Kathia smiled warmly at Whispering Wind. "It is absolutely delicious. What sort of berries did you use to make the cakes?" she asked, hoping to show her interest, even though Kathia knew not the first thing about baking.

In her home, her mother had done all the cooking. She had never encouraged Kathia to learn how. Her mother had always had one thing on her mind as far as Kathia was concerned: ballet. Above all, she wanted her daughter to succeed as a ballerina.

"Would you please share your recipe for the cakes with me?" Kathia blurted out, knowing that this was the highest compliment to a cook.

"I am pleased that you enjoyed my cakes so much," Whispering Wind said, but she spoke without smiling.

In fact, Kathia noticed that Whispering Wind lifted her chin somewhat smugly, her dark eyes narrowing strangely.

"I never share the recipe for my berry cakes with anyone," Whispering Wind said.

Kathia was too stunned by the refusal to feel slighted by it. Her mother, who was a wonderful cook, had always been eager to share her recipes with anyone who asked. Whispering Wind's behavior was bizarre, to say the least. Kathia believed it was a way for Whispering Wind to demonstrate that she wanted nothing to do with Kathia.

"*Mah-sie* for your kindness in bringing the cakes," Kathia said, wishing she did not have to thank her. She was beginning to dislike this elderly lady with a passion, and that was regrettable, for Kathia cared for the woman's son with even more passion.

Kathia was taken aback when Whispering Wind gave her another cold stare, then left the longhouse without saying another word to Kathia or Bright Arrow.

"I don't know how I can ever repay you and your mother, and White Moon, for your kindnesses toward me," Kathia said, trying desperately to hide her awareness of his mother's rude behavior. "Had you not been there today, I would be in the water now, trapped beneath the ice, dead."

"You owe me nothing," Bright Arrow said. He reached for her hands and gently took them in his. "Your smile is worth everything. To me, that is payment enough."

"Really?" Kathia said, her eyes wide, her heart pounding, her face hot with a blush. She looked down at his hands holding hers, then gazed up into his eyes again.

"*Ah-ha*, that is enough," he said, then slowly slid his hands away from hers. He knelt down by the fire and gingerly touched one of her skates. "Tell me about these. They seem to be filled with a strange sort of magic, as though they give you wings."

Kathia smiled at his description.

She lifted one of her skates and held it out before them. "These are ice skates, and, yes, I sometimes do feel as though I am flying while I am skating," she murmured. She smiled. "It is a wonderful pastime. I love to skate. But what I truly love to do is dance. I am a ballerina."

"A ballerina?" Bright Arrow said, rising. He led her back to the rocking chairs, where they sat down opposite each other.

"From the time I was old enough to learn things, I wanted to be a ballerina," Kathia said softly. "And I am. I have performed all over America."

"I have been in Port Angeles and have seen advertisements on buildings for ballets, but I had no idea what a ballerina did."

He didn't want to prove the depths of his ignorance about such things by asking her to explain what such a thing was.

Instead he said, "You told me that your father is ill. What sort of illness does he have?"

Kathia sighed. She gazed into the dancing flames of the fire, then turned her eyes to Bright Arrow again. "It is a mysterious sort of illness," she murmured. "First he seems to be getting better, and then suddenly he is worse again. He can't walk. His legs just won't hold him up any longer."

She paused, then continued. "I brought a doctor from Port Angeles to examine my father, but the doctor was just as puzzled as I over what he found," she murmured. "Neither he nor anyone else can diagnose his illness. All I know is that I will stay with him until he recovers."

She gazed downward, then looked up at Bright Arrow again. "If he ever does," she blurted out. "I cannot even imagine how I would feel if I were to know for certain that my father will never be well again, or . . . be . . . able to care for his beloved lights. Another doctor is caring for him now, someone who lives much closer than Port Angeles. It is Dr. Michael Raley."

Wanting to change the subject, feeling sadder by the minute as she talked about her father, Kathia smiled at Bright Arrow. "Bright Arrow, I know that you are chief of this village of Makah, but what else do you do?" she asked. She glanced over at the harpoons, then at him again. "Do you, personally, go after large, powerful whales?"

He didn't get the chance to answer.

There was a sudden commotion outside the lodge.

There were loud voices.

Kathia became aware of a horse stopping just outside Bright Arrow's longhouse.

She knew that he realized this as well, for he had risen from the rocking chair just as Dusty Harper stormed into the longhouse, his right hand resting on a pistol holstered at his waist.

Dusty stared at Kathia and the Indian robe she was wearing.

His face flooded with color as his anger swelled. "You let this woman go," he growled as his eyes and Bright Arrow's met in silent battle. "You are taking advantage of Kathia after rescuing her from the water. Let her go. Do you hear? Let her go this minute."

Kathia rushed from the chair.

With flashing eyes and a firm jaw, she stepped up to Dusty. "This man is doing nothing of the kind," she said angrily. "He saved my life. I am here because I asked to be brought here instead of my home, where Father is so ill."

Realizing that she owed this man no explanation at all, Kathia leaned her face closer to Dusty's. "Who do you think you are, coming in such a way to Bright Arrow and making demands? Why do you act like my protector when you are nothing to me?" she said icily. "You know that I despise you."

She placed her fists on her hips and glared even more angrily into Dusty's squinting eyes. "Apologize to Bright Arrow," she fumed. "Apologize *now*."

Dusty was still reeling from all she had just said to him. "Me? Apologize?" Dusty said. He laughed cynically.

He glared at Kathia, then Bright Arrow, then stormed from the longhouse.

Kathia stiffened when she heard him ride away at a hard gallop.

She turned sad eyes to Bright Arrow. She now

knew that he, too, would become the target of Dusty's hate.

She hated to think what Dusty might do to avenge himself for the way she had just treated him in the presence of Bright Arrow.

She was not afraid for herself, for she didn't think Dusty would harm her.

But she knew that he would surely take much delight in harming Bright Arrow.

As Bright Arrow gazed deeply into her eyes, the thought of anything happening to him caused a sick rolling feeling in the pit of her stomach.

She cared. Oh, she cared so much for this handsome Makah chief.

And she was keenly aware that Dusty had guessed her feelings. She'd seen how jealous he was over her desire to be with Bright Arrow.

Chapter Ten

A violet by a mossy stone
Half hidden from the eye!
Fair as a star, when only one
Is shining in the sky.
—William Wordsworth

"I apologize for that man's behavior, and . . . how . . . he pushed himself into your home," Kathia said, despising Dusty more than ever now.

She prayed to herself that he wouldn't have to be at the lighthouse for much longer. A man like that might do anything.

She hoped that he didn't find a way to bring any more misfortune to her family than she was already dealing with.

Surely he wouldn't.

What could he really do? Today he had proved just how asinine a man he was.

"Dusty Harper has been assigned my father's lighthouse duties until he is well again," Kathia quickly added. "He has proved to be a very unpleasant man . . . and possibly even untrustworthy and evil."

"That sort of man is one who likes to look big in front of women, while all along he only makes himself look small and insignificant, even *cultus*, which in my language means worthless," Bright Arrow said. "So do not concern yourself with him for my sake. But I do believe that you should keep an eye on the way he operates the lighthouse. Soon many of my Makah warriors will be in the water, depending on the beams as the whaling season begins."

Suddenly Kathia had another worry, and a cold shiver went down her spine. She wondered if Dusty would tell her father where she was today and add his own little story to make her visit with Bright Arrow look bad.

Her eyes wide with sudden fear, she rushed into the bedroom where she had left her dress, glad that it had been close enough to the fire to have dried by now. But she winced when she saw how wet her heavy wool coat still was.

She couldn't wear it. But neither could she wait until it was dry. She had to get back to her father and reassure him that she was all right.

"I need to go home," she said as she returned to Bright Arrow. "I'm afraid of what Dusty might say to my father to worry him. I . . . I . . . should have been home much sooner than this. I never stay away long, not while Father is so ill."

She gazed down at her wet coat, then gave Bright Arrow a wavering look. "Might you have something warm for me to wear? My coat is still very wet," she murmured.

She glanced down at her skates, remembering that she had left her shoes beside the pond before putting on her skates. Her skates were still damp, and looked tight and shrunken from having been wet.

She smiled softly at Bright Arrow. "Might you have something that I can wear on my feet as well?" she murmured.

"I will go to my mother's lodge and get moccasins for your feet and a cloak for you to wear in place of your coat," Bright Arrow said. "I can also get you a skirt and blouse if you would rather not wear your dress."

"My own dress will do. It's dry now. But a cloak and moccasins would be wonderful," Kathia said, touched by this man's sweetness.

"*Mah-sie*, thank you so much, Bright Arrow. I know you have duties to your people to see to, and here I am taking up so much of your valuable time."

"Time spent with you is valuable, too," Bright Arrow said, noting how his words made her blush. He saw her as a complex woman. She was independent in so many ways, yet vulnerable and sweet in others.

He liked all of these traits in her. He only hoped that today would not be the last day they were together. He wanted more time with her, to know her more deeply. He believed he already knew her well enough to understand what sort of wife she would make.

He was taken aback by where his thoughts had led him. "I will leave now," he blurted out, then turned and left the longhouse without looking back.

Kathia was still stunned by his earlier comment, that time spent with her was valuable.

She didn't know how it could happen so quickly, yet it was very clear that they both were beginning to have special feelings for one another.

She felt giddy, something she had never felt before over a man.

"Stop this," she whispered to herself.

Yes, she must get hold of herself, for she had her father to think about, and then her career to resume. She had a performance scheduled at Port Angeles with a visiting orchestra soon.

She would disappoint both her brother and father if she didn't do this special performance.

She only hoped that her father would be well by then, so that he could sit in the audience, his eyes filled with pride, his smile, so wonderful to see when she looked at him from the stage.

"Yes, he will be there," she murmured. "My father will be well by then."

"My mother was happy to lend you her cloak and moccasins," Bright Arrow said as he came back into his longhouse.

He held out the cloak, made of some lovely, plush fur, then smiled and chuckled when he showed Kathia the moccasins. "My mother had to dig in her storage chests for these moccasins," he said. "She wore these when she was your size, not the size she is now. She said to tell you that you can keep them, for she doubts she will ever be able to fit her feet into them again."

"They are so beautiful," Kathia said, admiring the beadwork on the top, and the fringe.

"Mother is skilled at many things," Bright Arrow said as Kathia took both the cloak and the moccasins. "Sewing is one of her favorite pastimes."

"I have never . . ." Kathia said, but stopped before admitting that she knew not one thing about sewing.

She felt that she lacked many qualities that would be necessary for a Makah wife. She knew it was not best to advertise her deficiencies, especially to a man she wished to impress, not disillusion.

"I must hurry now," Kathia said. She looked over her shoulder at the corridor that led to the bedrooms.

Then she looked into Bright Arrow's eyes. "May I

use one of your rooms again, to change?" she asked softly.

"Yes, and I will wait for you here, then take you home when you are ready," Bright Arrow said, going to sit in a rocking chair as Kathia hurried away from him.

He rocked slowly as he gazed into the flames of the fire. He was getting used to this woman's presence in his lodge and knew that it would be something he would enjoy, were it possible for her to stay with him forever.

He had to remind himself how full her life was. Surely she would not want to give up her career to become a wife.

There! He had done it again. He had thought of her as his wife.

His heart pounded at the very thought of her being in his lodge in the evenings, rocking with him, watching the fire, then . . . then . . . going to his bed. . . .

"I am ready," Kathia said, appearing clothed in the dress and the cloak and moccasins.

Bright Arrow rose from the rocking chair just as she bent to pick up her skates. They accidentally collided as he took a step away from the rocker at the same moment that she bent low before him.

He reached quickly for her, to steady her, just as she rose to her feet, and they found themselves eye to eye, their hearts beating loudly within their chests.

"I want to kiss you," Bright Arrow said as he placed his hands gently on her shoulders. "I have longed for this since the first time I saw you."

He waited for her to refuse him, since they had known each other for such a short time, but when she didn't, instead leaning closer to him, he swept her fully into his arms and crushed his lips down on hers.

Everything within Kathia grew warm and deliciously yielding. She had never been kissed like this by any man. She knew deep down inside herself that she had fallen instantly in love.

Bright Arrow was shaken by the kiss, so much so that his knees went rubbery. He had never been so affected by a kiss, not even Sun Blossom's, the woman who would have been his wife.

But he knew why the kisses didn't compare. He had planned to marry his childhood sweetheart, not someone who sent his heart into a rush of passion every time he looked at her.

His and Sun Blossom's relationship had been sweet, yet not at all passionate.

With this woman in his arms, he finally knew the true meaning of passion, and he wanted it now and forever!

But he also realized something else. He stepped quickly away from Kathia. "I should not have done that," he said thickly. "Your life is already so full.

Why would you want me to be a part of it? I am a man who lives by the sea, who hunts for whales . . ."

Kathia's eyes widened. She gazed up at him and smiled. "I never thought much about wanting any man, or anything besides my career, until . . ." she murmured.

"Until . . . ?" Bright Arrow interrupted, drawing her closer. Their eyes locked, their lips again so close.

"Until I met you," Kathia said, sighing as he brought his lips down on hers once more, but this time not so heatedly, but instead sweetly, gently, just like the man he was, gentle and ever so kind and caring.

They kissed and clung, then were drawn apart when Bright Arrow's mother's voice spoke from outside the lodge. "Son, it is beginning to rain," she said. "If you are to get the woman home, it is best you do it now, before it begins raining harder. She has been wet enough today."

Kathia smiled, for she knew that the only reason his mother had come to warn them about the rain was because she was afraid that if Kathia stayed until it started to pour, she might have to remain in her son's lodge overnight.

"Thank you, Mother," Bright Arrow said. He slid the cloak around Kathia's shoulders and tied it at her neck. He pulled the hood up and over her golden hair, then could not stop himself from lowering his lips to hers again and stealing another brief kiss.

When they broke away from each other, their eyes held a moment before they hurried out into the grayness of the day and the slight mist of rain.

Bright Arrow helped Kathia onto his horse, climbed up behind her, then took the reins and sent his steed into a hard gallop.

They arrived at the lighthouse just as the rain began to fall in torrents.

Bright Arrow took Kathia as close to the front porch as he could, then helped her off his horse.

"Why don't you come in until the weather improves?" Kathia asked, looking up at him through the rain. "My father might even be awake. He would enjoy seeing you. You said that you are friends."

"We are friends, yes, but I will come another time and meet with him," Bright Arrow said. "I do hope that he is better."

"Me, too," Kathia said, blinking her eyes as the rain almost blinded her.

She stepped away from Bright Arrow.

They gazed at each another a moment longer; then he rode away and was soon lost to Kathia's eyes in the downpour.

Trembling, and knowing that it was not a good idea to get so chilled two times in one day, Kathia hurried inside and took off the drenched cloak, which she hung on a rack in the foyer.

She stood there for a moment to collect her

thoughts, and to relive the wonderful moments with Bright Arrow.

She would never forget his kisses. They had touched her in places she had not even known existed but were now very alive and so sensitive!

She now knew how a woman felt when she first fell in love. She remembered her mother's description of how she had felt when she had fallen instantly in love with Kathia's father. Her mother had told her how precious and sweet and unforgettable those moments had been.

Kathia wanted her first love to be as long-lasting as her mother's.

"And it will be," she whispered as she hurried toward her father's bedroom.

But as she stepped inside the room, she stopped abruptly. Dusty was standing there, leaning over her father's bed. She wondered what it was he thrust into his front breeches' pocket.

When Dusty turned and found her standing there, his face drained of color and his eyes filled with a look of guilt.

Chapter Eleven

Never seek to tell thy love,
Love that never told can be;
For the gentle wind doth move
Silently, invisibly!
—William Blake

"What were you doing?" Kathia asked suspiciously, her eyes still on his pocket, where his hand lingered. She looked quickly up at his eyes again, still seeing an expression of guilt in them. "What did you just put in your pocket?"

"There's no reason for you to act as though I've committed some sort of dark sin," Dusty grumbled, easing his hand from his pocket. "I came to check on your father, to talk with him. But I chose not to bother him. Not while he's sleeping so peacefully."

"And you think I would believe that?" Kathia said, laughing sarcastically. "The only person you care about is yourself. You only wanted Father to be awake so that you could tattle on me, didn't you? You wanted to tell him that I was at the Indian village, that I went there instead of here after my fall in the pond."

She went farther into the room. She stopped a few feet from Dusty, but close enough to her father that she could see if he was still asleep.

Her heart sank when she saw that he was.

It troubled her that he was sleeping so much. It seemed to be a strange sort of sleep, as though he was drugged.

But she knew that the doctor who came and looked after him had not given him any drugs.

"I still don't understand why you went to the Indian village instead of coming here," Dusty said.

"Why do you continue to think that anything I do, or why I do it, is any of your business?" Kathia said, placing her fists on her hips. "You have wiggled yourself into our lives like a snake. I wish you would wiggle yourself out just as quickly."

"And if I did, who would take care of the lighthouse?" Dusty said, chuckling darkly. "You're stuck with me, pretty thing, so cheer up. It's not all that bad. *I'm* not all that bad."

She gazed at his pocket again, then looked guardedly into his eyes. "You never said what you slipped into your pocket when you saw me," Kathia said flatly.

"As if that is any of *your* business," Dusty said, firming his jaw.

"You are in my father's room, and up to something, so, yes, it is my business," Kathia said, her eyes flashing. "I don't trust you. None of us do. I don't like finding you alone with my father, especially when he isn't even awake."

"And what would you expect me to do?" Dusty said, placing his fists on his hips. "Are you accusing me of something?"

"Should I?" Kathia blurted, her heart thumping.

"If you must know, I was putting my handkerchief back inside my pocket," he said dryly. "I had just come in from outside. My face was wet. I was drying it."

She glanced down at his clothes, then again questioned him with her eyes. "Your clothes aren't wet," she pointed out.

"I only stuck my head out of the door to check the color of the sky," Dusty said quickly.

"You said that you had been outside," Kathia snapped back at him. "So which is the lie? You were outside? Or only your face was?"

"It was just my face, damn it. The rain splashed

on my face," Dusty said, his eyes narrowing angrily. "And I'm getting damn tired of this interrogation."

"Then leave," Kathia said, stepping aside. "Get out of where you weren't invited in the first place."

He took a step closer to Kathia so he stood towering over her. "You're making a big mistake treating me so badly," he warned heatedly.

Kathia could feel the color drain from her face.

She knew now, without a doubt, that this man had an evil side. She had no idea how far he might go in his anger.

But she wouldn't let him think he could intimidate her. "You'd best not do anything foolish," she said. She took a step away from him. "If you do, I'll not hesitate to report you. I could have you jailed for any wrong you might do while you are in charge of the lighthouse. If you do anything to harm my father's beams, I'll . . . I'll . . ."

"You'll do what?" Dusty interrupted in a low, slow growl. His eyes gleamed. "Don't you think you are taking on a bit too much, first interrogating me and now threatening me? I came here to help in time of need. And now you are making me feel like a criminal."

"Perhaps because you behave as though you are one," Kathia retorted.

She flinched when he leaned his face down into

hers. "Little Miss Prissy, little Miss *Celebrity*, you are a fool to continue this cat-and-mouse game with me," he snarled. "You are a fool to threaten me."

He glared at her for another moment, then turned and stomped from the room.

Kathia's pulse raced as she stood for a moment, too shocked to move. Then she hurried to the door and closed it.

Breathing hard, she leaned her back against the door. Tears pooled in her eyes when she looked at her father. He had not moved an inch during the heated exchange.

He obviously had not heard or, if he had, was not capable of responding. Kathia only hoped that one day soon he would awaken and tell her that he was going to be all right, and that soon Dusty would be sent packing!

But at the moment, there he was, lying so still, his eyes closed, his face pale. She even noticed a little drool rolling from a corner of his mouth.

"Oh, Papa," she cried, hurrying to him.

She reached into a basin of water for a cloth that was kept beside the bed for wiping her father's brow from time to time.

She wrung it out, then gently dabbed away the drool. Her eyes widened when his lips quivered slightly, as though he might be on the verge of saying something, or possibly even awakening.

But the quivering stopped as quickly as it had begun. Once again he lay as still as he had for so many days.

His eyes were still behind his closed lids. His breathing was slow, shallow, yet even.

Sighing heavily, Kathia put the cloth back in the basin, then, shivering with foreboding, went to the window. She slid the sheer white curtain aside and peered out into the pouring rain.

It had not let up at all. She hated thinking of Bright Arrow riding home in such a rain as that. With any luck, he had reached home by now and was dry and resting beside one of his fireplaces.

"The rain . . ." she whispered.

Yes, the rain would melt the ice on the ponds, lakes and rivers. Spring had definitely arrived. Soon Bright Arrow and his warriors would be out at sea, hunting whales.

It might be difficult to see him again, but she must. How could she ever forget the wonders of Bright Arrow's arms and lips?

Then she recalled Bright Arrow's warning. What if Dusty *did* purposely lead the Makah astray with the lighthouse beams?

If Dusty did something underhanded like that, Bright Arrow could find himself dashed against the rocks!

"Kathia . . . ?"

Hearing her name, Kathia felt her heart skip a beat. She turned quickly.

Her eyes widened when she saw that her father was awake. He was smiling at her. He was beckoning to her with a quivering, lean hand.

"Oh, Papa," Kathia cried.

She hurried to him and sat down on the edge of the bed beside him.

"Oh, Papa, thank the good Lord! You are finally awake," she said, gently hugging him.

Then she leaned away from him again and gazed down at him as his hand reached for one of hers and held it.

"Papa, this time you have been asleep for so long," she murmured. "This time was much longer than the others. How . . . how . . . do you feel?"

"Suddenly, strangely enough, I feel stronger," he said. He tried to sit up, but gasped and fell back down on the bed.

"Papa, don't try anything like that so soon," Kathia said, again taking the cloth from the water. She bathed his brow with it. "You must take everything slowly. You are too weak to do much. Just relax. Please try to relax."

"I am so anxious to get to my beams," Melvin said, breathing hard. "I have missed them so. And . . . and . . . how has Dusty treated them? I've been told that he's skilled at keeping the beams steady at sea."

Kathia dreaded this question, for she wasn't certain what to say. She couldn't bring herself to tell her father all that she thought about Dusty Harper.

Right now she had to be careful about everything she said to her father. If it was something that would upset him, it might cause another setback, and the most important thing now was for him to get well, and as quickly as possible.

"Things'll be fine, Papa," Kathia murmured. "Just you rest now. Everything is being taken care of. Soon you'll be able to go up the stairs and see for yourself. But for now, please just rest. You must regain your strength first."

"All right. I'll do as you say. It's nice to have people to depend on," her father said, patting her hand. "Yes, it's nice. That Dusty fellow will take good care of my beams until I can get back to work."

Kathia smiled awkwardly at him.

Chapter Twelve

The desire of the moth for the star,
Of the night for the morrow,
The devotion to something afar,
From the sphere of our sorrow.
—Percy Bysshe Shelley

Night had fallen. Bright Arrow slid another log on the fire, then sat back in his rocking chair and gazed into the flames.

As he listened to the rain falling softly on his roof, his thoughts were torn between anticipation of the coming whale hunt and eagerness to see Kathia.

Everything within him warned that he should not pursue his attraction to her. He was aware that their worlds collided in many ways. She was a woman of numerous talents who did not seem to be the marrying kind.

Yet when they had kissed, he had felt her response. And in her eyes, there were those silent messages that reached inside his heart.

"Bright Arrow?"

Outside his door, a quivering, old voice called his name, bringing Bright Arrow instantly out of his chair.

It was the voice of his uncle White Moon, who should not be out in this rain. He knew the shaman must have something on his mind that he wanted to share with Bright Arrow.

White Moon and Bright Arrow had always had a specially close relationship, and it saddened Bright Arrow to see his uncle's health slipping away. He seemed to be more frail each day.

Bright Arrow hurriedly opened his door and smiled at White Moon as he entered, the hood of his cloak covering his white hair and a good portion of his face. The cloak was sleek with rain, and as Bright Arrow lifted it away from White Moon, drops of water went everywhere.

"I should not have come tonight, bringing this wetness into your lodge," White Moon said as he stepped away from the cloak.

"Do not concern yourself with the water," Bright Arrow said as he spread the cloak near the hearth so that it would be dry when White Moon left again. "I look forward to our talks, especially on dreary, rainy evenings. You fill my lodge with the sunshine of your smile and knowledge."

He turned and gazed in wonder at what White Moon had been holding beneath the cloak. He gazed at it a moment longer, then looked into his uncle's faded eyes.

"I have brought something to show you. I began making it in response to a dream that I received during my recent illness," White Moon said, holding the cloth canoe out for Bright Arrow so that he could hold and study it. "You remember the coughing ailment that had me in my bed for many sleeps?"

"*Ah-ha*, I remember that very well," Bright Arrow said, gingerly taking the canoe, whose cloth was stretched tightly across thin sheets of wood, so that it was in the shape of a *can-im*, a hunting canoe. There were many designs painted on the cloth, those of the *eh-koi-i* or whale and other water creatures, but a two-headed sea serpent was the most prominent.

Inside the canoe lay miniature harpoons, floats, and paddles. It was a showpiece of his uncle's carving skills.

Although Bright Arrow was anxious to know more about this *can-im*, he first had to see that his uncle was comfortably seated. His wobbly legs could hardly hold him up any longer.

"*Mit-lite*, sit, uncle," Bright Arrow said as he nodded toward his two rocking chairs, upon which were two comfortable cushions filled with the down of seagulls.

Bright Arrow gently placed his free hand on one of his uncle's elbows and led him to the rocking chairs. "We can sit and rock and talk," he said. "You can tell me about your dream and the canoe."

White Moon nodded, then eased himself down onto the chair. As Bright Arrow sat down, still holding and silently studying the miniature canoe, White Moon began slowly rocking.

"Uncle, you are a remarkable artist as well as a spiritual leader," Bright Arrow said, smiling at his uncle. "What you have made here is another of your masterpieces."

"*Mah-sie*, nephew. A canoe song came to me in the dream," White Moon explained. "In the dream I died, but before I died, I was with family in the sky. They said they were going to take me home. In my dream, I put my gear in my personal canoe, and then I awakened. I discovered that I was singing the canoe song out loud. I awakened *well*."

Bright Arrow was always in awe of his uncle, and White Moon's words only increased his reverence for the shaman.

His dreams had told him so many things that later came to pass. But this time, fortunately, the dream had been wrong.

His beloved uncle still lived.

"The *can-im* that I made is a replica of the canoe I saw in my dream, the one in which I placed my belongings to ready myself for the long journey to the stars," White Moon said, nodding toward the tiny canoe. His lips quivered into a slow smile. "I am glad that it is a tiny replica of a canoe with replicas of my belongings that I am showing you today, not the real thing."

"I am also glad of that," Bright Arrow said, gingerly setting the canoe aside on the table beside his chair. "I am not ready yet to say a final good-bye to you."

"Nephew, I might not look strong, but inside I am still as young at heart as you," White Moon said, chuckling softly. He brushed his long, lean fingers through the coarse hair that hung over his shoulders. "Nephew, I will not be singing my true canoe song for some time."

"It would sadden all of our people if you did," Bright Arrow said.

His uncle was much respected by their people, but also sometimes feared for the tremendous powers he harnessed in order to cure his patients.

The Makah had both male and female doctors who obtained their healing powers through contact with a supernatural being, but Bright Arrow's clan only had one healer . . . one doctor. His uncle.

Bright Arrow loved White Moon dearly. He had

become a substitute father for him, since Bright Arrow's powerful chieftain father died.

He tried not to think about that tragic day three moons ago. Someone had rammed his father's whaling canoe, capsizing it. All within had died.

"Uncle, my heart pounds like thunder inside my chest over my excitement to hunt for the great gray *eh-koi-i,*" Bright Arrow blurted out. He leaned forward, his eyes looking into his uncle's. "Uncle, it will begin very, very soon, now that the rains have come and the sun has become closer and warmer. I have been preparing myself well, as have my warriors. If the weather permits, it should be a good hunting season."

White Moon slowly nodded. He gazed at a window, at how water droplets clung to the glass, then rolled slowly downward.

"Nephew, it has been a long winter, but spring is upon us. I can taste its sweetness," he said thickly. "The *eh-koi-i* will return to our waters. And there will also be many clams under the sand. There will be mussels on the rocks. Roots and berries of the forest will be thick and juicy. Ah, but how this world of land and sea and life are tied to the world of spirits! The spirits are everywhere, smiling and seeing that the world of the Makah is *kloshe*, so good!"

White Moon reached over and patted Bright Arrow's knee. "According to our custom, the right to lead our people passes from father to son," he said, nodding. "But if any *tyee* cannot handle a harpoon skillfully enough, he must step down and allow the warrior who can to become chief. *You* will never have to give up your title as chief for any reason. You listened well to the teachings of your chieftain father."

"And *you*, uncle. I have prepared myself a new harpoon for my first hunt this spring," Bright Arrow said, always filled with pleasure at his uncle's pride in him.

"Will you show your new harpoon to me?" White Moon asked, his eyes searching over his shoulder for the weapon.

"It would please me so much to let you be the first one beside myself to see it," Bright Arrow said. "It is kept where no one can see it until the day I first use it. But you are special. I will show it to you."

Bright Arrow rose and went to the bedroom farthest from the living room. In that room he stored most of his personal things.

He came back from the room carrying the harpoon between both his hands. He held it as though it were some delicate, precious jewel. In his eyes was his pride in what he had made during the long, cold nights of winter.

"It is the best you have ever done," White Moon said as Bright Arrow stood over him, his own eyes assessing the worth of the weapon.

White Moon reached out and gingerly touched the shaft.

"Made of the loveliest mussel shells I have ever seen, and sharpened well. This will be a powerful weapon for you," White Moon said, slowly drawing his hand back and resting it on his lap.

Bright Arrow held the harpoon for a moment longer, then took it back to the room where it would remain until the day he brought it out for all to see. How proud he would feel when his warriors gathered around him, their eyes wide with wonder.

As far as he knew, there were none among his warriors who were jealous or envious of him. His warriors were all like brothers to him, linked, heart and soul.

He came back and sat down beside his uncle again after placing another log on the fire. "As you taught me, I will navigate by reading the sea's currents and sounds," he said softly. "It is something I look forward to. I feel doubly alive when I am in my powerful canoe holding my harpoon."

"Had I been a hunter, I would feel the same as you," White Moon said, then slowly pushed himself up from the chair. "But I can only live such moments in my dreams. You can live them in real life."

Bright Arrow rose from the chair and walked his uncle to the door, surprised when White Moon stopped and turned to look him square in the eye. Then he asked a question that Bright Arrow never would have expected.

"The white woman," White Moon said thickly. "Will she interfere with your hunt?"

Bright Arrow was so taken aback by the question, he almost gasped aloud. He knew that his uncle had many mystical powers, but it was hard to believe that he had seen inside Bright Arrow's heart, and divined that his thoughts had strayed sometimes to Kathia while they had been talking this evening.

"Why would you ask?" Bright Arrow asked guardedly.

"I know you well, nephew, and I have seen your thoughts wandering tonight, even when we were discussing what you have always loved more than life itself . . . the whale hunt," White Moon said. He reached a hand to Bright Arrow's shoulder and rested it there. "I saw how you looked at the woman called Kathia when she was here. There is a connection, is there not?"

"I believe so, yet she has her life . . . and I have mine, and they are totally opposite from each other," Bright Arrow said, his voice drawn. "So, no, uncle, I do not believe she will interfere in any way with my hunt."

He knew that White Moon doubted the truth of that statement but would not challenge it.

"Your cloak," Bright Arrow said, quickly getting it from the hearth. "It has dried."

He gently placed it around his uncle's frail, bent shoulders, then drew the hood in place over his head. "There has been no woman since Sun Blossom," he said, his voice drawn. "I have not wanted any inside my heart. But this time? I cannot help feeling something for *this* woman."

"She is white," White Moon reminded.

"*Ah-ha*, she is white," Bright Arrow said, nodding.

"Always remember that when she comes into your mind's eye," White Moon said. He looked past Bright Arrow, at the tiny canoe that he had brought into his nephew's lodge, then smiled into Bright Arrow's eyes. "The *can-im* I made with my hands is now yours. Let it always be a reminder to be cautious in all things, especially the hunt. *You* do not want to sing *your* canoe song anytime soon."

"No, I do not wish to leave you, nor my people," Bright Arrow said. He embraced his uncle. "*Mah-sie*. I will cherish the gift because it was made by your hands."

White Moon returned the embrace, then stepped away from him. "Always remember, too, that although some of our people could shift allegiance and demand another chief for our clan, the majority will be true to you, even if you love a woman with another skin color," White Moon said thickly.

Bright Arrow gave his uncle another hug. "*Mah-sie*, thank you, uncle," he murmured. "*Mah-sie*."

His uncle stepped away from him, turned, then, without another word, stepped out into the darkness of the night.

Bright Arrow watched his uncle until he got safely home. Only when he saw White Moon enter his longhouse did Bright Arrow close his own door and go to stand near the fire. He glanced over at the tiny canoe and knew he would always remember its meaning. He would be careful in the hunt. He would be careful with . . . his . . . heart.

He gazed into the dancing flames.

His heart. Was it already stolen away? How could he know unless he saw Kathia again and tested his feelings for her?

Troubled by his conflicting feelings, Bright Arrow went to the back room where he kept his personal belongings and his whaling supplies.

His gaze went over everything . . . his older harpoons, his older lances, buoys, and even his bright arrows in their quiver made from the skin of a seal.

He reached for a yew-wood club that he had been making. It already had a thunderbird's head carved at each end.

The Makah, both men and women, loved to carve.

The symbols of their clan were carved into wood and bone, creating a visible link between the realms of the supernatural and the everyday. Using special tools, like Bright Arrow's own whalebone chisel and beaver-tooth knife, they fashioned objects of great spiritual power.

Yes, carving gave form to the unseen. And the

thunderbird had its own secret meaning to Bright Arrow, a meaning not even his uncle knew about.

He sat down on the floor before the fire, letting the shavings fall around him. The mess would easily be cleaned up later.

He thought of Kathia as he worked on the club. He had seen her silently admire the woodwork he kept in the outer room. It made his heart swell with pride to know that she seemed to understand the worth of his carving.

He recalled his uncle's warnings of only moments before. He reminded himself that she was white.

"Yes, she is white, but when we kissed that did not seem to make a difference to her. It certainly did not matter to *me*," Bright Arrow whispered to himself. He paused and gazed into the flames of the fire. "And she is free. The man with the camera contraption is her brother."

But he found himself frowning when he thought of another man . . . the man who had come to try to claim her from this very longhouse.

Now *that* man *was* a threat.

Chapter Thirteen

Why should two hearts in one breast lie,
And yet not lodge together?
Or love where is thy sympathy,
If thus our breasts thou sever?
—Sir John Suckling

Kathia sat on one side of her father's bed, Fred on the other. She was so relieved that her father was awake and alert as her brother fed him his soup.

"I'm sick to death of this rain," Fred grumbled, dipping the spoon into the chicken soup, gathering on it a piece of chicken along with several noodles. "It rained yesterday. It rains today. Of course, I'm used to it. It rains just as much in Seattle. I guess I'm just missing Magdalena."

"Big brother, quit grumbling," Kathia softly urged. "Magdalena will be back before you know it, and the rain is bound to stop."

"But I had planned to go into the Makah village today and introduce more of them to the art of photography," Fred said, his voice gentler as he fed his father another spoonful of soup. "I was going to try to get more adults interested, and then I shall include the children."

"Son, you're too impatient," Melvin said as Fred placed the spoon in the empty bowl and set it aside. "You shouldn't rush things with the Makah. They are gentle and caring. Also, their lives are filled with the supernatural. They might see the camera as evil."

Melvin lay back down against the feather pillow Kathia had just plumped for him. He sighed heavily, closed his eyes for a moment, then looked at Fred again. He chuckled. "Some say that Bright Arrow is like the Thunderbird, a supernatural being," he said, drawing Kathia's keen attention as she leaned closer. "Some say that he even changes into the bird to hunt or rescue loved ones."

Kathia gasped and paled.

Melvin noticed her reaction. He reached out and took one of her hands in his. "It's only a story, daughter, only a story," he said to reassure her.

"Well, my camera is no story," Fred said. "I am making certain that the Makah know up front what the camera is, and what it does. Thus far, most seem interested. There are only a few that I have not been able to win over."

Kathia was still thinking over what her father had said about Bright Arrow and the thunderbird. It was true that she knew little of this handsome Makah chief, but to say that he was part man, part bird, was ludicrous. She would not let herself think for one minute that it was anything but a story that perhaps the Makah told in order to frighten whites from their village.

Yet when she was there she did not feel threatened, nor did she feel as though the people were anxious for her departure. No one had referred to Bright Arrow having the ability to change into a bird.

She rose from the chair and went to the window, wishing it was possible to see Bright Arrow again.

She drew aside the sheer white curtain and peered into the sky. This was a new day, with all of its promises, yet, just like yesterday, it was still raining.

She looked heavenward. It was as though day had turned to night as dark clouds rushed across the sky and rain pummeled the earth.

Kathia jumped with alarm when a lurid streak of lightning lit the heavens and thunder rumbled beneath her feet.

"And so now it is going to storm, not only rain?"

Melvin said. "Look how dark it is." He tried to get off the bed, then fell back down, exhausted.

"Papa, you shouldn't . . ." Kathia gasped as he struggled again, then finally managed to stand.

He started walking across the room toward the door, clinging to things. Even on the best of days he limped, having injured one leg several years before. "I've got to see if Dusty is on the job," he said, his legs wobbling. "My beams. They are needed now. The skies are as dark as night."

"Papa, please . . ." Kathia said, a part of her glad to see that he could walk again, even if his legs were scarcely holding him up.

Yet part of her knew that he shouldn't rush into anything. She hurried to him and grabbed him by an elbow, then slid an arm around his waist.

"You are too frail," she insisted. "You mustn't try going up those stairs."

Breathing hard, Melvin nodded. "Yes, you are right. Get me back to my bed," he said.

"I'll go and see how things are for you," Fred said, but first he went to his father's other side and, along with Kathia, helped him back to his bed.

Once his father was settled comfortably, the patchwork quilt drawn up to his armpits, Fred moved toward the door. "If Dusty isn't there, Papa, doing his duty, I know enough to light the lamps and send the beams out to sea. I've watched you often enough through the years to at least know how to do that for you."

Kathia watched her brother leave the room, then followed him.

"Papa, I won't be long," she said across her shoulder. "While Fred goes up to the lights, I'll check on Dusty and see if he is in his room. He sleeps at least half of the day so that he can be at the lights at night."

She hurried from the room.

She could hear Fred going up the steps, his footsteps echoing back down to her as she walked toward Dusty's room.

When she got there, she found the door ajar. She gingerly pushed it open some more, but soon realized that Dusty wasn't there.

She hurried to the spiral stairs that led up to the lights. Just as she took one step on them, she saw Fred at the top, peering down at her.

"He isn't here," he shouted. "Was he in his room?"

"No, he's not there," Kathia said, hurrying on up the steps.

"I'll get the lights lit," Fred shouted so that Kathia could still hear him as he scurried around the room, lighting one lamp at a time.

Breathing hard after the steep climb, Kathia rushed into the room.

Fred looked over his shoulder and saw her standing there, then focused again on what he was doing. "Kathia, when lightning lit up the sky and everything at sea, I saw a canoe in the water. I couldn't see who was in it. All I know is that it is in danger of capsizing in the high waves, or being dashed against the rocks. The lights . . . if I can just get them lit, I might save the person's life."

Kathia panicked.

She rushed to one of the wide windows and peered out to sea. What if the person in the canoe was Bright Arrow?

But surely not. He knew not to travel during storms. Yet perhaps he had been far out at sea when the storm blew in!

Finally all of the lamps were lit. The canoe would now have a point of reference by which to navigate.

A figure in the canoe waved at Fred as he guided the vessel away from the treacherous rocks.

The lights were so bright, Kathia was able to see that Bright Arrow was not the one in the canoe.

She turned to her brother. She was so proud of him for having the skill to save a man's life.

"That was wonderful," Kathia murmured, then gave her brother a big, warm hug. "You could take over the beams, Fred. We could send Dusty away. He's not worth anything. Today proved it."

"Being a lighthouse keeper is the last thing I'd want," Fred said as he returned her hug, then stepped away from her. "It keeps a man too confined in one place for too long. I don't see how Papa has been able to stand such isolation."

"He loves his beams and he loves the sea," Kathia said, watching the path of the lights as they reached far out to sea.

She wondered how soon Bright Arrow would go on his first hunt. Would she be able to look from these windows and see him in his huge canoe? Would he look up at the windows and see her there, watching?

Or would he have nothing on his mind but the hunt? Would he forget she even existed?

Had he . . . already?

Chapter Fourteen

My true love hath my heart, and I have his,
By just exchange one for another given
I hold his dear, and mine he cannot miss.
There never was a better bargain driven.
—Sir Philip Sidney

"The time for our hunt is almost here," Bright Arrow said as he stood before his warriors in the huge council house that sat near the center of the Makah village. It was a longhouse, only much larger than most, even larger than Bright Arrow's home. It had a high, slanting roof, sixty feet long and forty feet wide.

It was large enough for all of the Makah people, men, women, and children alike, and even visitors from other clans, to be able to enter and sit comfortably when they gathered for celebrations.

Today there were no fires in the fireplaces that sat at each end. All of the windows were open to the wondrous, sweet spring breeze, and to the sight of the ocean that was as blue today, as the sky.

Ready and waiting for the hunt, many brightly painted canoes lined the beach.

"Have you all completed your own personal preparations?" Bright Arrow asked. "To ready yourself, have you gone often to your private praying places? Is all of your equipment ready for a full season of hunting?"

Before anyone had a chance to respond, which they usually did in unison, as one voice, a commotion outside the longhouse drew their attention. Wondering what was causing all the excitement, Bright Arrow went and opened the door. What he saw made his eyebrows rise.

It was the man with whom he had had a confrontation that day when he had first seen Kathia skating on the pond. It was Kathia's brother.

He was mingling with the Makah, showing them his camera . . . and coins.

The coins were what was causing the most commotion, as the children crowded around Fred, their voices excited, some even reaching out for the money.

His jaw tight, Bright Arrow stepped from the

longhouse just as he heard Fred tell the people that he would pay them if they posed before his camera.

"I mean you no harm," Fred said, especially enjoying the excitement of the children, for he knew now that if the adults refused to pose, the children would. "I truly mean you no harm. Believe me when I say that only good will come from my pictures. Please trust me. Please let me prove myself to you."

Bright Arrow's thoughts returned to that day when he had grabbed the contraption called a camera away from this man and stamped on it with his foot.

It seemed that Kathia's brother had been able to put it back together again, for there it was, in his hand, held up for all to see and wonder at.

Bright Arrow felt torn. This was Kathia's brother. He didn't want to alienate him, for if he did, he might also alienate Kathia.

He was determined to see her again. He wanted to talk with her.

But Bright Arrow had to put his people before his own needs and desires. He could see his people were fearful and distrustful of the contraption just as he had been.

He started forward to ask Fred to leave, but Bright Arrow stopped when several elders approached him.

"Chief Bright Arrow?" an elder named Sea Breeze said. "We have discussed this thing the man wishes to do. We have decided that we would like for our likenesses to be captured in pictures. Do you not see that it would be a good way to show future generations the ways of the Makah today?"

He raised a carved club for Bright Arrow to look upon. "Do you see?" Sea Breeze said, his old gray eyes smiling into Bright Arrow's. "I would like, too, for my prized club, which I carved with pride, to be in the picture taken of me. Our Makah clubs are important. It would be good for the future generation of Makah to see them. In pictures, they could."

Bright Arrow's gaze went from man to man; each of them meant so much to him. He often went to them for advice.

Wearing their best long robes today, their gray hair hanging down past their waists and carefully brushed, they had prepared themselves to pose for the camera.

"You have thought this over carefully?" Bright Arrow asked, surprised that they would want to be a part of something so new and mysterious.

But surely Kathia would not have allowed her brother to come to the Makah village if there was truly any harm in his contraption.

"I shall see about this," Bright Arrow said, placing a gentle hand on Sea Breeze's frail shoulder. "I shall talk to the man. I must hear his explanation of the camera before I allow him to use it in our village, on our people."

The elders nodded, Sea Breeze's nod the most energetic of all as he smiled into Bright Arrow's eyes. Seeing their sincere wish to participate in the picture taking, Bright Arrow left the elders and drew near to Fred.

Fred turned to him, his eyes searching Bright Arrow's. "Do you give your permission?" he asked hopefully. "Since you are chief, I imagine my project must have your approval."

"You are right to believe that," Bright Arrow said. He gazed down at the camera. He wondered how this man had put it back together again after Bright Arrow had stomped on it.

He then gazed into Fred's dark eyes. "Come with me into the Thunderbird clan's council house," Bright Arrow said, gesturing with a hand toward the large building. "You can explain everything there to my people. But wait until those who want to hear you get inside as well."

Fred was stunned that Bright Arrow was being so cooperative. After their first confrontation, he had thought that Bright Arrow would send him away as soon as he saw him there.

"Thank you, Bright Arrow," Fred said, then stepped aside as the *tyee* told his people his plan.

Soon the council house was filled with curious Makah as Fred stood before them all.

He began his explanation of photography, a craft that consumed all his waking hours. He told them about his camera, and how it could produce images that would last for future generations of the Makah people to see.

Fred had cleverly learned some of the Makah language from the elders, who had been delighted and astonished to see their likenesses in photographs. He planned to use this knowledge to help describe what he was doing to those who asked.

They called the camera a *cataqeuyak*, which translated literally as a thing for making photographs. The word for photograph was *cataqcu*, which meant a finished design. The negative they called *dadacswi*, a thing you could see through.

Yes, he would use these words when he needed them. But for now he had other things to explain.

Feeling a confidence that he had not had before, he told the Makah about the book he planned to make with the photographs. But his optimism waned a bit when he saw a guarded look enter their eyes at the idea of a book.

He now wished that he had not said anything about that until later. Still, none of those who frowned said anything negative out loud, so he continued. When he was through, he was pleased with the outcome, for he was given full permission to continue taking photographs.

One elderly man, whose old eyes were faded yet filled with life, teasingly told Fred that when he looked into the camera, he looked like someone peering through the wrong end of a telescope. Everyone laughed, but the old man finished by asking Fred to take a photograph of him.

Everyone went outside, where the light was bright. Happily, Fred started taking photographs of those who came to him. And all his subjects had broad smiles on their faces, trust in their eyes.

Chapter Fifteen

Thy eyes are gazing upon mine,
When thou art out of sight,
My lips are always touching thine,
At morning, noon, and night.
—John Clare

Kathia was enjoying the beautiful, sunny day as she rode on her midnight black stallion toward the Makah village. The skies were blue overhead, with not one cloud in sight.

Finally! A day she could enjoy.

And there was much more to give her pleasure than just riding her horse. With her father's health so improved that she could leave him, comfortably in bed and reading a novel, Kathia had decided that she might be gone long enough to visit Bright Arrow.

Just as she rode into the outskirts of the village, she saw Fred step from a large wooden building, bigger even than Bright Arrow's personal lodge.

She drew rein and watched, stunned that Fred was smiling as the people followed him, then stood watching as he arranged several children for a photograph.

She was stunned that they were actually agreeing to be photographed. Even the adults, who had as much anticipation in their eyes as the children.

She was proud that Bright Arrow had given her brother a chance when he could still show resentment and distrust, as he had that day at the pond when he had grabbed the camera and dashed it to the ground.

She searched until she found Bright Arrow. He stood in the shadows of the door of the large building, just now noticing her presence.

Their eyes met and held. They exchanged smiles.

Bright Arrow met her halfway as she rode onward into the village, then helped her from her horse.

A young lad took her reins and led the horse away, to a large corral just outside the village.

"Come with me to my lodge," Bright Arrow said. He glanced at Fred and the two children he was photographing. He forced himself to look away, for if he thought too much about what Fred was doing, he might change his mind.

Bright Arrow did not feel completely comfortable with the camera's ability to capture images of those it was aimed at.

It was not a weapon, yet in a sense he saw that it might be. If it harmed the Makah at all, it was just as dangerous as a weapon, and he would hold Fred accountable.

He hoped it would not come to that, for he would not want to hurt Kathia's feelings. He could tell by the way she smiled at him that she was glad he'd allowed her brother to take the pictures.

"Thank you for letting my brother take his pictures," Kathia said, surprising Bright Arrow, for it was as though she could read his thoughts.

"He explained his camera to my people and they seemed excited about what he wanted to do, so who am I to say no?" Bright Arrow said, leading Kathia into his home.

He closed the door after them and guided her by an elbow to the rocking chairs, even though no fires burned in the lodge today. The air was kept comfortably warm by the sun.

"Again, thank you," Kathia murmured as she settled down onto the soft cushion of the chair. "My brother's life is his photography."

Bright Arrow sat down opposite her. "Your brother seems skilled at more than taking pictures with the camera," he said. "He has the ability to put his contraption together again after it has been broken."

Kathia laughed softly. "No, not quite," she murmured. "The camera he is using today is not the one you stepped on the other day. He tried, but he could not make it work again."

"I am certain he must resent me for that," Bright Arrow said, slowly rocking in the chair.

"Perhaps a little," Kathia said softly. "But the fact that you are allowing him to take photographs in your village is enough for him to forget what you did. You did it for the right reasons. You thought he was going to harm me. You had no idea he was my brother and that it was a camera he was holding, not a weapon.

"I noticed all of the canoes lined up along the beach," Kathia said.

"Come. I shall point my canoe out to you," he said, rising and reaching a hand out for her. He was glad when she took it and came with him to the door, for it proved that she was truly interested.

"The end canoe to the far right is mine," Bright Arrow said. He turned to her and saw that she was admiring his canoe. He smiled at her reaction.

"It is huge," Kathia said, truly in awe of it and its carvings. "It is beautiful!"

"*Mah-sie*," Bright Arrow said. "I am proud to say that it is mine."

"The carvings," Kathia said, continuing to study them. "I see that the largest one is of a bird."

"The Thunderbird," Bright Arrow said. He was

gazing at the carving himself, so he did not see how what he had said brought a look of curiosity to her face. "The Thunderbird is our people's totem. It is carved on many things."

"I see . . ." Kathia murmured, finding herself studying Bright Arrow now instead of the canoe. Again she was thinking about what her father had said about the Thunderbird story and how it included Bright Arrow.

When their eyes met, she felt suddenly awkward, for if he knew where her thoughts had just taken her, how would he react?

"Come and sit again," Bright Arrow suggested, trying to read the look in her eyes but unable to.

Kathia went with him back to the rocking chairs and sat down opposite him.

"Soon all the canoes will be filled with my warriors and their hunting equipment," Bright Arrow said, glancing past her at the calm blue sea and thinking that this was the perfect sort of day for whaling.

Soon, ah, soon.

When news reached him of a whale sighting, then they would launch the canoes.

"Tell me about it," Kathia murmured, truly interested. She was amazed that men in canoes could actually catch whales. She would think that the whale would capsize the canoe!

"Whale hunting brings wealth to our people,"

Bright Arrow said, in his mind's eye already seeing the whales in the water, already feeling the thrill of the hunt. "Whales give oil, meat, bone, and sinew to my people. If there were no more whales, there would be no more Makah."

Kathia paled. "Truly?" she asked, her eyes widening.

"Well, there *are* trees to be carved into useful objects, and there *are* other fish in the sea that can be caught and sold at the market, but the whale is what makes my people rich," Bright Arrow said, his voice serious.

"Now, tell me more about *your*self," Bright Arrow said, his eyes slowly raking over her.

Today, he noticed, she wore a heavy-looking skirt and blouse, and boots. She was dressed for riding, not skating.

He was more impressed by this woman each time he saw her. She seemed skilled at so many things.

"My life as a dancer is exciting for me," Kathia murmured. "I'm not certain if I could live without it. I have been a dancer for so long, it is so much a part of me."

"Then you would find it hard to give it up for any reason?" Bright Arrow asked guardedly, wishing to hear her say that she would give it up to marry him.

But he was premature in thinking such things.

Although he would take her as his wife in a heartbeat, it was not so easy a thing for her to do. When he brought a wife into his world, marriage would change only one thing for him. He would have someone to love and depend on for the rest of his life.

But it would not change his duties as a chief, or his activities as a hunter.

But if she were to choose marriage over what she now did, she would leave behind something that obviously meant a great deal to her. He doubted that she would make such a sacrifice, so he must learn not to envision them together in any capacity.

"I have never considered giving it up," Kathia murmured. "I . . . I . . . have never had any reason to."

"Then a man's love could not change your mind about such a thing?" Bright Arrow dared to ask. Before she could respond, he blurted out another question that seemed to come from out of the blue. "Have you ever been in love?"

Kathia felt the abruptness of the question and was caught off guard. How could she confess to him that she had not loved until she met him?

She knew, deep down, where her desires were formed, that she had fallen in love with him.

But would she be able to give everything up for him? She couldn't even imagine giving up dancing!

Yet . . . when a woman loved a man, did she not sacrifice much for him?

"Have I ever been in love? Well, no, I . . . don't . . . think so . . ." she murmured. "Have . . . you . . . ?"

"When I was young, there was a maiden. I had always thought I would marry Sun Blossom when we reached the marrying age," Bright Arrow said, his voice drawn. "Five winters ago, when we did reach that age, a wedding was planned. Before . . . before . . . the ceremony, a winter storm came suddenly and trapped Sun Blossom where she had gone to pray and meditate. She became disoriented. She . . . she . . . fell over the cliff into the raging waters of the ocean."

"No . . ." Kathia gasped, growing pale.

"Your father's beams caught her fall," Bright Arrow said, his voice breaking. "Your father saw her falling. He went, himself, and recovered her body. That . . . that . . . was how your father injured his leg, that is why he now walks with a limp."

Kathia was stunned speechless. Her father had never told her about that.

He could have bragged about his good deed, but he was not the sort to brag. Since he had not actually rescued Sun Blossom before she died, he might have felt it was not something to be discussed.

"So you see why I am fond of your father and wish him well in his time of sickness?" Bright Arrow said. "You can understand why we have such a kinship?"

"Yes, I can see . . ." Kathia murmured.

She was touched deeply by his story, and saddened that Bright Arrow had lost someone so important to him. In her mind's eye she could see her father carrying the lifeless form of the tiny woman in his arms.

It brought tears to her eyes. She hurriedly brushed them away with her fingertips.

"Your father talked of you to me, how proud he was of you. He explained why you didn't live with him, or come home all that often, that first your schooling kept you away and then your career," Bright Arrow said. "When you did come for a visit, it was brief, as were your brother Fred's . . . not long enough to take the time for your father to bring you or Fred to my village. He said that when his children were at the lighthouse, he wanted every moment of their time to himself."

"Yes, I know that is how my father felt," Kathia said, nodding. "I feel ashamed sometimes for not having come back any more often than I did. But my schedule was so busy. How I wish I had visited my mother more often. But I didn't expect her to die so suddenly, either."

"And now you feel regret for things left unsaid between you," Bright Arrow said, nodding slowly. He would suffer no such regret, he decided.

He leaned closer to Kathia. He reached out and took her hands in his. "Had I met you under any circumstances, even for only a moment in passing, I would have known immediately that I loved you," he said thickly. "You see, Kathia, my feelings for Sun Blossom were those born of friendship and devotion. These feelings I have for you are born of passion . . . of intense love . . . and need."

"Truly?" Kathia said, moving to her feet as he stood and urged her up.

She trembled as he swept her against him, his arms holding her there, their lips meeting in a tender, sweet kiss. She was afraid of her feelings . . . the passion. She knew that such feelings usually led to marriage, and marriage was the last thing she had ever thought of wanting for herself.

She eased away from him. She cleared her throat nervously when she saw the disappointment in his eyes.

How could she explain her hesitation? The passion between them was real. She *did* care for him, and her heart ached for more than a kiss.

She did not know how to respond to him, so instead, she changed the subject.

"My father . . . my father . . . told me that some say you are like a thunderbird," she murmured. "He says that some believe you . . . you . . . change into a bird."

She saw how strangely he looked at her then, his eyes wide with feelings she could not interpret.

She wished now that she hadn't repeated that ridiculous story to him, and started to apologize, but he spoke first.

"The thunderbird *has* appeared in my visions and dreams many times and has taught me many things," he said. Again he took her hands and gently held them. "By both the creatures of the physical world and the creatures of the supernatural, I have been shown how to take care of what I have been given . . . my people."

Again he drew her into his arms. "I need to kiss you again," he whispered against her lips. "I need you, Kathia, as I have never needed a woman before."

She twined her arms around his neck, for she was now so lost in her love for him, she could no longer deny him what he asked of her. "Yes, yes, please . . ." she whispered back to him.

As he kissed her, she clung to him. But once again she remembered the future that she had mapped out for herself. It had not included a man.

Again she left his arms.

She gazed up at him, her heart pounding, for her body accepted him completely. Her body ached for him!

She saw hurt in his eyes, and saw how quiet he had become. "I . . . I'd best get back home to see if my father is all right," she said, her voice soft, her eyes searching his. "But . . . I will return soon. I cherish these moments with you."

That was all Bright Arrow needed to hear to erase the doubts of moments before.

He understood that she wanted to be with him. He realized that she was battling many things within her.

She was a woman of dedication. Until she had met him, she had been dedicated to her career, and now to her ailing father.

He believed that, in time, if he was patient, she would dedicate herself to him.

They were meant to be together.

"I shall walk you to your horse," Bright Arrow said thickly. He took her gently by the elbow and walked her outside, then took her to the corral where her horse awaited her.

Kathia had quickly noticed that Fred was no longer in the village. No doubt he was anxious to go to his darkroom and develop the photographs he'd taken today. His pictures and darkroom brought excitement into his life just as dancing brought it into Kathia's.

She allowed Bright Arrow to help her into her saddle, then gazed down into his eyes and felt a sensuous tingling throughout her body.

"Come again soon," Bright Arrow said, then watched her ride away.

Kathia felt torn now between many things: Bright Arrow . . . her career . . . and wanting to be sure her father was totally well before she returned to her normal life.

But could she ever return to that life, now that her heart was pulled in two directions?

She loved Bright Arrow. Oh, how she did love him. How she wanted to share the ultimate bliss with him.

She had never given herself to a man before. She had never even desired to.

But now? Every beat of her heart told her that she wanted to make love with Bright Arrow.

But could she sacrifice one love to have another?

She had to decide which was the most important to her now. Love . . . or career . . . ?

Chapter Sixteen

I told my love, I told my love,
I told her all my heart.
—William Blake

"I'm amazed at how the Makah reacted to your offer," Kathia said as she met her brother in front of their father's house. "They actually let you take pictures of them."

"Only because Bright Arrow allowed it," Fred said, stepping up on the porch. He turned to Kathia. "Sis, at first I disliked the man because of what he did to my camera, and because of his obvious interest in you. But I see now that he is a fine fellow, yet . . ."

"Yet what?" Kathia asked as Fred opened the door and they both stepped into the foyer.

"Yet I don't like how you two have been drawn together," Fred said dryly. "Kathia, he's an Indian. You're white. There's something taboo in a red man showing such an interest in a white woman. I especially don't like what I see in your eyes when you look at him. Kathia, remember who you are, and what your future holds for you."

"Big brother, I think you'd best concentrate on your photography," Kathia said. "And if you can't concentrate on photography, think of Magdalena. Think of anything but me. I can take care of myself," she tossed back at him.

The day had been so warm a wrap had not even been required.

It had felt good to ride free on her horse today, without the encumbrance of a coat or hat.

She loved the scent of the wind in her hair. She loved even more how she suddenly could feel Bright Arrow's lips on hers, making her face grow hot with a blush.

She didn't dare turn to Fred or he would see the blush and surely know what had caused it.

If Fred knew that her and Bright Arrow's relationship had gone as far as a kiss, he would probably order her back to Port Angeles.

Fred walked past her and into their father's bedroom.

"Kathia! Hurry in here!" Fred said.

She heard the alarm in her brother's voice. Was something wrong with her father?

Kathia had made certain that he was comfortable and had smiled to see him sitting up, reading a novel. It had been several days since he had been strong enough to sit up in bed.

She hurried into her father's bedroom, noting that the book now lay beside the bed, its pages awkwardly spread on the floor. Her father seemed to have slumped over suddenly, for he was positioned awkwardly in the bed.

"What is it, Fred?" Kathia said, alarm in her voice. "What could have happened? Papa seemed to be so much better before we left."

"Well, he isn't better now," Fred said as he rearranged Melvin on his back, resting his head on a pillow and bringing the patchwork quilt up over him.

"Oh, Lord, look," Kathia softly cried as she covered her mouth with a hand.

"The drool," Fred said, finishing what she was about to say.

He plucked the cloth from the water in the basin on the table beside the bed. Wringing it out, he gently washed the drool away from his father's mouth.

"What in hell is causing our father to drool?" he said, his voice drawn. "Look at his mouth. There is a strange sort of chalkiness around it. What could it be, Kathia? The medicine that Doc Raley gave him to take?"

"It did look chalky when Dr. Mike first poured it out in a spoon," Kathia said, recalling the white-haired, elderly doctor. Dr. Mike had retired several years ago, yet he had come to call on Kathia's father since the other doctor did not seem to be able to give a diagnosis.

Kathia and Fred had rowed over to the tiny island called The Point, where Michael Raley made his residence now that he was retired. He had been the Parrish family doctor when they all lived in Port Angeles. He was someone they trusted.

But even he could only guess at what might be wrong with their father. He had called it a long word that neither Kathia nor Fred could remember now.

"Fred, I'm afraid," Kathia said, clutching her throat. "Papa might . . . might . . . not make it."

Fred turned to her. He went and placed gentle hands on her shoulders. "Don't talk like that," he said flatly. "Sis, it won't do any of us any good to start thinking negative thoughts. Papa will get well. He has to!"

"Fred, do you know what this means?" Kathia said, searching her brother's dark eyes.

"What?" he asked, raising an eyebrow.

"That terrible Dusty will have to stay longer," Kathia said softly. "Oh, Fred, I had so hoped that Papa could return to what he loves, especially now, when his precious beams are going to be needed so badly. The beams are particularly necessary when the Makah go out to sea. I can't help thinking that Dusty is evil enough to purposely let the light go out if it would mean harming Bright Arrow."

She stepped away from him and stood over her father, gazing worriedly down at him. "But, oh, surely not," she murmured. Tears filled her eyes at seeing her father in that strange sleep again. "Surely Dusty's anger toward me and Bright Arrow can't go that far . . . so far that he would actually want to see Bright Arrow dead."

"Sis, you don't look so good," Fred said as he stepped up beside her. "Your face looks flushed. Are you all right?"

"Fred, I'm fine," Kathia said, but her throat felt even worse than it had just moments ago.

She bent down and picked up her father's book from the floor. She closed its pages and laid it on the nightstand, then leaned against the bed when she suddenly felt a strange sort of dizziness.

She knew now that she did have a fever. She felt hot all over.

"Well, I want you to sit down anyway," Fred said, scooting a chair close to the bed for her.

"Thanks," she murmured, appreciating his kindness.

She didn't want to admit that she might be sick, so she would put it from her mind as best she could.

Perhaps if she concentrated hard enough on not being sick, she wouldn't be.

There was much power in positive thinking, her father had told her when she was a child, prone to worry about this or that too often.

"A worrywart," he had teasingly called her.

So she would practice what he'd preached about the power of positive thinking and hope for the best.

All Fred needed on his hands was two family members sick. Now that he had made progress with the Makah, he needed to return to the village before they changed their minds.

That would dash all of Fred's hopes to publish a book of Makah photographs.

"I'll sit beside you," Fred said as he pulled another chair closer to the bed, next to Kathia's.

"Fred, Bright Arrow told me something today," Kathia murmured, carefully watching her father for any signs of his awakening.

"What did Bright Arrow say?" Fred asked, glancing over at Kathia.

She told him about Bright Arrow's bride-to-be falling from a cliff into the ocean, and how their father had risked his life to retrieve her body from the water.

"Papa was injured while performing a heroic act, Fred," Kathia murmured. "That's how his leg was injured. That's why he has to walk with a cane now, and has such a limp."

"Papa never told us how he injured his leg," Fred said, awed by his father's bravery. "I wonder why he didn't."

"Papa has never been one to brag, that's why," Kathia said. "And . . . perhaps he felt not all that heroic after all. He was not able to save the woman. He was only able to rescue her body from the water and take it back to her people for burial. Otherwise, she would have been washed out to sea."

"It was a heroic act even if he wasn't able to actually save her life," Fred said flatly. "He could've lost his own by diving into that fitful ocean to retrieve her body, for as you said, he did it during a terrible storm." He gazed admiringly down at his father. "Yes, Sis, our father is a true hero."

Suddenly a chill raced across Kathia's flesh. She grabbed at her arms, hugging herself.

"Sis, what's wrong?" Fred asked as he noticed how she was hugging herself and trembling.

"Fred, I'm coming down with something," Kathia said, her throat aching unbearably. "I guess I'm catching a cold from my spill in that icy pond. I must get away from Father or he might catch my cold. And . . . and . . . I feel dizzy. I have to go and lie down."

"Let me help you," Fred said, hurrying from his chair. He helped Kathia up and held her against him as he walked her to her room.

"I'll be all right," Kathia murmured, yet she wondered if she would be. She could almost feel the heat of her fever when she held a hand an inch from her flesh.

"I can help you get into your gown," Fred said when they had reached her room.

"No, Fred, I can do it myself, but you might check in on me in a little while, for I do feel pretty bad," Kathia said, swaying as she walked toward the chifferobe where her gowns hung from wooden hangers.

"I'll have Mariah prepare some fresh chicken soup for you for supper," Fred said, turning to leave the room.

"Fred, the last thing on my mind is food," Kathia whispered, shuddering at the thought. "Just go on. Be sure to check on Dusty. Make certain he takes care of the lights. I worry about Bright Arrow and his warriors. I hope they will be safe when they . . ."

"Sis, there are many more things for you to worry about than Bright Arrow," Fred said, his voice drawn. "Get to bed. Rest. I'll take care of everything."

"All right," she replied, giving him a weak smile over her shoulder.

Fred walked from the room, closing the door behind him, then stopped and leaned against the wall, sighing. He looked sadly toward his darkroom, a closet he had converted into a workroom where he could develop his photographs. He would have to wait and work on the photographs he'd taken today later.

He moved away from Kathia's door and gazed at it, and then at his father's. He didn't know which to sit with first. His father? Or his sister?

He hurried to Dusty's room and knocked on the door.

When Dusty opened it, bare-chested and barefooted, a cigar hanging lazily from the corner of his mouth, Fred's jaw tightened with disapproval at the man's slovenly habits.

"Yeah?" Dusty asked, lifting an eyebrow. "What do you want?"

"Dusty, I'd like to ask a favor of you," Fred said, nervously shuffling his feet, for he hated to ask anything of Dusty Harper.

"What sort of favor?" Dusty asked, idly taking the cigar from his mouth.

"My sister is suddenly ill," Fred said solemnly. "Before you begin your duties at the lighthouse tonight, would you row over to The Point, the island where Doc Raley makes his residence? You know; he's the doctor who's been caring for my father."

"Kathia is ill?" Dusty gasped out. "What's wrong with her? How bad is she?"

"She has a temperature and a sore throat, that's all I know," Fred said curtly. "Will you do that for me, Dusty? I don't want to leave Father or Kathia for the length of time it would take to go for the doctor. You go and tell Doc Raley that he's needed again, but this time for my sister."

"I'll be ready in a jiffy," Dusty said, showing a sincere concern for Kathia. "Let me get dressed. I know where the island is. I'll get there in no time flat. I've rowed over that way a couple of times, but never gone ashore. I was just looking around."

He stepped away from Fred, pulled on a shirt, and then his shoes. He turned then and left his room, stopping momentarily to look at Kathia's closed door.

He turned to Fred. "Take care of her, Fred," he said thickly. "Don't let nothing happen to that princess. I'll get Doc Raley as quick as I can."

Fred felt a coldness in his heart to hear this man actually speak as though he might have some claim on Kathia. It rankled to hear Dusty call Kathia a princess, as though he truly meant to say, instead, *his* princess.

It took a lot of willpower for Fred not to put the man in his place, but he made himself hold back. He wanted to do nothing to stop Dusty from going for Doc Raley.

He watched Dusty leave the house. Then he went to the window and watched him run down to the beach, where Fred's father kept a small boat. Dusty pushed the boat out into the water, then climbed aboard.

"You bastard, don't think I'll be in your debt for this help," Fred grumbled to himself. He meant to pay Dusty for his trouble.

But Fred was afraid that Dusty would expect more

than that. He might feel as though Kathia owed him something.

"Never!" Fred whispered as he clenched his fingers into tight fists at his sides.

Chapter Seventeen

Since there's no help, come let us kiss and part;
Nay I have done, you get no more of me,
And I am glad, yea, glad, with all my heart
That thus so cleanly I myself can free.
—Michael Drayton

Although Bright Arrow had immersed himself in prayer and meditation in preparation for his first whaling expedition of the year, he had not been able to stop thinking about Kathia. Several days had passed since he had last seen her. She had not come to him, nor had he seen her anywhere else.

He had begun to wonder if he had rushed her too much, kissing her and telling her his feelings for her.

She had left right after his declaration. But she *had* said she would be back.

So why hadn't she come?

Trying hard to put her out of his mind as he sat working on his club just inside the open door of his house, he again thought about the hunt.

The night before the hunt he and his warriors would sit on the beach in the evening. They would watch the color of the sky and study the direction of the wind. They would listen to the sound of the water.

Ah-ha, he and his men would sit on the beach watching these signs, and nobody would be allowed to bother them, for their lives depended on the knowledge they would gather on the evening before their first hunt.

They knew how to read the weather. They also knew the position of the stars and moon in each season, and could guide themselves to shore if night fell upon them before they completed the hunt.

During the day, natural landmarks helped them to navigate on clear days. They guided themselves by the way two islands lined up with each other, or the disappearance or appearance of certain mountain peaks.

If fog came in upon them, his men could steer by the direction of the ocean swells and the feel of the familiar tide rips. Surf breaking against headlands or rocky islets sounded different from waves against sand. Even the call of nesting seabirds could identify certain islands.

"Hunting the *eh-koi-i*, the gray whale, is the core of my people's culture," he whispered to himself.

Ah-ha, the gray whales were the traditional target of his tribe. The *eh-koi-i* would surely bless his people with their presence again this year. Their lives depended on it.

"My son, your club looks finished," Whispering Wind said as his mother stepped into his house, blocking his view of the outdoors, where his people were busy at work doing their individual chores.

He enjoyed watching the children the most; how carefree they were. Too soon they would have the duties of adults as their parents did. These past two days Bright Arrow had watched the children more carefully, for he had begun thinking about how blessed he would feel to have a son or daughter of his own.

Bright Arrow desired first a son, and then a daughter.

But first . . . he must have a wife!

Kathia! She was all he desired in a woman.

"Bright Arrow, you must be careful with that knife," Whispering Wind said as she knelt down beside him. "Son? Do you even know that I am here with you? You are so lost in thought. Dare I ask what you are thinking of?"

Bright Arrow turned his head toward her, suddenly aware of how he had been ignoring his mother as his thoughts strayed again to Kathia.

"I am sorry, Mother," he said, laying aside his club and knife. He stood and helped Whispering Wind up before him, then drew her into his gentle embrace.

"Is it the hunt that has taken your mind away from everything and everyone today?" she murmured, enjoying this special moment with her son. "Were you envisioning yourself already in your beautiful, huge *can-im* with your new harpoon ready to throw?"

She eased herself from his arms and placed a gentle hand on his face. "I have been picturing that often myself," Whispering Wind said, smiling up at him. "Although I have never accompanied you on a hunt, when you hunted close to home, I have watched and admired you. No mother could be any prouder than I am of you. You are responsible for feeding our people and also giving them warmth from the whale's oil."

"*Mah-sie*, thank you, Mother," Bright Arrow said, smiling down at her.

He stepped away from her and stood at the door, looking toward the ocean.

Its waves were gentle today. Its briny smell made him long to be there even now, riding the waves, feeling the splash of seawater on his face, tasting its saltiness.

He enjoyed every aspect of the hunt. As soon as

he paddled out on the ocean, he always felt an excitement so keen it could not be described to anyone who had not experienced it.

"The hunt?" he said, nodding. "*Ah-ha*, I have been thinking of the hunt."

He started when far out at sea he saw the sudden leap of something huge, then sighed to himself when he realized it was only a large dolphin.

Then another dolphin splashed upward, and gracefully dove back into the water.

Bright Arrow knew all about dolphins, how they whistled, jumped, teased, wrestled, and played with their food, and how they breathed air through a blowhole on top of their heads, extracting enough oxygen to stay submerged for a lengthy amount of time.

He had also watched these interesting water creatures from a bluff, noticing how when they dove, muscles seemed to close their blowholes, and how their rib cages seemed to compress.

They hunted in groups. They preyed mainly on the blue whale—a massive species more than twenty times their size.

He had witnessed the way they communicated through clicks, whistles, and the movements of their body.

Seeing so many dolphins today, he knew that the gray whales were not far behind.

He turned to his mother again. He looked deeply into her eyes and read her thoughts, realizing that she was aware he had been thinking of more than the hunt.

"You were thinking of her, too, were you not?" Whispering Wind said, walking heavily toward a rocking chair and sighing as she settled down on its soft cushion.

Bright Arrow followed her and sat down in the other rocking chair, where he began to slowly rock back and forth, his gaze on the cold ashes in the grate.

He now only lit fires on the coolest of evenings. And since food was not prepared in his dwelling, but in the lodges of the women who had volunteered to keep their chief fed, no cooking stove had ever been brought into his home.

But perhaps there would be one soon. If he married Kathia, wouldn't she want a stove? Surely she could cook delicious food.

Of course, she would not know the Makah foods that he was accustomed to. But he hoped that his mother might teach her, or the women who were known for their cooking in his village.

"I cannot help thinking of Kathia," Bright Arrow said, moving his eyes to meet the question in his mother's. "She has not returned since her last time here. I hope she is all right. Do you think she might have become ill from her fall through the ice?"

He had another worry that he would not speak aloud to his mother. He feared that Kathia might have told her father about a Makah chief's feelings for her. If so, might he have forbidden her to be with Bright Arrow again?

Although Bright Arrow and Melvin Parrish were friends, it was one thing to be friends, another to see one's only daughter courted by a man of a different race and culture.

He suddenly realized that even her brother had been missing from the village.

Troubled, Bright Arrow made a quick decision. He must go to the lighthouse and find the answers to all his questions. He could not go another day, not even an hour, without knowing.

He jumped to his feet. "Mother, I must leave for a while," he said, going to help her from the rocking chair. "I am truly concerned about Kathia. If she is ill, I want to know."

"It is not your place to know," Whispering Wind said, her voice drawn. "Son, you are only listening to your heart, not to what is logical. You are a smart man, a great leader. Why would you bring a complication like this into your life? It is time for the first hunt. Think about that . . . not . . . this woman."

"I have prepared myself well enough for the hunt," Bright Arrow said, placing gentle hands on her shoulders. "But I have not prepared myself for being in love. I must, though, Mother, because I am. I am in love."

He saw shock enter her eyes. "You speak of love as though it . . ." she started, but stopped.

"*Ah-ha*, as though it is very important for me to pursue my feelings. It is. I must see if the woman can love me as much as I love her," Bright Arrow said, realizing that his mother was truly unhappy with him. Her jaw was set and she stepped away from his hands.

"My son, you have always been astute in all things, but where women are concerned, you are not as practiced," Whispering Wind said softly. "You have loved only once, and that love was taken from you in such a tragic way. Do you truly want to . . . ?"

"Mother, you know that my relationship with Sun Blossom was not created out of feelings of love," Bright Arrow said, interrupting her. "Our feelings were born of a sweet friendship that we had shared since childhood. At the time it seemed only right that we should marry. Now? As I look back at how it was, I know that even had she lived, we should not have married. We should have sought true love, not settled only for sweetness."

"She was all sweetness," Whispering Wind said, lowering her eyes.

"And so is Kathia," Bright Arrow quickly interjected. "And you know this is true about her. You have been with her only a short time, yet long enough for you to see that she is gentle and sweet, and *good*. I want her for my wife, Mother. If she agrees, she will become your daughter."

"My daughter . . ." Whispering Wind said, heaving a deep, heavy sigh. She reached up and placed a gentle hand on her son's cheek. "I have never fought your decisions about anything. Nor shall I say any more against this. I see how important it is to you. Go. Go and see if she is all right. Go with your mother's blessing."

Hearing her sincerity, and rejoicing in the smile she now gave him, he swept her into his arms and gave her a big hug.

"She will be such a friend to you, Mother," Bright Arrow said. "You shall see."

"If she marries you," Whispering Wind said as Bright Arrow stepped away from her.

"*Ah-ha*, if she marries me," he said thickly.

Brushing another kiss across his mother's cheek, he hurried from his lodge, mounted his horse, and rode from the village. He was beginning to feel that Kathia was calling out for him, that she *was* ill.

He drummed his heels against the flanks of his roan and rode harder toward the lighthouse. He saw it in the distance, as though it were a sentinel, beckoning him onward.

Yet even as he watched vapor was rising from the earth and massing against the distant hills, until a hazy fog hid the lighthouse from his view.

He hoped that was not a bad omen.

Chapter Eighteen

> O hurry to the ragged wood, for there
> I will drive all those lovers out and cry
> O, my share of the world, O, yellow hair!
> No one has ever loved but you and I.
> —William Butler Yeats

A thundering sound that Kathia could not immediately identify awakened her from her feverish sleep. Blinking her eyes in the semidarkness, Kathia leaned up on an elbow.

She listened more intently. The sound seemed to be coming from outside the French doors of her bedroom, which led onto a side porch of the house.

Now more fully awake, Kathia gasped when she

realized that the sound was being made by the wings of a huge bird. The flapping of the wings sounded almost like thunder.

She watched as a huge bird with eyes like flashing lightning landed outside the French doors.

Fear leaped into Kathia's heart. Trembling, she pulled her blanket up to her chin and blinked her eyes to see if what she was seeing was an eagle.

She had seen huge eagles circling around the lighthouse on beautiful, clear days.

But no.

This was night, and this bird looked like no eagle she had ever seen.

Could it be a thunderbird, the kind she had heard legends of? Was there truly such a bird? Could one have landed just outside her doors, the moon's glow defining it against the black forest that grew right up to the lighthouse?

Disoriented from the fever, and so ill she could not hold her eyes open any longer, Kathia eased her head back down onto her soft feather pillow and fell into another feverish sleep.

Again Kathia slowly awakened. She felt a cool cloth on her brow. She felt a presence.

Suddenly she remembered having seen the huge bird.

She looked quickly up to see who or . . . what . . . was sitting beside her bed, placing the cool cloth on her forehead. She was startled to find Bright Arrow sitting on a chair beside her bed, a damp cloth in his hand.

She gazed questioningly at him, then looked toward the French doors, which still stood open. Her brother had opened them for the fresh evening air before he left her alone earlier in the evening.

The bird. It was no longer there. Had it ever been?

Had she been dreaming? Was she dreaming even now?

Was Bright Arrow truly in her bedroom, sitting beside her bed, his eyes filled with concern?

She turned her eyes to him again. She recalled what her father had said about the legend that Bright Arrow could change into a mystical Thunderbird.

But no. It just couldn't be.

"How . . . did . . . you get here?" she asked softly. "Did my brother let you in? Did he leave you alone with me like this?"

Bright Arrow laid the cloth back in the basin, then sat down on the edge of the bed. He leaned over Kathia, then drew her gently into his embrace. "Do not concern yourself about how I happen to be here. I have just arrived," he said softly. "The important thing is that I am here, and that I want to hold you. I want to help you."

"I am so sick," Kathia murmured, clinging to him. "I've such a fever. And my throat hurts so. It feels as though it is on fire."

"*Ah-ha*, I feel the heat of your fever, even through your clothes and mine," Bright Arrow said, slowly stroking her back through her cotton gown. "But you will be all right."

Kathia felt herself drifting again.

She closed her eyes and fell into another deep sleep in his arms.

When she awakened she looked beside the bed, surprised that Bright Arrow was still there. "You . . . *are* here," she murmured. "I thought that I had dreamed it."

"No, I am no dream," Bright Arrow said, smiling down at her as he took a small vial from a pouch. "I have brought something for you. It is my people's medicine for fever. It was made by my uncle."

"What is it?" Kathia asked, watching him open the top of the vial. "Are you sure . . . ?"

"Had I not been certain it would help you, I would not have brought it," Bright Arrow replied. "And what is it made from? From the bones of the lingcod, a fish that is normally eaten by sharks and seals. The bones wash up on the beach in the winter. My uncle collects them for his medicine. He has boiled these into a delicious broth. Drink. You shall see that it has a taste that pleases you."

Kathia winced at this description of exactly how the medicine had been made, expecting it to taste as awful as it sounded.

But trusting everything Bright Arrow did, she nodded. "Yes, I will drink it," she murmured. "Thank you for bringing it. Nothing Doc Raley has done yet has helped my throat, or my fever."

As Bright Arrow lifted her head slightly from the pillow, then placed the tip of the vial to her lips, Kathia drank the tangy-tasting liquid.

She felt a quick relief, surprised at how soothing the brew was to her sore throat.

Bright Arrow took the vial from her lips, easing her head back down onto the pillow.

He smiled down at her as she closed her eyes and drifted back to sleep. He kissed her, then left through the side doors.

Up in the lighthouse, where Dusty was in control of the beams, he jumped in alarm when he saw a huge bird flying over the water. The beams of the lighthouse caught it just before the mysterious creature flew into the dark shadows of the forest.

Dusty swallowed hard. He was frightened. Never in his life had he seen such a huge bird.

And its eyes. They seemed to blaze with fire.

He shuddered as a fear he could not control spiraled through him.

The lighthouse beams fell upon the sea and the rocky shore just as he saw Doc Raley beach his small boat. Fred stood waiting on the beach for him.

Surely Kathia was no better, or the doctor would not have been summoned at this time of night.

He gazed skyward again and followed the trail of the beams as they lit up low-hanging clouds, his eyes searching for any sign of the huge bird.

A part of him was glad that he didn't see it any longer. Yet a part of him would have liked to have seen it again so that he could be sure he had not gone temporarily insane.

There could *not* be such a bird. Surely it had been his imagination.

A noise behind him made Dusty turn abruptly.

He sighed heavily with relief when he saw that it was only Fred. "What are you doing here?" Dusty breathed out. "I saw you only moments ago meeting Doc Raley's boat."

"You saw right," Fred said, ambling into the room, where lighted lanterns sat on his father's oak desk. "But I came up to check on you and my father's equipment."

"There you go again, calling the equipment your father's, like he bought and paid for it, when you know that it is no more his than mine," Dusty said arrogantly.

He sank down into a comfortable leather chair. He propped his feet on the desk, crossing his legs at his ankles.

He pulled out a cigar from his shirt pocket and lit

it. "Just can't trust me, can you?" he asked, his eyes gleaming strangely.

"Nope," Fred said, slowly walking around the room, checking the instruments.

"Why did you call for Doc Raley?" Dusty asked, taking the lit cigar from his mouth. "Is Kathia no better?"

"As if it's any of your damn business," Fred growled, stopping to lean his back against the wall. He folded his arms across his chest. "But since the news is good, I will share it with you."

"Good? How so?" Dusty asked, placing the cigar between his lips and drawing lazily on it.

"When Doc Raley went to check my sister, he found her sleeping peacefully and saw that her fever was gone," Fred said. "Just like that, she has improved dramatically. Doc Raley said that he expected her to be able to get out of bed tomorrow."

"Well, don't that beat all," Dusty said, again yanking the cigar from his mouth.

"While Doc Raley went to check on Father, I came here to check on you," Fred said. "I imagine Doc is through by now. I'll be escorting him back to his boat."

Dusty rose quickly from his chair. "When you were out on the beach, meeting the old doctor's boat, did you happen to see something strange in the sky?" he asked guardedly.

"Strange in what way?" Fred asked, arching an eyebrow.

"You didn't see it," Dusty said, then turned from Fred and went back to the controls.

"What did you see?" Fred persisted.

"Nothing," Dusty said. "Absolutely nothing."

Fred shrugged, then went down the spiral stairs to his father's bedroom, where Doc Raley was just closing his satchel. "There's improvement here, too," Doc Raley said, turning to smile at Fred. "Your sister is better. Your father is better. I think my medicine is doing a good job on them both."

"This morning Papa was so bad," Fred said, gazing down at his father, who was awake again and smiling. "Papa, are you certain you feel okay?"

"Tomorrow I'll be climbing those stairs up to my beams. That's how much better I feel," Melvin said. He eased back down on his pillow. "But for now? I need a few more winks of sleep."

Fred made certain the patchwork quilt was covering his father, then left the house with Doc Raley. As they walked toward the beach, Fred's eyes widened as he saw a strange sight. For an instant, he thought he saw a huge bird with gleaming eyes, then there was nothing but the darkness.

"Doc Raley, did you by chance see something unusual in the sky?" Fred asked guardedly.

"Can't say that I did," the doctor mumbled. He

was too absorbed in watching his footing on the loose rock beneath his feet to look up.

"Maybe I didn't either," Fred said, shrugging.

Sometimes the lighthouse beams made strange shadows in the sky and water and forest. If one did not know better, one could imagine all kinds of crazy things.

He helped Doc Raley into his boat.

"Thanks for coming this time of evening," Fred said as the doctor took his oars from the bottom of the boat.

"Any time, Fred, any time," Doc Raley said, then rowed away from the shore.

Fred watched the doctor for a while, to make certain he was far enough from the rocks to be safe. Then he looked into the forest again.

He idly scratched his brow when he saw nothing unusual, then hurried back to the house and went to his sister's bedroom.

He drew a chair up close to his sister's bed and sat down beside it.

He planned to keep vigil there for a while. For some reason he felt that he needed to make sure she was safe tonight.

His gaze moved to the French doors that led out to the side porch. Feeling uncomfortable about leaving them open now, he rose from his chair and locked the doors.

He went back and sat down beside Kathia's bed. "Sis, I'll be here when you wake up," he whispered, leaning over to brush a soft kiss across her brow.

Hearing a sound behind him, he turned his head quickly. He found nothing there, yet still a strange fear rode his spine.

Chapter Nineteen

You and I
Have so much love,
That it burns like a fire.
—Tao-sheng

The sun came softly through the window next to Kathia's bed, awakening her. She reached up to her throat, surprised that it was no longer sore.

She placed a hand on her brow. The fever was gone. She could hardly believe it. She was well.

After having been so ill and suffering from such a high temperature, she was amazed that she had recovered so quickly.

She sat up and looked out her window. It was early

morning; the sun was just now rising. It was such a beautiful day, it was good to be alive.

She got out of her bed and hurried to the French doors that led out to the small porch outside her bedroom.

She opened them and stepped out into the morning air, breathing it in. Then, suddenly, she remembered having seen the large bird there last night just before Bright Arrow appeared at her bedside.

She once again recalled what her father had said about Bright Arrow turning into a thunderbird. Then just as quickly, she told herself that it was only a legend.

"No, it *couldn't* have been him," Kathia whispered as she went back into her room and closed the door behind her.

Most of what she remembered from the previous night must have been a feverish dream, except for when Bright Arrow had been in the room.

That *had* been real, very, very real. She remembered him holding her, how she cuddled close to him. His nearness alone had given her comfort as nothing else could have during her time of sickness.

She also remembered taking medicine that Bright Arrow had brought to her. It had had a tangy taste, yet not so horrible that she could not drink all of it. She couldn't recall now what Bright Arrow had said was in the medicine. Was it some sort of bones?

It didn't matter. What was important was that she was well.

She went to the window and drew aside a sheer white curtain so she could look in the direction of his village. She was anxious to tell Bright Arrow that she was all right.

She turned and gazed at her closed bedroom door, for she was anxious, too, to see how her father was. She hoped to discover that her father had improved, as well.

Anxious to get the day started, she went to her chifferobe and chose a pretty, yellow silk dress, slipped into it, then brushed her hair until it shone.

Smiling at her reflection in the mirror, she drew her hair back into a long golden braid, one of her favorite ways of wearing it. Then she hurried from her room to her father's.

Slowly she opened the door and found that he was still asleep. She was uncertain what to do. Allow him to sleep longer? Or wake him before she left for Bright Arrow's village?

But she had someone else on her mind, too. Her brother. She wanted him to know that she was all better.

Deciding that she had to know whether her father was all right before she left the house, she bent low over him and kissed his brow, then spoke his name.

When his eyes opened and he smiled up at her,

she knew that he, too, was improved today. Not completely well, but improved. That was all she asked for, to know that he was again feeling better.

"Well, seems Doc Raley did a good job with you," Melvin said, slowly moving to a sitting position. "Just look at you. Your color is normal. Your eyes are beaming. And your smile makes my old heart sing."

Her smile faded at the mention of Doc Raley. "Papa, I don't remember Doc Raley being here to see me," she murmured, easing down on the edge of the bed.

"You were asleep," Melvin said. "He didn't want to awaken you. Whatever he did, it worked."

She smiled quietly at him, for she did not believe that her being well had anything to do with Doc Raley. She was convinced that she was better because of what Bright Arrow had given her, and because he had held her in his arms.

He was her medicine!

But of course, she could not tell her father or Fred that Bright Arrow had been at the lighthouse in the middle of the night. They wouldn't approve, or understand.

"Doc Raley is good for both of us," Melvin said, nodding. "I am much better today, but not yet strong enough to go up the stairs to my beams. My old legs just won't get me there. Dusty will have to stay awhile longer."

Kathia hugged her father, then sat down on the

chair next to his bed. She held his hand as she gazed into his eyes. "Papa, please quit referring to yourself as old. You're as young as you allow yourself to be. And Papa, I am so glad that you have improved so much, but I can't understand how you can be better one hour and so ill again the next," she murmured. "It's truly mysterious. But the important thing is that you are better today. I won't complain, that's for sure."

"I don't understand it either, but I am glad for these moments when I *am* feeling better," Melvin said. He patted her hand with his free one. "Honey, sometimes when one gets older, strange things happen to one's body. I guess I'm proof of that. But I tell you one thing, I'm fighting this with all my power. I'm not one to give up easily."

Kathia smiled softly at him. "I know," she murmured. "You've always been a fighter."

"Yes, a fighter," Melvin said, then sighed heavily. "Honey, you go on and do what you have planned today. Mariah will bring me my breakfast soon and see to my bath. Don't let this old fogy get in the way of what you want to do. Lord, it's good to see that sparkle in your eyes again, and the flush gone from your cheeks that the fever caused. I love seeing the rosiness that is your normal color."

"Papa, there you go again," Kathia said, sighing heavily. "That word 'old.' You might feel old now, but one of these days real soon you'll be as fit as a fiddle. I know how anxious you are to get upstairs to check things out."

She shuddered. "Papa, I hate it that Dusty has to stay longer. But I understand why he must. I know you believe he's capable of controlling the lights. He's not done anything yet to prove that he isn't. It's just his attitude. It stinks, Papa. It stinks."

She took her hand from his and stood up. She bent low and kissed his brow. "Papa, please don't rush back to work," she murmured as she stood and gazed worriedly down at him. "Although I know how badly you want to climb those stairs and get back to your business, you just can't rush into doing things yet. You could have another relapse."

"Yes, another relapse," Melvin said, nodding. "I'm going to get another wink of sleep. What does the morning hold for you?"

"It's a beautiful day, so I plan to go horseback riding," Kathia said. She glanced over at the window, where it was raised just enough for the gentle breeze to blow over her father's bed. She smiled again at him. "Papa, spring seems to have arrived overnight. The rains have woken the flowers from their winter sleep. I am ready to experience it all."

"Be careful, hon," Melvin said, scooting down, getting his head comfortable again on the feather pillow. "Don't go to places that are unfamiliar to you. Be sure to watch where you are riding. There is quicksand in some areas."

"I know," Kathia said, again brushing a kiss across his brow. "When I return home, I'll let you know that I'm here. I don't want to worry you needlessly."

"That's good," Melvin said, yawning.

His eyes were already shut when Kathia left the room, softly closing the door behind her.

She glanced down the corridor at the door to Dusty's room. She could hear him snoring even from this distance. That meant he was still in the room, not somewhere else where she might bump into him. She avoided him as much as possible.

"Sis!"

Fred's voice behind her made Kathia turn and smile at her brother.

"Sis, I'm so glad to see you are up and about," Fred said, coming to hug her. Then he placed his hands at her waist and held her away from him. "What sort of miracle is this? You look a hundred percent well. Last night I was very concerned about you."

"As Papa always says when he feels better, I feel as fit as a fiddle," Kathia said, laughing softly.

"How about eating breakfast with me?" Fred said. "I'm smelling some mighty good aromas coming from the kitchen. I think I detect pancakes."

"Maybe I should take time to eat, but I truly don't have my appetite back just yet," Kathia said. "I think I'll take a ride on my horse. I'd love to have the morning air in my face. I love the forest smells."

"Sis, be careful," Fred said.

"Big brother, how can anything happen to me when I have two men keeping such a close eye on me?" she said, laughing softly, thinking that she actually had three men watching out for her, for Bright Arrow was the third.

"After breakfast I plan to go to the Makah village and see if they will let me take more photos today," Fred said, walking down the corridor with Kathia. "Every day more and more are willing."

"Fred, be careful not to go too quickly with this," Kathia urged. "Don't take advantage of their innocence. Please?"

"Sis, must I remind you that what I am doing will help, not harm them?" Fred said, stopping at the front door. "When my book is published, I will be teaching all white people about the Makah, and how they have been taken advantage of by the white community."

"And how do you know that?" Kathia asked. She grabbed a knitted shawl from a coatrack and placed it around her shoulders.

"I've made friends with several Makah children," Fred said. "They talk openly with me."

"You know that friendship is based on the coins you give them for posing," Kathia said, tying the shawl at her throat. She opened the door, again inhaling the fragrance of the morning air.

"For now, that's all I need," Fred said, leaning

down to kiss her. "Be careful, Sis. You might not be as strong as you think you are."

"You worry too much," Kathia said, then swung away from him and hurried to the corral.

A minute later she was riding her horse across the countryside. She loved this feeling of freedom. She loved the idea that she might see Bright Arrow soon.

She smiled at the thought of how he would react when he saw that she was well enough to ride.

She headed the horse in the direction of the Makah village. She had just entered the thick forest, when she heard a familiar voice.

Her heart skipped a beat, for the voice was Bright Arrow's. She dismounted and tethered her horse's reins to a low tree limb, then walked until she saw Bright Arrow. He was sitting beside a creek, praying.

Touched by the sight, and by the sound of his voice and what he was saying, Kathia stopped and watched him.

He looked so spiritual. She truly didn't feel that she should interfere in his private moment. She started to leave, but stopped in midstep when her horse whinnied.

Bright Arrow's steed whinnied back to hers.

Bright Arrow leaped to his feet, turned, and saw her. He smiled and reached a hand out toward her.

"You are well," he murmured.

Smiling, Kathia nodded and went to him. He took her by the hand.

"Yes, I am well, and I have you to thank for it," Kathia said, laughing softly. "Had you not come . . ."

She noticed the fingers of his other hand were closed over something.

"I feel as though I am interfering," she murmured. "I'd best go."

"No. Please stay, at least for a moment," Bright Arrow said. "All of my people pray at every sunrise. My Makah people know their lives depend on the Great Spirit above, so each prays in secret at sunrise. Each has his or her own way of praying."

He opened his left hand and showed her a black rock. "I hold this rock as I pray, so that I will be strong like the rock," he said thickly.

She found that symbolism mystical and beautiful.

"It works," she said, smiling at him. "I have never met such a strong man, yet one who is also kind, generous, and filled with love and compassion. Thank you for coming to me last night with your people's medicine. As you can see, it worked. I am well."

"And how is your father?" he asked softly.

"He is better, too," she murmured.

He slid the rock into his left front pocket, then embraced her. He kissed her, then stepped away from her.

He held her hand as he led her down beside him on a soft bed of moss near the creek.

"When will you go whale hunting?" she murmured, loving the way he slid his arm around her waist and drew her closer to him.

"Tomorrow," he said. "My heart pounds at the thought of boarding my hunting canoe for the first time this season."

He turned to her. "I wish that I could stay longer with you today, but my warriors have been told to meet me in council after their morning prayers," he explained. "We are to make final plans for the great whale hunt tomorrow."

"I understand," Kathia said softly. "I should return home, anyway, and make certain Father is still doing well."

"I wish I could go with you and give your father my good wishes, but I truly must get back to my duties as chief," Bright Arrow said. He drew her into his embrace again. "My woman, when I am not with you, I feel incomplete."

His words made Kathia's insides melt. She twined her arms around his neck, and when he kissed her, she felt as though she were floating.

When he released her, she wanted to fling herself into his arms again and never let go, yet she knew that his duties called him, and she did wish to see if her father's improvement was a lasting one.

Hand in hand, they walked to her horse. He helped her into the saddle, and before letting go of her hands he kissed the palm of one, then stepped away from her.

"I shall see you again soon," he said to her.

"Yes, soon," Kathia said.

She wheeled her horse around and rode from him. She was scarcely aware of being in the saddle, for she was still floating rapturously. She was hardly aware of anything until she found herself at the corral.

She laughed softly at her behavior, and how different it was for her. Normally she was absorbed in her career, not a man.

After leaving her horse unsaddled, with its nose buried in a bucket of fresh oats, Kathia almost skipped to the house, then rushed up the steps and hurried inside.

She slung her shawl over the coatrack, then stopped abruptly when Fred came from their father's room, a frown creasing his brow.

"What is it?" she said, rushing to him. "What's happened?"

"I just checked on Papa," Fred said, taking her hands. "Sis, he is in that damn semi-coma again. He . . . he . . . won't awaken. He doesn't respond to his name, not even when I raise my voice while speaking it."

"No," Kathia gasped.

She hurried away from Fred and went inside her father's bedroom.

She paled at the sight of her father. He had been all right when she had left him. But now his skin had a strange sort of pallor to it.

She bent low and whispered his name in his ear. He didn't respond.

"He won't wake up, Sis," Fred said as he came to her side. "No matter what I do, he won't wake up."

"Before I left, he was okay," Kathia said, tears filling her eyes. "What could have happened in such a short time?"

"I'm going for Doc Raley," Fred said, hurrying from the room.

Kathia paced, her eyes never leaving her father.

Dusty had stood outside in the corridor and heard Fred and Kathia's alarm over their father's failing health.

He stood in the kitchen now, smiling as he rinsed out the cup that Melvin had used to drink the tea Dusty had made for him.

Snickering, pleased as punch at what he had just done, he replaced the cup with the others in the cabinet, then slid a hand inside his front right breeches' pocket. He smiled evilly when he circled his fingers around a small bottle.

He brought the bottle out and laughed as he

looked at the white powder inside it. Just a few sprinkles of that powder, and puff, like magic, Melvin was worse again.

He chuckled as he put the bottle back into hiding in his pocket and hurried to his room, closing the door behind him. He went to the window and watched Fred rowing his boat out toward The Point, to get Doc Raley.

So far the idiot doctor hadn't gotten suspicious about what was causing Melvin's health to change so abruptly. Dusty had made certain to use the right amount of the powder, for if anyone ever suspected what he was doing, he would be hanged for the deed!

"I'll do anything to make certain my services will still be needed at the lighthouse, at least for a while longer," he whispered to himself.

No sirree. He wasn't finished here. Not just yet, anyhow.

Chapter Twenty

Wild nights! Wild nights!
Were I with thee,
Wild nights should be
Our true luxury.
—Emily Dickinson

Kathia could hardly quell her excitement. She knew that this was the first day that Bright Arrow and his warriors would be out in their huge canoes, hunting whales.

Kathia watched from the lighthouse windows, glad that Dusty was asleep, so she could be there alone.

Today, her father was better again. She was relieved, yet puzzled more and more by the strange pattern of his illness.

Doc Raley was at the end of his rope, for he had no idea what to do next for her father. It was a mystery to everyone, but all that mattered now was that her father was better today, and had even tried to leave his bed to take a few steps.

The doctor had told him that he must exercise his legs if he was ever to climb the stairs again to get to his beloved beams.

Lifting the binoculars to her eyes, Kathia slowly scanned the sea for Bright Arrow's canoe. He had told her that he would be hunting today. The men would not go far out to sea, for he had spied whales much closer to land than usual.

He had got his first sighting of the mighty gray whale yesterday after his council with his warriors.

The thrill of possibly seeing him at the hunt made Kathia's heart pump wildly within her chest.

But so far, she had not seen any canoes, only huge ships far out at sea, probably on their way to and from Seattle, or Port Angeles, her home.

She could not deny missing Port Angeles. And because she did, she could not help wondering if she could truly give up the life she had known for so long. Could she live in a longhouse with none of the luxuries that she was accustomed to?

She forced such concerns from her mind, for at this moment just the thought of glimpsing the man she loved was enough to have her jumping out of bed with eagerness.

She could hardly get up the spiral staircase quickly enough, for she did not want to miss seeing Bright Arrow and his warriors should they come in this direction for their hunt.

She held the binoculars steady, glad that the day was pretty and calm, without clouds, wind, or high waves at sea. She wanted the man she adored to be safe on his first hunt of the season.

Just before dawn, Bright Arrow and his fellow hunters had left their village together, heading out toward the feeding grounds of the great gray whale a few miles off shore.

Bright Arrow's new yew-wood harpoon was held in his tight grip, ready for the first sighting. His eyes watched the water, where yesterday whales had been seen passing by on their spring migration north.

Bright Arrow knew that whaling was a most dangerous endeavor. Few took up the quest. Few enjoyed the prestige of a successful hunt.

He hoped that enough rituals had been performed to ensure his warriors' safety, and that the whales would consent to be taken, giving the Makah plenty to eat and enough oil to trade.

Strong, silent paddling had quickly brought Bright Arrow's thirty-six-foot cedar canoe to the area where the whales had been sighted. There were eight men in his canoe, each one strong, each hoping they would soon be floating their catch right onto the sandy beach by the village.

His people would meet them with songs and ceremony, welcoming the whale as an honored guest so others would come.

Bright Arrow had been patiently waiting for favorable weather for his first day of hunting. This day *was* that perfect day. Surely the whales would surface again.

Suddenly his heart skipped a beat. He had spotted an *eh-koi-i*, a gray whale.

So had the men in the canoe with him, as well as the warriors in other close-by canoes. But Bright Arrow's was the lead canoe today. It was Bright Arrow's place to hurl the first harpoon of the hunting season.

His warriors paddled slowly and as silently as possible toward the spot where the whale had surfaced, then disappeared back into the water.

Still paddling silently, the whalers studied the breathing pattern of their quarry. They knew from experience what to expect.

As the whale appeared again, spouted and returned underwater, Bright Arrow directed his crew to where it would next surface. Once there, they waited.

When the whale rose from the water again, the

paddlers held the canoe just to its left, then followed it, their speed matched to the animal's.

Again it made a deep dive. Again the hunters hurriedly paddled to where they believed it would surface again.

Then, as the back of the whale did break the surface, Bright Arrow raised his harpoon and took his first catch of the season.

After going through all the rituals known by many generations of Makah, in order to ready the whale for its arrival on land, the next step was to tow the dead whale home. It was not far, for the spirit of the whale had heeded the Makah's prayers to swim close to their village.

With the whale's heavy carcass secured at the side of the canoe, the Makah warriors broke into song to ease the struggle of paddling.

The warriors' songs also welcomed the *eh-koi-i* to the village, as did the songs of Bright Arrow's people, praising the power that made it all possible.

Bright Arrow was proud to again prove his importance to his people. Many of them, men, women, and children alike, dove into the water and swam toward his mighty canoe and the whale that meant everything to them.

The winter had been long. The spring was not as long. It would pass by quickly.

Many hunts were necessary to get the Makah through another long winter! But the first one was the most important. It gave the people confidence that there would be many more successful hunts.

Kathia had not actually seen the capture of the whale, but the sound of songs coming from the direction of the Makah village told her that the people must have something to be happy and to sing about.

"The hunt must have been successful," she whispered to herself as she lowered the binoculars and set them on her father's oak desk.

She longed to go to the village and see the excitement there that a successful hunt would bring.

She hadn't seen Fred today and wondered if he was going to the village to take photographs again. Would the Makah allow him to be among them at such a time as this? Or was it a private celebration?

And would they ever allow her to be among them at such a time? She decided that until she was asked, she would stay home.

She would help her father learn to walk again, since he was so eager to regain his mobility. She understood. He had been away from his beams for far too long already.

She made her way down the spiral staircase, then went to her father's room. She was relieved to see that he was still all right. These past days it seemed that just as she had hope of her father's full recovery, he would worsen again.

She was afraid that one of these days he would not survive one of those relapses. The thought of losing him made her shudder, for her father was everything to her and Fred.

Although they led their separate lives now, which took them away from their father, they both idolized him. No man could ever be as good and kind as Melvin Parrish.

"Except Bright Arrow," she whispered, again aware of the singing coming from the direction of Bright Arrow's village.

It took all her willpower not to leave the house and join in the excitement. But today she would center her full attention on her father.

"Bright Arrow," she whispered, and just the sound of his name made a sensual thrill course through her veins.

She smiled when she recalled a time when she was a schoolgirl of ten and had a crush on a boy in her class. She would spend a lot of her time in that class just writing his name over and over again in her notebook. Seeing the name brought him closer to her.

Now speaking Bright Arrow's name was much more exciting than those innocent moments of puppy love so long ago.

She hurried down the corridor, then stopped when again the singing wafted through a window in the parlor.

"Should I?" she whispered, wavering. "Or shouldn't I?"

"Kathia!"

The sound of her father's voice stiffened her resolve.

She wanted to spend a lot of time with her father today to keep an eye on him. If he worsened while she was there, perhaps she could figure out why.

It always seemed to happen when she and Fred weren't around.

She hurried into her father's room and caught him standing beside his bed, fully clothed, his cane in hand.

"Papa, should you have dressed?" Kathia asked, crossing to him. "I think you should remain in your sleeping gown, so that when you tire yourself out trying to walk, you can go immediately back to bed."

"I can go to bed and rest just as easily in my clothes as I can in that damnable gown," he fussed. "I'm tired of being puny, especially looking puny. In clothes, I feel almost human again."

"Well, if you insist," Kathia said, taking him gently by an elbow. "Come on. Let's start with short walks here in the room, just back and forth for a while, and then to bed you go again."

"No, I want to go to the stairs," Melvin grumbled. "Let me at least give it a try."

"Papa, that isn't wise," Kathia softly argued. "Please listen to me. Today, let's just stroll around the room for a while. Tomorrow? Perhaps if you are still as strong, and continue to improve, you can go to the steps and take a couple, but not all of them."

"You should've been a nurse, not a ballerina," Melvin said, chuckling.

"Well, I don't know about that," Kathia said, laughing softly. "Come on, Papa. Please let's just take a few steps at a time, rest, and then take some more."

"Well, all right," Melvin said.

As he took his first step, with Kathia helping him, Melvin glanced over at the window, which was half open, the breeze wafting through the sheer curtains and bringing in the singing that came with the breeze, as well.

"What's going on at the Makah village?" Melvin asked, raising an eyebrow. "It is the Indians singing, isn't it?"

"I imagine their whale hunt has been successful," Kathia said. "I imagine they are celebrating."

"Ah, yes, I do recall how they like to sing after the first successful hunt," Melvin said, groaning when his lame leg almost buckled beneath him. Determined to get well, he didn't give in to the pain, or weakness.

Holding her father's arm firmly, Kathia pictured the Makah village. She could almost see the pride in Bright Arrow's eyes. He had told her that he would be the one to cast the first harpoon.

How she longed to be there in person. Perhaps tomorrow?

Chapter Twenty-one

I love thee to the level of every day's
Most quiet need, by sun and candlelight.
I love thee freely, as men strive for Right;
I love thee purely, as they turn from Praise.
—Elizabeth Barrett Browning

Trying again to see Bright Arrow as he hunted the mighty whale, Kathia positioned herself at the window the following day with her father's binoculars.

Like yesterday, so far she had seen no sign of any canoes. She had only seen the brilliant sky, gentle waves, and soaring seagulls.

Until now!

Her eyes widened and she peered more intently through the binoculars as she finally saw movement down below in the water. She saw canoes. Many of them.

But those aboard weren't hunters. There were women and children, as well as warriors in the canoes. And they were headed in the direction of the Makah village.

Her eyebrows rose in surprise when she suddenly heard singing and realized that this time it was not coming from the Makah village, but instead from the canoes that were passing below her.

"Why are they singing?" she whispered to herself.

Perhaps there was to be some sort of celebration at the Makah village and these people were going there to join the festivities. Could they be celebrating the first successful whaling expedition of the spring?

She felt sad that she had not been invited to be a part of it. She had not heard from Bright Arrow since their chance meeting two days earlier, when she had came upon him praying.

She was puzzled that he had ignored her since, especially after their wondrous embrace and kiss. She had expected him to come last night to tell her about his hunt . . . to share his experiences with her.

Had all their moments together—so precious to her—meant nothing to him?

Or was she wrong to feel slighted? Perhaps no one but his people could attend celebrations at the Makah village. Perhaps she would be intruding.

Then her heart skipped a beat. Fred! He had already left today. He had not told her where he was going, but she could only surmise that he would be headed for the Makah village.

If he'd gone there, had they allowed him to stay?

Or was he even now down in his room, having returned home while she was gazing out at sea.

She started to go check his room, then stopped when she saw Bright Arrow on his horse, riding toward the lighthouse.

Her heart warmed at the sight of him. Her pulse raced. He had not forgotten about her after all!

He was coming this morning to see her, even as the canoes arrived at his village.

Breathless with eagerness to see him, Kathia set the binoculars aside and hurried down the steep spiral steps. She rushed outside just as Bright Arrow drew rein and stopped.

As Kathia walked toward him, her knees weak from the passion he always aroused in her, he dismounted, then met her halfway. He reached for her hands and took them in his. They gazed at each other, their eyes searching.

Kathia longed for him to kiss her, yet knew that this was not the right place, or perhaps even the right time.

He had surely come for a reason and probably would be at the lighthouse for only a short while, for he would be needed at his village when everyone arrived there.

"Why are you here?" she blurted out.

"I have come for you," Bright Arrow said softly. "Will you come with me to my village? I would like you to see how my people celebrate the first successful whaling expedition of the spring. I would like you to be a part of it."

She was stunned to know that he had left his village at such a time to get her.

That he had thought about her when he surely had so many other things on his mind made her feel very special. Her earlier doubts were banished. She now knew that he cared for her.

Sharing such an important day as this with him was an honor.

"I watched for you through my father's binoculars yesterday to see if I could witness your first catch of the season," Kathia murmured. "I did not see you, but I did hear singing coming from your village. I was almost certain then that you had taken your first whale and brought it home to your people."

"As I had thought, our hunt did not take us as far out to sea as it often does," Bright Arrow said, smiling at her. "And yes, my warriors sang as they rowed homeward with our catch, and my people sang when they saw us approaching. It is a happy time at our village. And that is why we are having a potlatch, a celebration."

"I saw many canoes full of people headed toward your village," Kathia said. "The people in the canoes were singing. Are they going to join your people for the celebration?"

"Many will join our people," Bright Arrow said. "They are arriving for the potlatch, which I, the one who brought in the whale, am hosting."

"Potlatch?" Kathia asked, lifting her eyebrows. "You spoke that word twice to me. I am not familiar with it."

"A potlatch is a gathering where much food will be eaten, many games will be played, and where I will give away many gifts to those of other clans who join us," Bright Arrow said. "My guests will be given the best food, the finest blankets, and the most handsomely carved boxes."

He smiled somewhat mischievously. "My gifts will be reciprocated at future potlatches at other villages," he said. "Will you come and join my people? I did not send you a *hidata beys*, a formal invitation. Instead I am inviting you personally. Is your father well enough for you to leave for a while today? You might not want to stay for the entire celebration, for it will go long into the night, and perhaps even into tomorrow. But please come and be with me for a while."

"My father is doing very well," Kathia said, her eyes dancing. "And Mariah is here for him if he needs anything. Yes, I would love to go with you. But I must first let my father know."

She started to hurry away, to tell her father, then

turned and gazed at Bright Arrow again. "Have you seen my brother?" she asked. "Is he possibly at your village?"

"I have not seen him, so, no, I doubt that he is there," Bright Arrow said. He frowned slightly. "Should he come, though, it is best that he does not bring his camera. It would not be good to capture pictures during the celebration, especially with so many there who have not become acquainted with your brother and his camera, as my people have. If you see him, you might tell him that he is welcome at the village today, but not with his camera."

"I truly don't think he's home, but I shall look in his room," Kathia murmured. "And I understand about the camera. I hope that *he* will."

She turned to hurry up the steps, but stopped and turned toward Bright Arrow again. "Bright Arrow, you and Father are friends, so would you like to join me this morning as I tell him my plans?" she asked softly. "He does admire you so much."

"As I do him," Bright Arrow said, nodding. "I keep his kindness inside my heart for always. He did for me what no other man would risk doing. If not for your father, Sun Blossom would not have a true grave."

"I am so sorry about her," Kathia murmured. "But I'm so glad that Father did have the courage to recover her . . . her . . ."

"Her body," Bright Arrow said when he saw that

she was having trouble saying it. "Yes, Kathia. I would like to see your father today. I would like to give him my best wishes."

He walked up the steps with her. Inside the house, he stopped and grabbed her by the hand, turning her toward him.

"I would also like to thank him for having such a daughter as you," he said.

Kathia felt the heat of a blush rush to her cheeks.

She laughed softly, stood on tiptoe, and brushed a soft kiss across his cheek, then went on to her father's room, stopping to knock before entering.

"Enter," her father said from the other side of the door, his voice sounding so strong, so healthy, it made Kathia feel that things were finally going to be as they normally were.

Her father would be in control of the lighthouse. He would be in control of his life.

Kathia opened the door.

When she found her father fully dressed and sitting in a comfortable chair, a novel perched on his lap, she smiled broadly at him. It was such a wonderful sight. He looked so well, his cheeks their normal color, his eyes sparkling when he saw Bright Arrow with her.

"Well, what do we have here?" Melvin said, gesturing with a hand to Bright Arrow. "Come over here, young man. I've missed your hugs these past weeks."

Kathia watched as Bright Arrow gave her father a warm hug, then knelt before him as Kathia came and stood beside him.

"And how are you feeling?" Bright Arrow asked, his eyes searching Melvin's. "Kathia told me about your failing health. It looks like you are doing much better now."

"I do feel much stronger. Fit as a fiddle, as my father always said when he recovered from a long illness," Melvin said. He glanced up at Kathia, and then at Bright Arrow. "I hear you two are hitting it off mighty fine."

"We care for one another," Bright Arrow said, rising and standing beside Kathia. "Your daughter is special. I find her refreshing and wonderful."

"Refreshing and wonderful, huh?" Melvin said, chuckling. "Well, seems I agree with you a hundred percent."

"Papa, Bright Arrow has come to ask if I would like to join him at his people's potlatch," Kathia said, drawing his eyes to her again.

"Potlatch, eh?" Melvin said, nodding. "Yep, I've been to a couple, haven't I, Bright Arrow?"

"It was good to have you there so that you could receive the gifts I made especially for you," Bright Arrow said, smiling. "Have you enjoyed the box I carved for you?"

"I keep it upstairs where I control my lights," Melvin said, nodding. His thoughts went to the box. A superb craftsman, Bright Arrow had explained to him how he had bent a plank of wood cut from a soaring straight-grained cedar into a box by grooving and steaming the corners.

The container bore the image of a Thunderbird and an intriguing wooden figure of another supernatural being that had come to Bright Arrow in a dream.

Melvin considered it a masterpiece.

"I don't use the box, Bright Arrow," Melvin quickly interjected. "I keep it near as a reminder of our friendship. Thank you again, Bright Arrow. I do appreciate the gift. But more than that, I appreciate your continuing friendship. If you ever need anything that I can help you with, you know I'll give it to you."

"Right now I would like the company of your daughter for the rest of the day," Bright Arrow said, slowly sliding an arm around her waist. He noticed that Melvin's eyebrows rose at such an open gesture of affection.

"Well, son, you have it," Melvin said, feeling that for a moment he had made Bright Arrow uneasy by questioning the way the young man placed his arm around Kathia's waist. But he truly did not mind, for he knew how honorable a man this chief was. He knew Bright Arrow would never do anything that could harm the dignity of his daughter.

"Papa, Mariah will be checking in on you,"

Kathia said, bending low to kiss his brow. "And should you see Fred, you might tell him that he is invited to the potlatch, too, but not to bring his camera."

"Sis, you can tell me yourself," Fred said as he sauntered into the room.

Kathia turned with a start. "Fred, where on earth have you been?" she asked, seeing the mud on her brother's usually spotless leather boots.

"I've been exploring, I guess you could say," Fred said, shrugging idly. "I took a long stroll on the beach. When I saw that long procession of canoes and heard the singing coming from them, I headed back. I've come to change my shoes and then go on to the village. It will be a great opportunity to take many photographs if those people are all going to your village, Bright Arrow."

"They are even now at my village," Bright Arrow said, stiffening at the realization that he would have to deny Fred the "opportunity," as he called it, to use his camera today.

He did not want to anger any of Kathia's relatives, but he had no choice.

He knew that the visiting clans would not want the camera there today, for none knew what it was, and today was not the time to explain it.

It was Bright Arrow's day. He hoped his potlatch would give pleasure to many people, not cause tension because of a white man's contraption.

"I'll hurry to my room and change my shoes, then grab my camera equipment so I can accompany you to your village," Fred said, stopping when he saw a frown crease Bright Arrow's brow. "Did I say something wrong?"

Kathia stepped toward him. "Fred, you can't take your camera," she said tightly. She glanced over at Bright Arrow, and then at her brother again. "There is a celebration today at the Makah village . . . a potlatch. Your camera has no place there."

"But you are invited," Bright Arrow was quick to add. "Come with me and your sister. I shall even challenge you to a canoe race."

"Canoe race?" Fred said, raking his long, lean fingers through his coal black hair. "How can I think of a canoe race when I have just been put in my place?"

"No one has put you in your place," Melvin said firmly. "Son, Bright Arrow just doesn't want your camera at his village today. That's that. Now, either you go with your sister and Bright Arrow or you don't."

Fred glanced from his sister to Bright Arrow, his gaze holding on Bright Arrow. "All right, I'll accept the challenge," he said, his lips curving into a slow smile. "And I understand about the camera. I appreciate your allowing me to use it at all, so I am not going to argue about not being able to bring it this one day."

Kathia flung herself into her brother's arms.

"Thank you," she whispered in his ear. "I know how disappointed you are. Thank you for not spoiling the day."

"Sis, you don't need to thank me," Fred whispered back, so that no one but she could hear. "I'm going to make Bright Arrow pay by beating him in the race."

Kathia found that very humorous, for she had never seen her brother man any canoe, much less those used by the Makah, which were huge and heavy.

"There is one thing I did not tell you," Bright Arrow said, smiling at Kathia as she stepped away from Fred. "Fred, you will not be alone in the canoe. I will make certain three of my strongest warriors are in the canoe with you. But understand this, Fred, those with me will be just as strong."

"And may the best man, or should I say *men*, win," Fred said, looking down at his father and seeing the delight he was taking in this. His interest warmed Fred's heart through and through. His father *was* on the road to recovery. Today Fred would be able to truly relax and enjoy himself, as would his sister!

"Hurry, Fred, and get out of those muddy shoes," Kathia said, shooing him away with her hands. "We'll be right here, waiting for you."

"It does my old heart good to see you youngsters enjoying yourselves after worrying so much about this old codger these past weeks," Melvin said. He sighed heavily. "Let me tell you, it's wonderful to feel good again. I want you to go today and have barrels of fun, Kathia. Do you hear? Don't you take one moment of your time worrying about me. I'm going to be able to go up those stairs real soon and see to my beams."

"I will feel safer at sea if you are there," Bright Arrow said, glancing toward the door when he thought that he saw someone lurking in the corridor.

He hurried past Kathia and looked from side to side, then stared at a door at the far end of the corridor. It was just closing. Whomever that room belonged to had been eavesdropping outside this door.

He turned to Kathia. "Come and tell me whose door that is at the far end of the corridor," he said.

"That's Dusty's," she said, then glanced quickly at Bright Arrow. "Why do you ask?"

"I believe he was sneaking around, up to no good," Bright Arrow explained. He gazed into her eyes. "That man is not trustworthy. I will be glad when he is no longer in charge of the lights. I do not like to think of him being under the same roof as you, Kathia."

"He won't be here for much longer," Kathia said, then soon forgot the conversation when Fred came from his room, his boots changed, and a broad smile on his face.

"I'll challenge you to a horse race as we head toward your village, Bright Arrow," he said, his eyes twinkling.

"No, no more challenges today," Kathia interrupted. "It's too beautiful outside to ruin it by getting all sweaty and rumpled in a horse race."

"Ah, well, I guess I can wait until we get in the canoes," Fred said, chuckling.

They all took turns hugging Melvin, then left, and were soon on their horses headed toward the village.

Something made Kathia turn and look back at the house.

When she caught Dusty standing at a window, his eyes peering at her, she got an eerie, uncomfortable feeling, but knew that she had to shake it off. She had no choice but to accept his presence in the house, at least for a few more days.

But once her father was well? She would be the one to place Dusty's suitcase outside the door and bid him a sincere, heartfelt adieu!

Chapter Twenty-two

Love? I will tell thee what it is to love!
It is to build with human thoughts a shrine,
Where Hope sits brooding like a beauteous dove;
Where time seems young, and Life a thing
divine!
—Charles Swain

The aroma of food wafted through the air from several small fires, where women stood preparing an assortment of dishes for the crowd to eat once the gift-giving and games were finished.

Bright Arrow had told Kathia that today many favorite foods from the Ozette fishing grounds would be served. There would be sweet rock cod, halibut, and blueback.

Some of the fish would be eaten raw, while others would be roasted or boiled in a water-filled box or steamed in a wrapping of salal leaves.

Kathia sat beside Bright Arrow on a mat filled with the down of cattails. She was in awe of the gifts he was giving to the visitors from other villages. They had received the finest blankets, food, bolts of cloth that he had bought for this purpose in Port Angeles and Seattle, and beautiful carved boxes, made by his own hands.

As she continued to watch, she recalled what he had said about giving so many gifts . . . that his gifts would be reciprocated at future potlatches. She guessed he meant potlatches that would be held elsewhere.

She glanced over at him, at his broad smile as he continued to give things to those who stepped up for them. Today he was dressed in what appeared to be his finest clothes: fringed buckskins that were beautifully embroidered on the front. His black hair shone from a brushing and flowed down his straight back to his waist.

Kathia loved to touch his hair, to feel its thickness, its sleekness.

She trembled with passion when she thought of how she had twined her arms around his neck, how her arms rested against his hair as they embraced and kissed.

And his smell. It was so clean, as though he was bathed with the sweet air of the forest.

"The gift-giving is finished," Bright Arrow announced, bringing Kathia's thoughts back to the present. "There now will be games!"

"Foot races!" a young brave shouted from the crowd. "Let us first have foot races."

"Foot races it will be," Bright Arrow said, standing. "Those who wish to participate, gather together down on the beach."

He turned to Kathia. "I will not join in this game," he said. "Come with me to watch?"

"Yes, I'd love to," she murmured, then followed Bright Arrow's gaze as he looked past her at Fred. "Do you wish to stand with us? Or would you prefer to join the foot races?"

"I don't think I want to participate in foot races, but, yes, I would like to join you and Kathia to watch them," Fred said, smiling from Bright Arrow to Kathia.

They followed along with the crowd toward the beach.

"And when will the canoe races begin?" Fred asked, bringing Bright Arrow's eyes back to him.

"So you still wish to challenge me?" Bright Arrow said, his eyes gleaming.

"Fred, you haven't been in any canoes like the Makah's," Kathia said quickly. "Surely you aren't serious about the race."

"Yes, I am," Fred said, his eyes gleaming as eagerly as Bright Arrow's.

"The canoe race will come after the foot races," Bright Arrow said, then leaned low next to Kathia's ear. "Do not worry about your brother. As I said earlier, he will not be alone in this race. Three of my strongest, best canoeists will be with him."

"You act as though you might want him to win," Kathia replied so that only he could hear.

"I only give gifts away, not races," Bright Arrow said, laughing softly.

"And you gave away so many gifts," Kathia said, her voice no longer so low that Fred couldn't hear. "I was amazed at how much you gave, and at *what* you gave."

"It is necessary," Bright Arrow said, watching as the young braves congregated on the beach, choosing partners. "In the process of giving gifts, the potlatch cements relationships between families, as well as economic ties between villages."

"Maybe that's what the United States Government should do to make things better in the world," Kathia said, stopping with Bright Arrow at the front of the crowd. Fred had stepped farther back, to watch alone.

Kathia saw Fred eyeing the canoes worriedly.

"White missionaries and Indian agents see the potlatch as wasteful," Bright Arrow said, his smile gone. "So, no, potlatches will never be practiced in the white world."

Suddenly the festivities were interrupted by the sound of a horse approaching at a fast gallop, and by someone shouting Kathia's name.

She turned and felt the color drain from her face when she saw Dusty Harper riding hard toward the beach. People parted to allow him through the crowd, sweat streaming from his brow.

Her eyes met his as he stopped, then dismounted and hurried to her. "Kathia, your father has taken a turn for the worse," he said, glancing over at Fred as he came and stood beside Kathia. "Mariah came to me and asked me to fetch you. She says that Doc Raley is needed. Do you want me to go for him?"

Stunned by the news, especially since her father had been so well these past two days, Kathia was at a loss for words.

"How could this be?" Fred demanded, stepping up to Dusty.

"I don't know," Dusty said, shrugging. He wiped sweat from his brow with the back of his hand. "I was in the control room shining the instruments. I heard Mariah shouting my name at the foot of the stairs. I hurried down and found your father slumped over in his chair."

"And . . . ?" Kathia finally found the words to say.

"I put him in bed and left immediately to come

and tell you," Dusty said thickly. "Should I have gone for Doc Raley first, you second?"

"No, you did the right thing," Kathia said, brushing past him and running toward the corral where her horse had been turned out with the Makah's. "Fred! Come on! Time is wasting!"

Fred grabbed Dusty by the collar. "Something smells mighty fishy here, and I don't mean the smell of fish coming from the ocean," he growled out. "It's strange how Father always worsens when Kathia and I are gone, and that you . . . seem . . . to always be there."

"I didn't do anything," Dusty choked out. "Let go, Fred. This isn't the time to take your frustrations out on anyone, especially not me. I came for you. I didn't have to, you know."

"No, you didn't have to, but you did, perhaps to cover up your guilt for something you might be doing to Father," Fred said, tightening his grip on Dusty's collar.

"Fred!" Kathia screamed as she mounted her horse. "Leave him be. Come on. We must get to Father. Now!"

Bright Arrow was not sure what to do. He knew that he was expected to stay for the rest of the potlatch. But he also wanted to go with Kathia.

Yet he knew that was not where he belonged, not when so many of his people depended on him.

He could, at least, give her encouragement. He

ran to her just as she grabbed her reins and was ready to ride off.

"I will come later," he said quickly. "After everyone is settled in and eating. I won't be missed then."

"Bright Arrow, I appreciate your wanting to be there with me, but I feel your people would resent me and my brother if you were to leave," Kathia said softly. "Please wait until your guests are gone, and then come. I only hope that when I get home I will find my father not so ill, after all. Dusty might only want to frighten me. He enjoys my misery."

"He is a man without a conscience," Bright Arrow said, then stepped back when Fred rode up beside Kathia. "My heart and prayers go with you both."

"Thank you," Kathia murmured, tears splashing from her eyes.

She so badly wanted to blurt out that she loved him but knew she could not reveal such serious feelings before so many witnesses.

Instead, she gave him another soft smile, then rode off with Fred. Dusty soon caught up with them as they raced for home.

When they reached the house, Kathia went breathlessly to her father's room.

Her knees almost buckled beneath her when she saw his condition. Mariah had changed him from his clothes into his gown and his face was so pale, it looked as though all color had drained from it.

He was in a deep sleep. And there was drool again coming from one corner of his mouth.

"Papa," Kathia sobbed as she fell on her knees next to the bed and took his hand in hers. She quickly released it when she found it clammy and cold. She gave Fred a quick, worried glance. "Go for Doc Raley. Quick!"

"I can send Dusty," Fred said, his eyes wavering.

"No, Fred, you go," Kathia said. "I don't want that snake involved in our personal problems. Yes, he came for us; I'm grateful for that. But I don't trust him, otherwise. He might take his dear sweet time going for Doc Raley. I don't want to chance it."

"I'll hurry as fast as I can," Fred said, rushing from the room.

"Yes, hurry," she whispered as she again took her father's hand, this time clinging to it.

A sob caught in her throat, then she whispered, "Big brother, pretend you are in that race with Bright Arrow. Go as fast as you possibly can!"

Bright Arrow.

Tears spilled from her eyes as she recalled the concern on his face when she rode away from him. She could tell that he had wanted to accompany her.

But she knew his departure would have begun her relationship with his people on the wrong note, for they would blame her for his leaving the potlatch.

"Kathia?"

Her father's voice made Kathia jump with alarm,

and then she felt hope once again when she saw his eyes opening.

"Papa, you had another relapse," she murmured. "Do you know what might have caused it?"

"No . . ." he said weakly. "I was . . . I was . . ."

Without finishing what he was saying, he closed his eyes and fell into that same strange sleep that she had seen too often of late.

"Papa, you were *what?*" Kathia softly cried as she tried to get him to respond.

When he didn't, tears streamed from her eyes. "Oh, Papa, Papa," she whispered, choking on a sob.

She hurried to the window and gazed out to sea. "Hurry, Fred," she whispered. "Hurry!"

Chapter Twenty-three

His heart in me keeps him and me in one,
My heart in him his thoughts and senses
guides.
—Sir Philip Sidney

"He is so much better today," Kathia murmured as she walked with Bright Arrow toward her father's room.

When Bright Arrow had come the previous evening to see how her father was, he had not stayed for long. Melvin was too weak for visitors.

Kathia was glad that he had come again today, which proved just how much he did care about her father, and *her*.

When she was with him, she felt as though she were glowing, she felt so wonderful and warm.

It was so strange, though, how only weeks ago she would never have thought she would be in love, much less with a powerful Indian chief, and yet there she was.

She was in love and actually contemplating giving everything up for him.

To be able to wake up every morning and to go to bed each night in his arms would surely be paradise.

But she did have to make certain she would not miss her dancing once she was married. If she pined over her career, her dissatisfaction could tear them apart.

And when she got married, she wanted it to be forever and ever, as it had been for her parents.

"I could not stay away," Bright Arrow said, stepping up to Melvin's door with Kathia. "Last night I did not rest for worrying about your father, and *you*. I saw how his illness was tearing you apart."

"Thank you for caring so much about both of us," Kathia murmured. Before opening the door, she turned to him and twined her arms around his neck. "I care so much for *you*. I . . . I . . . love you, Bright Arrow. So very, very much."

He swept his arms around her waist and drew her even closer to him. "As I do you," he said thickly. "When I go to sleep at night, you are there in my dreams. When I am awake, you are there in my mind's eye. You are in my heart, both day and night."

He lowered his lips to hers and gave her a tender, sweet kiss. Her lips responded, her heart singing.

But when they heard footsteps coming down the spiral stairs that led from the lighthouse control room, they moved quickly apart.

They turned in time to see Dusty Harper step into view, his eyes narrowing when he saw them together. No words were exchanged, only glares. And then Dusty hurried on to his room.

"I have such strange feelings about that man," Kathia said, her voice drawn. "I am so afraid that he has something to do with my father being ill so often. But what could he be doing?"

She turned to Bright Arrow. "Let's go on inside and see how Father is doing now," she said, her voice breaking. "Thank you again for coming."

She reached for the doorknob, then turned back to Bright Arrow. "Did your guests leave?" she murmured. "Was your potlatch all that you wished it to be?"

"All were gone by this morning," Bright Arrow said. "And, yes, it was all that I had wanted it to be. My people enjoyed themselves." He took one of her hands in his. "It would have been much better, though, had you been there to enjoy it all with me."

"I shall be there with you the next time you have a gathering," Kathia said softly. "I do so want to share everything with you. I want to learn everything about your people."

"I will teach you," Bright Arrow said, leaning to brush a kiss across her lips.

Sighing contentedly, feeling as though she were walking on clouds, she opened the door.

When she stepped into the room, Bright Arrow at her side, she was relieved to see her father sitting up in bed, enjoying the breakfast that Mariah had brought to him on a tray. The smell of bacon and eggs wafted across the room toward them.

"Well, look who's here again to see this old, ailing man," Melvin said, smiling at Bright Arrow. "I heard that you were here last night, too. Sorry I didn't know. Usually I welcome your visits."

"Yes, I know, and I enjoy our time together, too," Bright Arrow said, walking over to the bed with Kathia. He gazed down at Melvin. "You are very much improved. That is good."

Melvin reached a hand up for Bright Arrow.

Bright Arrow took it and held it for a moment, then released it.

"I'm not sure what's going on with me," Melvin said, nodding toward the tray, so Kathia would remove it.

She was pleased that he had eaten almost everything on his plate, and had drunk a full cup of hot chocolate, his favorite drink.

"Papa, it's so strange the way your condition flip-flops from well to sick to well again," Kathia said, placing the tray on the bedside table. "Maybe this time you will stay well for good."

"I feel weaker from this last attack," Melvin said, scooting down to rest his head on the pillow. He closed his eyes. "I'm not certain how many more of these strange attacks my poor old ticker can stand."

"Papa, *please* don't talk like that," Kathia said. She leaned down and placed her hand on his brow, to see if he had a temperature. She was relieved when she discovered that he didn't.

"Doc Raley is here," Fred said as he came into the room with the old doctor.

"And I'm staying a good portion of the day," Doc Raley said, pulling a chair up beside the bed and plopping down onto it. "So, Kathia and Fred, if there's anything you want to do, do it. You can rest easy knowing that I'm here to look after your father. I'd like to get to the bottom of this once and for all."

"You are so kind to come and stay with him," Kathia said.

"The fish I'd be catching today at home, will be there for me tomorrow," Doc Raley said, chuckling. He waved a hand toward the door. "Get on with you. Have a good day." He glanced at Bright Arrow. "You, too, young man. It's good to see you. It's been a while."

"Yes, it has been too long since you came and sat with me and talked," Bright Arrow said, smiling down at the older man. "Come soon. The children enjoy your stories."

Doc Raley chuckled again. "I miss the children," he said, then turned to Melvin when he coughed. "You all right?"

"Just tired; other than that, I'm as fit as a fiddle," Melvin said, but Kathia guessed that he was saying it only for her and Fred's benefit.

"You youngsters go on," Doc Raley said, this time more sternly. "I'm here. Nothing'll get past me. Your father will be fine."

Kathia's eyebrows rose at those words. Obviously Doc Raley was suspicious of something, or . . . someone . . . but was keeping it to himself.

She guessed that he thought it was best not to accuse anyone until he had definite proof.

She was pretty sure he was thinking that Dusty might be the culprit.

If Dusty was the one who'd caused her father such pain, she would not rest until he was incarcerated for the crime, perhaps even hanged.

"Fred, are you going to the village today?" Kathia asked as she turned to him.

"No. My camera is on the blink," Fred grumbled. "I've got some fixing to do before I can take any more photographs."

"How'd that happen, son?" Melvin asked, lifting an eyebrow as he gazed at Fred.

"I don't know," Fred said, idly scratching his brow. "I took it out of the case today and tried to take a photograph of the sunrise and it just wouldn't work."

Kathia heard an uneasy note in Fred's voice, and saw through his ploy. There was nothing wrong with his camera. He was just uneasy about leaving the house under these circumstances.

She wondered for a moment whether she should leave, but with both Fred and Doc Raley there to keep an eye on things, surely it would be all right if she left, at least for a while.

She ached to be with Bright Arrow. Never in her life had she felt such longings as she did now, and all awakened by the handsome Makah chief.

"Can you fix it, son?" Melvin asked, propping himself up on an elbow.

"Always do," Fred said. He glanced over at Bright Arrow, a slow smile lifting his lips. "Except for recently, when someone took it upon himself to stamp on one of my cameras."

Bright Arrow returned the smile with one of his own. "I am sorry about that," he said. "Had I known then that it was a camera, not a weapon, I never would have done that."

"I know," Fred said. He shrugged. "It was an old-timer, anyway. The one I'm using now is new."

"If it's so new, why isn't it working?" Melvin persisted.

"Papa, things happen," Fred said, forcing an idle shrug. "It's complicated equipment. Thank God I have studied cameras since I was a little boy, so that I know how to fix most anything that happens."

Bright Arrow turned to Kathia. "There is no whale hunt today," he said. "The hunters are preparing for tomorrow's hunt. I will go later and help them. But for now I would like to spend my time with you. It is a beautiful day. Would you like to go riding?"

"Riding?" Fred interjected. "How about a canoe ride, Bright Arrow? Do you want to have that race today?"

"Perhaps another day?" Bright Arrow suggested, turning to Fred.

"Yep, another day," Fred said, giving Bright Arrow a half salute.

Kathia leaned down to give her father a soft kiss on the brow, gave her brother a hug, then smiled at Doc Raley. "Keep a close watch, do you hear?" she said.

"I plan to," Doc Raley said, nodding.

Bright Arrow and Kathia left the room.

She turned to him. "I'm so anxious for that ride," she said, her eyes dancing.

"I will take you to a beautiful place where spring flowers are abloom," he said softly. "We will tie our horses there and sit and talk."

"Yes, let's," Kathia said, a sensual thrill sweeping through her at the thought of being alone with him.

Bright Arrow waited for Kathia to saddle her horse, then they rode from the lighthouse together. Kathia didn't look back, for she was afraid that as usual she would see Dusty watching from his bedroom window.

As each day passed, she was more uneasy with his presence in her father's home. She was afraid of what his next move might be, afraid not only concerning herself, but for her father.

For now, she would force such uneasy thoughts from her mind and enjoy her moments with Bright Arrow. They were finally going to be alone.

Chapter Twenty-four

Go, lovely rose!
Tell her that wastes her time and me,
That now she knows,
When I resemble her to thee,
How sweet and fair she seems to be.
—Edmund Waller

Riding beside Bright Arrow on her father's favorite steed, a proud strawberry roan with a thick mane and bright, alert eyes, Kathia felt as though she were in a dream. Her feelings for him were so strong, it was like a dream come true every time they were together.

She would have never guessed in a million years that she could feel this intensely about someone, especially since she had met him such a short while ago.

But the moment she had gazed into Bright Arrow's eyes, even though they had met under awkward circumstances, she had known that she was looking into her destiny, for he was her future.

She gazed over at him now, loving the way his long, black hair bounced along his straight back, the way he held his chin proud and high as he kept his horse moving at a slow trot.

Her gaze moved to his muscled shoulders. His magnificent physique was as mesmerizing as his face and his voice. When he spoke to her, especially when he called her by name in his deep, masculine voice, her insides melted. When he held her, when he breathed her name in her ear, ah, how electrifying it was to her senses.

"Kathia, be wary of this area," Bright Arrow said, bringing her out of her reverie.

She noticed that they had reached the mouth of a river. Bright Arrow was guiding his horse far back from the beach.

"Our Makah children have been warned, over and over again, never to come here," he said.

"Why?" Kathia murmured, her gaze scanning the rocky terrain of the beach and noticing a long, wide stretch of sand just past the rocks. "What is there about this place that warrants such a warning?"

"Do you see the small stretch of sand over there?" Bright Arrow asked, pointing to it. "That is quicksand. Remember to warn your brother about it and tell him not to go there. It is tricky, because this sandy part of the beach looks so inviting. It lures one to walk there instead of on the rocks, which hurt the feet."

"I will most definitely warn Fred, for only yesterday he was exploring along the beaches," Kathia said, involuntarily shuddering at the thought of how her brother could have wandered into quicksand.

"Come on with me, for we have almost reached the spot I promised to take you," Bright Arrow said. He sank his moccasined heels into the flanks of his steed and rode at a harder trot away from Kathia.

Kathia kicked her horse and was soon riding beside him again. They reached the ocean together and rode along beside it.

She inhaled the fragrance of the seawater and the pines and cedar trees just beyond her and Bright Arrow. The forest and its shadows were only a few feet away.

Then she became aware of other smells, which were even more pleasant than those she had just been enjoying.

Flowers.

Surely they had almost reached the place where they would stop and rest beside the sea, where they would . . .

"Just beyond that rise in the land," Bright Arrow said, pointing toward a small hillock. "It is a place where one can enjoy nature to the fullest. On one side is the great expanse of the ocean, and on the other a great field of wild flowers that bloom only once a year, and that is now, in springtime."

Anxious to get there, to inhale, Kathia rode onward with Bright Arrow, then sucked in a breath of pure pleasure when they rode up and over the slight hill and she saw the huge field of flowers. There were many varieties of all colors and sizes.

The wind was softly blowing today, and the flowers swayed in the breeze, as though they were dancing.

Their smell was sweet and heady. She felt it actually embracing her.

"It is more beautiful than words can describe," she said, drawing rein beside Bright Arrow when he stopped his own steed.

Just past the field of flowers there was a shaded area, where pines and spruces grew high, and spread their branches wide to create a sheltered nook.

"Come," Bright Arrow said, dismounting.

He walked his horse over to the low-hanging limb of a tree and secured his reins. Kathia followed his lead and did the same.

When he took her hand, she smiled sweetly up at him, hoping that he could not hear the pounding of her heart, for at that moment she was so in love and anxious to be with him, she could hardly breathe.

They walked in silence past the flowers, over to where the land dropped off. Below them the ocean's waves splashed onto the rocky shore, and seagulls congregated.

"Here is a soft place to sit," Bright Arrow said as he motioned with his other hand toward a thick stretch of green moss that was shaded by the trees.

As Kathia sat down beside him, she tossed her long golden braid over one shoulder. Today she wore a white blouse and a gingham skirt, with a matching bow tied around the end of her braid.

"I feel so free here," Kathia murmured, reaching back and untying her bow. She tossed it on the ground beside her, and then unbraided her hair.

When her hair was spread out down her back, she closed her eyes and enjoyed the breeze, the smells, the wonder of being alone with Bright Arrow. Finally, she could relax with him, because her father was not alone.

"As do I," Bright Arrow said, gazing out over the ocean, his heart skipping a beat when he saw a gray whale make a leap from the water, then dive again to be lost from sight.

"I saw it, too," Kathia said, opening her eyes and spotting the whale. She looked quickly at Bright Arrow. "Would you rather be out there in your canoe, chasing down the whales, instead of here with me?"

"There are many more whales," Bright Arrow said, sliding an arm around her waist and drawing her close to his side. "There is only one you."

That touched Kathia's heart, for she knew the importance of whales to Bright Arrow and his people.

She smiled sweetly at him. "I am so happy here with you," she murmured. "It is a moment I shall never forget."

"It is a moment I have waited for," Bright Arrow said. He turned to her, both hands at her waist, drawing her up before him. "If I go too fast for you, it is up to you to tell me. You have said you love and need me. I, too, love and need . . . want . . . you."

His lips came down upon hers in an explosive kiss.

Lost in rapture, Kathia twined her arms around his neck. Her heart soared when his body pressed against hers, gently pushing her down on the cushiony moss.

She melted as one of his hands swept up inside her skirt, causing ripples of pleasure along her flesh. She had never been with a man like this before.

A part of her warned against it, against being with a man so intimately before marriage, yet another part wanted to relax and enjoy these precious moments.

"I am yours as long as the grass shall grow," Bright Arrow whispered into her ear. "I love you, Kathia. I love you."

Again his lips came down upon hers, but this time sweetly and gently.

She was overcome by indefinable feelings when his hand reached that part of her that had never been touched by a man. When he gently stroked her there, she sighed against his lips and felt the wonders of bliss.

"Is it too soon?" he whispered against her lips. "Do you want to wait?"

Completely inexperienced with men, yet wanting what her body was craving so badly, Kathia gazed into his eyes. She knew that he would not be asking this of her if he did not truly love her.

"It is not too soon," she murmured. "And, no, I do not want to wait."

"You are not familiar with loving a man in this way, are you?" he asked, his eyes searching hers.

"No, I have never been with a man in such a way, nor have I ever felt as delicious as I feel now with you," she said, realizing that her face was hot with a flush of both anticipation and shyness.

"I want you for always, not only today," Bright Arrow said huskily. "I want you to be my wife."

Kathia sucked in a wild breath and realized at that very moment that she had a decision to make, and not only about making love with a man for the first time. This was a decision that would alter her future forever.

All of her life she had wanted only to be a dancer. She had never even thought about a man interfering in her career.

She had never thought about marriage even though she understood that a time would come when she wouldn't be as thin and as delicate as now, and would no longer be appealing to crowds as a ballerina.

Now she wanted nothing but Bright Arrow's arms around her, his lips on hers, their bodies pressed together.

"I want to be your wife," Kathia murmured, amazed at herself and how easily she had accepted this momentous change in the direction of her life.

"You are ready, then, to make love?" Bright Arrow asked, wanting to make certain she would not regret it later.

"I want you, yes, so badly," she murmured, her eyes smiling into his.

She closed her eyes when Bright Arrow began stroking her again. Each stroke brought her closer to an ecstasy that was completely new to her.

"We will be married soon?" Bright Arrow asked, pausing, his eyes searching hers more intently than ever before.

His seriousness made her even more conscious of what answering him would mean. Her heart skipped a beat, for this was truly the moment of decision-making, a moment that would change her life forever. If she went ahead, the destiny that she had thought was hers would no longer be there for her to work toward.

Her destiny was now. Yes, it *was* Bright Arrow.

"Yes," Kathia murmured. "We will be married

soon. I truly do want to be your wife. Please don't doubt my sincerity."

She was going to be a wife! Then a mother!

She had never thought about children and what it would be like to have one of her own. But now? The thought of having a child in Bright Arrow's image made her truly want it, and soon.

"Would you rather wait until vows are spoken?" Bright Arrow said, still hesitant about making love.

"I believe that if I waited, my heart might burst from wanting you so badly," Kathia murmured, placing a gentle hand on his smooth copper cheek. "Love me. Love me now. Teach me the wonders of making love."

"There is one thing I need to warn you about," Bright Arrow said.

"Warn me . . . ?" Kathia said, surprised that he was still holding back, especially after she had agreed to make love with him, not once, but twice.

She had always believed he was a gentleman. Now she knew it.

Most men would hurry into lovemaking. Yet this man wanted everything to be right. His patience, his respect for her, were wonderful to behold.

"There is a moment during the very first lovemaking when a woman has pain," Bright Arrow said, taking his hand from beneath her skirt, and pulling her up to sit on his lap. "Let me explain."

"You are so sweet," Kathia murmured, framing his face between her hands. "Do you realize just how wonderful you are to take the time to explain everything to me first? I shall remember this always, my love. And I now know what to expect from you as your wife. You will always be patient and understanding with me."

She lowered her eyes, then looked into his again. "In the future I may express some sadness that I am no longer able to dance before an audience," she murmured. "But always know, my love, that I will not be feeling regret. It will only be normal that someone like me, whose life was the stage until we met, would have a need to look back and talk about my former life."

"I will always be patient and understanding with you, even when you and I are old and gray," Bright Arrow said, brushing a soft kiss across her brow.

"You were about to tell me about a moment when a woman experiences pain when she makes love the first time," Kathia murmured. "My love, I already know about it. I have already experienced that pain."

She saw a look of shock and horror enter his eyes, and felt the anger in his hands as he placed them at her waist and set her away from him. He placed her on the ground, then rose and stared out at the ocean, his back to her. Kathia knew that she had just said something that might have damaged their relationship, but only for a moment.

When he heard the full truth of how she understood what he was referring to, surely he would not think of her as a whore. Obviously he had interpreted her words to mean that she had been with a man already.

She rushed to her feet. "Bright Arrow, let me explain . . ." she said, reaching out to take one of his hands.

When he pulled his hand away and turned to glare into her eyes, she grew cold, for she saw a man who was looking at a woman he no longer respected.

He thought that she had lied earlier when she said she had not been with a man in this way.

She took a step away from him, the color having drained from her face.

"Please let me explain," she murmured.

He turned from her again, as though he never wanted to hear her voice again.

Chapter Twenty-five

All tastes, all pleasures, all desires combine
To consecrate this sanctuary of bliss.
—Charles Swain

Knowing that what she said in these next moments might mean her happiness for the rest of her life, or a loss she was not sure she could bear, Kathia trembled.

She swallowed hard, taking in Bright Arrow's muscled physique, his long and flowing raven-black hair, and his . . . yes . . . his hands doubled into tight fists at his sides.

She could not believe that she had spoken so carelessly. Now she had to find a way to correct her error or lose this wonderful man forever.

Surely once he understood he would take her into

his arms again and hold her. Surely he would apologize for being so cold toward her without giving her a chance to rephrase her sentence!

"Bright Arrow," she murmured as she stepped up to him. "Please listen to what I have to say. I did not mean to make you think badly of me. I . . . I . . . did not explain my problem correctly, for, yes, it is a problem. Mother told me that it would be once I found the man of my dreams. At the time I didn't take her seriously. I . . . I . . . had not planned to fall in love. All I wanted out of life was the stage. Now . . . now . . . I only want you."

When he continued to stare out at the ocean, his jaw tight, she knew what a battle she had before her. If he thought that she was making up a lie to cover up a horrible mistake, then she doubted she would ever be held by him again.

"Please look at me, Bright Arrow," Kathia said, reaching over and touching his hand, then flinching when he drew it away from her.

"All right, don't look at me, but at least listen," she said, her voice catching in her throat. "Bright Arrow, long ago, when I was only ten, I was practicing my ballet on a stage unfamiliar to me before performing later that evening. It was early in the morning. My mother and I were alone on the stage. She was instructing me, telling me which leaps to do, and encouraging more perfect pirouetting. Always anxious to please my mother, I put my whole heart into my practice that day. I practiced my leaps over and over again. Then . . . then . . . during one of those leaps, I slipped. I came down hard and awkwardly onto the stage floor. I . . . I . . . did a wide split with my legs. I felt instant pain. I felt torn apart inside. I couldn't get up, the pain was so severe. I couldn't even move. Mother came to me and helped me over, onto my back. Then I felt warmth between my legs, and she saw blood seeping through my tights. She screamed for help."

As she spoke she noticed that Bright Arrow's expression was softening. She saw his fingers unwinding out of the tight fists that they had been moments ago.

She knew that he was listening and believing.

She had never told anyone about that day before, for there was no need. Now everything depended on her telling, and on her listener believing.

"Bright Arrow, I was examined by a physician, and then a doctor specializing in women's complaints came and examined me, too," Kathia said, remembering that day so vividly. She would never forget how embarrassed she had been.

"Bright Arrow, after the exam, the doctor led my mother away from me and talked in a hushed tone to her," Kathia said, her voice catching again. "It was only later that night that my mother tried to explain what had happened. She told me that a thin barrier of flesh inside me had been torn due to my fall. She told me that she would explain the repercussions of it all later, when I was older."

She hung her head, unaware that Bright Arrow had just turned toward her, in his eyes a soft apology. "When I was old enough to know the truth about such things, Mother told me that I would have to explain to my husband about my fall, and how it would look as if I was no longer a virgin. She explained how some men might doubt me and think that I had been with a man before my husband."

She turned her eyes quickly up at him, relieved when she saw him gazing at her, his eyes proving that he believed her. She sighed when he reached out and drew her gently against him.

"You do believe me," Kathia sobbed, clinging.

"*Ah-ha,* I believe you, and I am sorry that I treated you callously, yet you used the wrong approach to tell me something so important," Bright Arrow said. He placed a finger beneath her chin and lifted it so that their eyes could meet. "Knowing you, I should have understood what you had to tell me, and also the awkwardness you were feeling. Will you forgive me for judging you too quickly?"

"Will you forgive me for having ruined such a beautiful moment between us?" she murmured.

"We both were in error," Bright Arrow said, smiling down at her. He swept his arms around her and drew her against him again. He held her close. "Perhaps we should wait now until later to . . ."

"No, please, let's not wait," Kathia said, leaning away, gazing into his eyes again. "I want to erase what I caused between us now, not later. I want to look back on this day and remember only the good. I want you, Bright Arrow. I need you."

His eyes swept over her, and then he lifted her into his arms and spread her out on the soft bed of moss. Kneeling over her, he slowly undressed her.

Nude for the first time ever with a man, feeling the sun warm against her flesh, Kathia shyly covered her breasts with her hands. Rapture shot through her when he reached for her hands and removed them, then knelt lower over her and flicked his tongue over one small breast, stopping to suck a nipple between his lips.

Kathia was totally lost to him, heart and soul; she gave herself up to the rapture.

His dark, stormy eyes moved over her with an urgent message. Then he stood over her and removed his clothes.

Totally nude now, he stood there for a moment longer, letting her eyes take him in.

"Come to me," Kathia murmured, reaching her hands out for him.

Awed by this man's body, not only his muscles but that part of his anatomy she knew was meant to send a woman to paradise, she yearned for him to make love with her.

She had waited a lifetime for this, without even knowing it.

In her midnight dreams, she had been on the stage, not in the arms of a man making love.

But now that she had looked fully upon this man for the first time, and imagined the paradise she would soon reach in his arms, she knew that only he would fill her dreams from now on.

"My woman," Bright Arrow said huskily as he stretched himself over her, a knee parting her legs, a hand guiding his manhood to where she eagerly awaited him.

He drew a ragged breath when he placed his manhood against her thigh, forcing himself to be patient just a little longer.

He wanted her to have time to get used to what was about to happen. She was new to all this.

He wanted her to enjoy every minute of it, so that she would hunger for more.

He lowered his lips to hers and kissed her, causing waves of liquid heat to pulse through him. He reached between them and cupped her breasts with his hands, his thumbs slowly circling her nipples.

Kathia's pulse was racing, the heat of her passion overwhelming her. She was experiencing desire, true desire, for the first time in her life, and ached to have him inside her.

Her body was growing feverish with rapture, and

her breath was stolen when he did finally place his manhood at the place where his hands had been earlier, caressing her.

She gasped with pleasure against his lips as he slowly slid himself inside her, yes, ah, so slowly, which she knew he was doing to prepare her for what was to come.

His patience, his sweetness, would always be remembered by her. It was just another example of the kindness she had known on that first day when she had met him.

"I love you so much," Bright Arrow whispered against her lips. "I have never needed anything as much as I need this now, with you."

"I, too, am filled with such need, such love," she whispered back against his lips.

She twined her arms around his neck.

She lifted herself up against him, then spread her legs, herself, much more widely open as he made one last plunge that took him deep inside her.

The pleasure was instant for Kathia.

She gasped and moaned as she clung to him, an erotic heat knifing through her body, stabbing deeply into that place where she had been deflowered so innocently long years ago.

She was glad now, because there was no pain at all with his entry, only luscious pleasure.

When he reached for her legs and urged them around him, at his waist, she complied and understood immediately why he had asked this of her. It brought him even more deeply into her.

She could feel his heat almost clean into her heart as he continued his deep thrusts, his hands now at her hips, lifting her closer and closer to his body.

His mouth scorched hers again when he kissed her.

She groaned against his lips, flooded with emotion that she would always remember. Waves of ecstasy washed through her as his steelly arms enfolded her again, crushing her breasts against his powerful, muscled chest.

The euphoria that filled Bright Arrow's being was almost more than he could bear as he continued thrusting inside her, rhythmically, demandingly, and then he was overcome with a feverish heat and knew that he could not hold back any longer.

He adjusted their bodies slightly as he made that one last plunge that spilled his seed into her. Her response was as heated as his, as her body quivered and quaked along with him, her moans of pleasure filling the morning air.

And then they lay quietly together, each clinging, their breaths rapid, their sighs long and leisurely.

"I never knew such bliss could exist between a man and a woman," Kathia murmured as Bright Arrow slowly rolled away from her.

She reached for him and slowly stroked his chest as he lay on his back beside her, his eyes closed, his breathing still rapid.

"It exists now and forever between us," Bright Arrow said, reaching up and taking her hand.

When he placed it on his manhood, which had lost some of its fullness, she watched in awe. Just touching him made it grow again to a size she knew must be greater than most men's.

"Just move your hand on me for a while," Bright Arrow said huskily as he took his hand away from hers.

He held his eyes closed as she did what he asked, her eyes watching her hand, and him, realizing that she had just stepped over an invisible barrier between what her life had always been and now would be.

This man, and the wonders of his body, and the beauty of his love for her, were her life now.

For only a moment she thought of being on the stage, pirouetting, feeling free, almost feeling immortalized by her talent as a ballerina.

But now?

Ah, now, this was her stage.

This was her pleasure.

He was her everything.

When he rose above her and slid his heat back inside her, and began moving inside her with slow, steady strokes, Kathia moaned with pleasure and again became lost in total ecstasy.

Chapter Twenty-six

If I meet you suddenly, I can't speak—
my tongue is broken;
a thin flame runs under
my skin, seeing nothing.
—Sappho

Feeling as though she were someone else, Kathia rode home toward the lighthouse.

Was what had just happened truly real?

Had she made love for the first time in her life?

Had she made love with someone she saw as the most wonderful man in the world, a proud chief who had professed his love for her in all ways possible?

"These were the most wonderful moments of my

life," Kathia whispered to herself, thrilled just to relive those moments of total bliss with Bright Arrow.

Always before, her ballet performances had brought her pure joy.

But now her performance as a woman outshone any moment that she had had while on the stage.

She looked over her shoulder, back in the direction of the spot where she had said her good-byes for the day to Bright Arrow.

He had told her that tomorrow he and his warriors were going farther out to sea to hunt. She hated thinking of going a whole night and a day without seeing him, without being held by him, without making love with him.

But she knew that he had his chores as a chief to see to. He had to leave for another hunt at sea. Being in love would surely always come second in his life; his people must come first.

Even when they became man and wife, she would have to accept that she could never be first to him, not as long as he was a chief to his people.

She turned and gazed at the lighthouse, which now was high above her as she rode toward the stable.

For now, she would concentrate on her father, and hope that by the time she saw Bright Arrow again, she would have good news to share with him, news about her father being able to climb the stairs to return to his beloved beams.

She knew that she would feel much more comfortable about Bright Arrow being far out at sea if her father was in the lighthouse. If a storm blew in, she knew the hazards of the Makah canoes being out at sea, even if they were large and heavily built.

"Kathia!"

A voice familiar to Kathia made her turn just as she dismounted. It was Kathia's childhood friend Magdalena, who now lived in Seattle. As usual, she had not sent any notice of her arrival.

"Magdalena!" Kathia shouted back as her friend hurried into the stable, her gorgeous red hair bouncing down her tiny, straight back.

Kathia only secured the horse's reins to a post. She would return later and take him to his stall in the stable.

Now she was too anxious to hug Magdalena.

"It's so good to see you," Magdalena cried as she flung herself into Kathia's arms.

"It's wonderful to see you, too," Kathia murmured, returning the hug. "I'm so glad that you came. I've much to tell you."

"Me, too," Magdalena said, giggling as she stepped away from Kathia.

Kathia's gaze swept over her friend. She was a tiny woman, a head shorter than Kathia. Her round face was flushed with excitement and her large green eyes were luminous. She wore a pale green velveteen skirt and a low-necked white blouse with matching velveteen trim down the front and at the cuffs.

A diamond necklace hung around her neck, sparkling in the late afternoon sun.

"What have you got to tell me?" Kathia said, taking her friend's hand and walking her back toward the house. "Don't keep me guessing. Then I shall share something wonderful with you."

"Sis!" Fred shouted from the porch. "I see Magdalena found you. I was beginning to worry. Doc Raley left ages ago. Where on earth have you been?"

Kathia felt a blush rush hotly to her cheeks as she started up the steps toward her brother.

She was ready to share her private moments with her best friend, but not with her brother. And she most certainly didn't want to tell him yet that she was going to marry Bright Arrow.

She felt that should wait until her father was well enough to hear the good news at the same time she told her brother.

"I was with Bright Arrow," Kathia said, stopping beside her brother and brushing a kiss across his cheek. "We went for a ride. And, big brother, he showed me a place that I want to warn you about. He showed me a place that has quicksand."

"Father has already told me," Fred said, idly shrugging. He stepped around her and took one of

Magdalena's hands in his. "Kathia, come on into the parlor. Father is there. I have an announcement I want to make."

"Father is well enough to sit in the parlor?" Kathia asked, her eyes wide.

"Well, he thinks he is, so I helped him there," Fred said softly. "He's fully dressed and sitting comfortably before the fire. He's reading."

"I'm so glad he loves books. Otherwise I don't know how he'd get through these days when he can't be upstairs in the control room," Kathia said, going inside with her brother and Magdalena.

They all went in to the parlor.

Kathia rushed over and gave her father a kiss and a hug as he laid his book on his lap to return her embrace.

"I'm so glad you are better," she said as she bent down onto her knees before him. "Papa, your color looks almost normal. Do you feel lots better?"

"Yes, lots," Melvin said, chuckling. Then he turned toward Fred, eyeing him suspiciously. "Well, don't keep us waiting any longer. What's this news you said you had for me and Kathia when she returned from her ride?"

"Magdalena came today for a specific purpose," Fred said, placing his arm around her waist and drawing her closer. "Father, Kathia, Magdalena has promised to marry me after she finishes her latest tour." He chuckled. He gazed down at her, smiling. "She's going to make an honest man outta me, aren't you, darling?"

"Yes, as will you, me," Magdalena replied, giggling. She held out her ring finger and showed off a large diamond. "Fred gave this to me today right after I arrived from Seattle."

Kathia was stunned speechless, for her brother had not shared the news about buying an engagement ring with her, and he told her almost everything. Just as she usually told him everything about herself.

But from this day forth, that would change. She couldn't tell him about those private moments with Bright Arrow.

And she wasn't ready to tell anyone about her plans to be married, either. Not until she knew that her father was totally well.

"What a stone!" Melvin said, gasping openly as he took Magdalena's hand and looked at the ring closely.

"Kathia, what do you think?" Magdalena asked, walking to her and lifting her finger so Kathia could examine the ring more closely. "You're surprised, I can tell."

Kathia admired the ring, then suddenly realized that she would never have one, herself, for none of the Makah women displayed diamond rings on their fingers, or even wedding bands.

But Kathia didn't care. Having Bright Arrow and speaking vows with him was all that mattered.

"Yes, surprised," Kathia murmured, smiling at Magdalena. "But wonderfully so. I'm so glad you are the one who will become my sister once you and my brother are married. You've always been my special friend. It will be even more special to have you as my sister."

She frowned then. "But Magdalena, what about your career?" she asked guardedly, knowing that she, herself, had wrestled with her own feelings about her career after realizing just how much in love she was with Bright Arrow. She had realized she would have to make a choice between him and her career.

She had chosen him.

Yet she had loved the ballet for so long, sometimes she wondered whether she could really give it up.

"Fred understands the demands of my career," Magdalena murmured. "As do I, his. We know that our careers will cause us to be away from one another at times, yet won't those absences make being together again that much more wonderful and exciting? I will have my career *and* your brother. It will be a perfect world, don't you think, Kathia?"

"I hope it works out that way for you," Kathia said, watching as Fred took a blanket and placed it over their father's legs, then handed Melvin his favorite pipe and helped him light it.

"I've got some darkroom duties calling me," Fred said, turning to Magdalena. "This will give you some time with Kathia."

Magdalena went to him and hugged him. "You be careful with those chemicals," she murmured.

"I've worked with those chemicals for so long, I can print photographs with my eyes closed," Fred said, chuckling.

"Then go on, and I'll see you when you're through," Magdalena murmured.

Fred walked briskly from the room.

"Now, Kathia, you and Magdalena go on to your room, where you'll have some privacy so you can talk without this old codger eavesdropping," Melvin said, picking up his book and opening it. "I'll be just fine while I smoke my pipe and read my novel."

Kathia went to him and kissed his brow, then led Magdalena to her room.

She had a fireplace in it, and Mariah had already started a small fire to make the room cozy.

Knowing how much Kathia loved popcorn, Mariah had brought in the popcorn popper and a bag of golden corn, along with a bowl and salt.

"Ready for some popcorn?" Kathia asked as she sat down on a stool before the fire.

"You know how much I love it," Magdalena murmured, settling down on the floor in front of the fire on a thickly braided rug. Kathia poured the corn in the popper, then slid the lid on and held it over the flames.

"I'm so happy for you and Fred," Kathia said, shaking the popper over the flames, the fragrance of corn already wafting through the air. "I always wondered what you would do when he asked you to marry him. Your career: I had thought it might stop any wedding plans."

"We talked it over and both came to the same conclusion, that it was not necessary for me to give up the ballet to be a wife," Magdalena murmured. "When we are ready for children, that will be something else. We do want children. I just don't know how long we want to wait."

Kathia continued to shake the popper over the flames, suddenly quiet as her thoughts went back to Bright Arrow, and those precious moments they had spent together.

Earlier she had been anxious to reveal this wonderful news to Magdalena, but now she hesitated. Might it take something away from Magdalena's special day to make such an announcement?

She flinched when she heard distant thunder, reminded of Bright Arrow's plans for tomorrow. He would leave early for the hunt.

She hoped the storm would stay farther out at sea than where Bright Arrow planned to hunt.

She glanced over at the window, then turned and watched the huge white popcorn filling the popper.

Strange how night had seemed to fall so quickly. Yet had not the whole day passed by just as quickly? Her moments with Bright Arrow certainly had.

She had lingered with him as long as she felt she should. But she had felt guilty spending so much time away from her father.

Again she heard the thunder. Again she looked over at the window, this time flinching when she thought lightning lit up the dark forest on the far side of the house. She laughed to herself when she realized it wasn't lightning at all, but instead the beam of the lighthouse.

"You seem so quiet suddenly," Magdalena said, moving to her knees facing Kathia. "What is it, Kathia?"

"I was distracted by the thunder," Kathia murmured, smiling at her friend.

Magdalena's beautifully shaped eyebrows lifted as she gazed at the window, and then turned back to Kathia. "I don't hear any thunder," she murmured.

"It's far out at sea," Kathia said, taking the popped corn from the fire, opening the popper, and emptying it into the large bowl. She set the bowl on the floor and shook salt onto it.

"I guess you are used to listening for thunder since your father's beams are more important during storms," Magdalena said, smiling a quiet thank you when Kathia held out the bowl of popped corn for her.

Kathia took a handful, herself, savoring the salty corn as she chewed it.

"Magdalena, do you truly believe Fred will understand the demands of your career?" Kathia asked. "Will you understand his?"

"We've talked about it often," Magdalena said as Kathia joined her on the rug. "It will work out. If you love someone enough, you can get past any obstacle to make a marriage work."

Kathia took another handful of corn and ate it as she gazed into the flames of the fire, wondering whether Bright Arrow would understand if she asked if she could perform sometimes after they were married.

But, no. He would need a full-time wife. His people's lives were vastly different from white people's.

Magdalena's eyes went to the window as the beams moved slowly past, lighting up the forest as though it were day.

She looked excitedly at Kathia. "Kathia, there's something that I think would be such fun," she said, her eyes bright with excitement.

"What?" Kathia asked, her own eyebrows lifting. "What is that you wish to do?"

"Let's dance in the beams, out on the beach," Magdalena said, searching Kathia's eyes. "What do you think? It's a warm night. Don't you think it would be fun?"

Kathia smiled. "I have never thought about doing

that, but, yes, it does sound like fun," she said, setting the bowl aside. She took Magdalena's hands. "Do you want to now? Do you?"

And then she dropped her hands away from Magdalena. "I don't think it's such a good idea after all," she blurted out before Magdalena had a chance to respond. "There's Dusty to worry about."

"Dusty? You mean the man who's taking your father's place in the control room?" Magdalena asked, somewhat taken aback.

"Yes, Dusty," Kathia murmured. "I'm not certain I want to let him see us perform. He always seems to be watching me, Magdalena."

"He does?" Magdalena said, her eyes widening. "And you? You don't care for him?"

"I can't stand him," Kathia said, visibly shuddering. "And I trust him even less. There's something about that man that gives me the creeps. I think he might be . . ."

She stopped before saying what she truly felt, that she thought Dusty might be doing something to harm her father.

"Don't even think about him," Magdalena urged. She took Kathia's hands again. "Come on. Let's go. It will be such fun dancing on the beach in the beams. They are much brighter than any we've danced before on the stage." She sighed. "And what a stage! The beach! Yes, Kathia. Come on. Let's do it. I brought my shoes in case Fred wanted me to dance for him."

"I brought my shoes, too," Kathia murmured. "I had planned to practice."

"Have you?" Magdalena asked as she jumped to her feet.

Kathia felt a blush rush to her cheeks, for, no, she hadn't practiced. Since she had met Bright Arrow that day while she was skating, she had not taken time to practice her ballet. All she could think about was him.

"No; not yet, anyhow," Kathia murmured.

"That doesn't sound like you," Magdalena said, searching Kathia's eyes. "Tell me the truth, Kathia. What else has kept you occupied besides your father? You are not the sort to let many days pass without practicing your leaps, your pirouettes. . . ."

"Let's go and get our shoes," Kathia said hurriedly, hoping to avoid any more mention of why she had ignored her practicing. She was not quite ready to tell Magdalena about her upcoming nuptials. It still seemed too new to share, even though she was bursting at the seams with the need to talk about Bright Arrow.

Again she reminded herself that this was Magdalena's night. She had had her own announcement to make. Kathia did not want to take away from it.

Perhaps tomorrow . . . ?

"Get your shoes and I shall go and get mine," Magdalena said, giggling. "I am so anxious to dance, aren't you?"

Kathia nodded.

Moments later they were out on the beach, their ballet slippers on, dancing beneath the shine of the beams as they swept over the sand, out to sea, and then back again.

"It is such a feeling of freedom, isn't it, to dance out here on the beach, with the sea air fresh on our faces and the beams even brighter than day?" Magdalena said, sighing as she pirouetted on the sandy ground.

Kathia didn't want to admit to just how wonderful it felt to be dancing again. She was lost in the joy of her graceful movements.

She realized she was looking forward to her upcoming performance in Port Angeles. She would keep that date and perform her heart out, for it would be her last.

"Kathia, aren't you enjoying yourself?" Magdalena said, stopping and staring at Kathia when the lights again drifted away. "You are so beautiful as you dance. Surely you feel as I, as though you are floating in this sea air."

"It's wonderful, yes," Kathia murmured as she stopped and took Magdalena's hands in hers. "I didn't mean to be so quiet. I . . . I . . . just had other things on my mind."

"You aren't still worrying about that Dusty person watching us, are you?" Magdalena asked as she glanced up at the tall lighthouse tower. "He's just seeing to his duties, that's all. He didn't let the lights linger on us once even though I wish that he had."

"I'm sure he's getting an eyeful during those moments the beams *are* on us," Kathia said, watching the slow sweep of the lights as they showed over the water, then began making their way toward the beach again.

As she looked into the beams, she gasped and took a shaky step backward. Once again she saw the same huge bird that she had thought she'd seen in a dream when she was ill and feverish. It was in the lights of the beams even now; then, as she looked again, it had disappeared.

Was it an apparition? Was she losing her mind?

She grabbed for Magdalena's hand. "Did you see a huge bird moments ago?" she asked hoarsely. "It was flying in the beams. Did you? Did you see it?"

"No, I didn't see it. Birds don't fly at night, anyway, Kathia," Magdalena said, frowning at her. She placed her hand on Kathia's brow. "Are you feverish? Perhaps we should go back inside."

"No, I'm not feverish," Kathia said, taking Magdalena's hand from her brow. "Perhaps daft, but not feverish. Surely it was my imagination tonight, as it probably was that other time I saw the bird."

"You saw it another time?" Magdalena asked as

she peered into the darkness, trying to see the bird Kathia was talking about.

"Yes, but let's forget about it," Kathia said. "Let's dance again. I feel like a schoolgirl, Magdalena. It has been such fun dancing like this with you."

She looked quickly away from Magdalena as she spotted something moving in the darkness. Her eyes widened when she saw Bright Arrow step out of the shadows.

She swallowed hard.

She remembered that the last time she had seen the huge bird, Bright Arrow had appeared moments later in the room with her.

Could he be . . . ?

No. It was foolish to even think such a thing!

"Bright Arrow," Kathia said, running to him and throwing her arms around him. Then she gazed into his eyes. "Why are you here?"

He smiled at her with a knowing look that told her he had been there for some time, watching.

"I saw you dancing," Bright Arrow said, taking her hands and holding them as he smiled at her. "You are beautiful. You are exquisitely beautiful."

"Kathia, who is this man?" Magdalena asked as she came and stood beside Kathia, her eyes never leaving Bright Arrow.

Kathia was uncertain what to say, for she had not yet confided in Magdalena about her deep feelings for Bright Arrow, or their plans to marry.

Before she had the chance to say anything else, Fred's voice broke the silence.

"Kathia! Come quickly! Father! He's ill again!" Fred shouted from the front porch. "Hurry!"

"Ill again?" Kathia said, feeling the color drain from her face. She glanced up at the beams, realizing that surely this time Dusty could not have had anything to do with her father's relapse, for he was tending to the beams.

"Go; we shall talk later," Bright Arrow said, then smiled at Magdalena. "I feel that our paths will cross again. If you are Kathia's friend, I know that we will see each other once more."

"Yes, we're friends, the *best*," Magdalena murmured, then watched him disappear into the shadows of the forest almost as quickly as he had appeared.

Just as Kathia started to run back toward the house, she stopped dead in her tracks and gazed up at the beams. The huge-winged bird was illuminated by them again.

She had never seen anything as mystical as that bird. *Could* it be the Thunderbird?

Was it not mythical at all, but real? Was that bird truly . . . ?

The wind began blowing. The lights moved out to sea again just as Kathia saw the huge bird fly into the dark shadows of the forest.

"Kathia! What's keeping you?" Fred shouted.

"Coming!" Kathia cried. Magdalena ran close beside her until they were on the porch, and then they ran together into the house.

"Where is he?" Kathia asked, her eyes wild as she met Fred's. "Where is Papa?"

"He's still in the parlor where we left him earlier," Fred said, hurrying there along with her. Magdalena stood back, just inside the door, a hand covering her mouth as she watched brother and sister run to their father.

"Papa!" Kathia cried as she fell to her knees beside the chair where she had left her father contentedly reading and smoking.

The book and pipe were on the floor now. Her father lay sagging sideways in the chair, his eyes closed, white drool coming from his mouth.

"Papa, please wake up," Kathia cried. Out of the corner of her eye she saw Fred pick up a teacup that had fallen on the other side of the chair.

"He was drinking tea," Fred said, bending to one knee and picking up the cup. "He passed out while drinking it, for look, Kathia. What was left of the tea was spilled on the floor when he dropped the cup."

"His breathing is so shallow," Kathia said, hardly even aware of what her brother had said about the cup. "Fred, carry him to his bed. And . . . he needs a doctor."

She ran to the window, and as the light swept out over the ocean, she saw that the waves had picked up. The wind blew hard across the water.

"It would be impossible to get over to The Point tonight to fetch Doc Raley," she said, her voice tight. "But Papa needs a doctor. He needs one now!"

She watched Fred lift their father in his arms.

She walked with him as he carried Melvin to his bedroom, Magdalena following quietly behind.

"Fred, I know of another doctor," Kathia blurted out as he placed their father on the bed and slowly began undressing him.

"Who?" Fred said, sliding his father's shirt off, and then his breeches. He then covered him up with the patchwork quilt.

"Bright Arrow's shaman uncle," Kathia blurted out.

"What?" Fred said, giving Kathia a quick, incredulous look. "Kathia, I'm stunned that you would even consider using a shaman for Papa. The Makah's way of healing is vastly different from what a white doctor would prescribe."

"Perhaps, but, Fred, I cannot help remembering how gentle White Moon was to me when I was taken to the village after my spill in the pond," she murmured. "I truly feel that he can be trusted to do what is right for Papa. I regret now having not asked him to come and look in on him earlier."

"Kathia, it's raining now," Magdalena said, as she went and held a curtain aside at the window. "And the lightning. It's fierce!"

"I have no choice but to go, rain or not," Kathia said. She took her brother's hands in hers. "Please accept him and his way of doctoring when he arrives; I am going for White Moon."

"Oh, Kathia, you are so hardheaded sometimes," Fred grumbled. He drew her into his arms and hugged her. "Perhaps I should go, not you. You'll get drenched."

"I won't melt," Kathia said, easing from his arms. She laughed softly. "I proved that when I fell in the pond."

"Then you insist on going yourself?" Fred asked, searching her eyes.

"Yes, and I'd best get to it, for as each moment passes, Father is getting no better," Kathia said, then left the room in a hurry.

After she changed into comfortable old clothes that would not be ruined in the rain and threw a hooded leather cloak around her shoulders, she ran to the stable and mounted her horse, then rode off in the thunder, lightning, and rain.

When the beams caught her in her flight, she realized that this time they lingered longer than they should have.

She frowned up at Dusty.

"Do your duty, you—" she shouted, not saying all that she wished to say, for she was not one to use profanity.

But she did know that there were ships out at sea that needed the beams tonight.

Tomorrow her beloved would be there on the ocean. She hoped the storm would have passed over by then.

Then, as she rode hard through the rain and wind, flinching when the lightning lit up the dark heavens, she thought back to the moment she'd spotted the huge bird.

This time it had not been part of a dream. It had been real!

Then moments later Bright Arrow had appeared on the beach. She would always wonder about how he chanced to appear almost at the same time as the huge bird had disappeared.

She was not even sure she wanted to know the answer. It might be too frightening!

Chapter Twenty-seven

When from the frowning east a sudden gust
Of adverse fate is blown, or sad rains fall,
Day in, day out, against its yielding wall,
Lo! the fair structure crumbles to the dust.
—Ella Wheeler Wilcox

The storm had passed quickly and clouds no longer covered the moon. Kathia sighed with relief as she rode into the Makah village.

Her cloak was heavy with rain. She yanked it off, shook as much water as she could from it, then laid it across her saddle.

She looked around her and quickly realized that her arrival at this time of night was causing a commotion. The Makah people came out of their homes, looking at her questioningly.

As Kathia glanced around, it seemed that she had drawn everyone's attention, everyone but Bright Arrow.

As she rode to his longhouse and dismounted before it, she noticed that he had not come from the house.

It seemed he was not there. She would have thought that he would be home by now.

What was she to do?

She gazed around her, at the glow of firelight coming from the open doors of the longhouses, then at the huge fire at the center of the village that had surely been lit only a short time ago, since the rain stopped. She saw several older men congregated near the fire, on blankets spread out on the damp ground.

They were smoking their long pipes, and were now quiet as they stared at her. Among them she saw a familiar face. White Moon's.

He was just now rising, struggling and groaning as he pushed his way up slowly from the ground. When he finally did get to his feet, he started walking in his twisted, strange way toward Kathia, the hump on his back seeming even more pronounced beneath the brilliant shine of the moon.

Kathia hurried to him and met him halfway just

as Whispering Wind appeared, her pale gray eyes silently questioning Kathia.

"I am so sorry I am disturbing everyone's quiet evening, but I had to come," Kathia rushed out. She looked over her shoulder at Bright Arrow's longhouse, then gazed into the shaman's faded old eyes. "I came for you, White Moon. My father is worse. I am so afraid for him. Will you go to him? Will you help him?"

"Why would you come to my people's village and ask this of our shaman?" Whispering Wind said, before White Moon had a chance to respond. "Do you not have your own doctor in your white world? Would you truly accept White Moon's healing? I have always heard how skeptical you whites are of our shaman."

"I am not at all skeptical," Kathia murmured. She smiled at White Moon. "I will always be grateful for how you came to my aid after I fell into the icy water of the pond. Again I thank you for caring enough to help me."

"I acted from the heart," White Moon said. He reached a trembling hand to Kathia's arm. "You say your father's health is worse. Tell me, what ailment has made him worse?"

"I have no idea what is causing my father's health to deteriorate so strangely," Kathia murmured. "First he seems to be on the road to recovery, and then almost as suddenly, he is worse again. I truly believe that he is at his worst now, White Moon. And . . . and . . . the waves are too high at sea for anyone to row over to The Point to get our white doctor. Can you come? Will you see what you can do for my father? Will you?"

"*Ah-ha*, I will come with you," White Moon said, nodding. He gazed over at Bright Arrow's longhouse. "Our *tyee*, our chief, is not here to accompany us to your home." He looked at Whispering Wind. "Will you alert him when he arrives as to where I am, and why? I would like him to come. He can help me return home, since Kathia will want to stay with her father."

"*Ah-ha*, I will tell my son," Whispering Wind said, then reached out and hugged White Moon. "Come home soon, White Moon. I will worry until you do."

"You worry about this old man too much," White Moon said, chuckling. He slid away from Whispering Wind, then turned and beckoned with a hand toward a young brave.

The boy ran to him, eyes wide as he stopped before his shaman. "You wish something of me?" he asked, his voice that of a child who was soon to be a man.

"Go and saddle my horse and bring it to me, Two Suns," White Moon said, nodding to the corral behind White Moon's longhouse. "Hurry, young brave. Someone is in need of my skills as shaman."

Two Suns nodded and ran to saddle White

Moon's white steed as the old man went to his lodge and brought out a buckskin bag that had a design of lightning and clouds embroidered on it.

Kathia was surprised to see the twisted, bent old man get on his horse and secure the bag at one side. He was soon waiting for her to mount her own steed.

Kathia fastened her cloak around her shoulders, then swung herself up.

"Ride with care!" Whispering Wind said to White Moon as she wrung her hands in concern.

White Moon smiled over his shoulder at her, then rode alongside Kathia through the forest. The leaves dripped rain from the trees. The moon broke through gaps in the branches overhead, giving the forest a surreal look to Kathia. She was not used to being out at night like this.

If only the shaman could find a way to help her father!

She kept looking over her shoulder, hoping that Bright Arrow would appear riding after them. She would feel much better if he were with her, for she doubted that the old shaman could do anything to protect her if someone jumped out at them from the shadows of the forest.

She was glad when the beams from the lighthouse came into view as they swept over the tops of the trees, filtering down onto Kathia and White Moon.

She could even see the ocean through the breaks

in the trees, the beams illuminating the swells of the waves, which were now not as huge, yet still too threatening for anyone to go over to the island for Doc Raley.

It did seem that her father's health tonight depended on the knowledge of a shaman.

She wondered how he would feel if he were to wake and find the twisted, white-haired man standing over him, doing whatever he would do to doctor him.

She hadn't thought about that earlier. What *would* her father do? Would it frighten him to know that his life lay in the hands of a doctor unfamiliar to him?

No matter her father's reaction, Kathia knew that she had done the right thing by going for White Moon. She could not have stood by and watched her father worsen by the minute without taking some action.

But what was the cause of this latest relapse? What on earth could be wrong?

"We are at your home now?" White Moon inquired, interrupting Kathia's train of thought.

She looked ahead and saw that they had only a short distance to go.

"Yes, we're almost there," Kathia murmured, leading the way to the porch, where she stopped and dismounted.

She went to White Moon and helped him from his horse, then untied his bag and handed it to him.

"Come inside," Kathia said, placing a gentle hand beneath one of his elbows and helping him up the stairs.

Fred came rushing into the hall when he heard the door open and shut. Magdalena stood aside, still only watching.

"Thank God you're here," Fred said, his face flushed with fear. "Father is even worse."

He gazed at the twisted old man, gave Kathia a questioning look, then led the way to his father's room.

Kathia paled when she saw that her father's color had turned an ashen gray. His breathing was even more shallow than before. He moaned as he slept.

Without hesitation, White Moon reached inside his bag, from which he took two sticks. They were grease-smeared, striped, painted, feathered, and embellished in other ways.

"These are power sticks," White Moon quietly explained. "They hold much healing magic."

Kathia's eyes widened when White Moon stepped closer to her father's bed and began rhythmically beating the sticks together against each other while he softly chanted. Kathia and Fred exchanged questioning glances, then looked at the shaman again as he stopped and put the sticks back inside his bag.

He turned to them. "Will you leave us alone now?" White Moon said as he stood over the bed, his old eyes examining Melvin closely.

Kathia questioned Fred with her eyes, then thinking that her hesitation might cause White Moon to think she did not trust his judgment after all, she took Fred by the hand.

"Yes, we will leave," she said. "We . . . we . . . will be out in the corridor."

"Kathia, I'm truly concerned now," Fred said, starting to pace back and forth in the hall while Magdalena stood with Kathia, as quiet as before. "I don't think Papa is going to make it." He raked his fingers through his thick black hair. "It doesn't look good, Kathia. It doesn't look one damn bit good."

"Fred, we're doing all that we can," Kathia said, reaching out a hand to stop his pacing. She stepped before Fred and took both of his hands. "Big brother, you've never been one to give up on anything. Don't now. I don't think I could bear it if you gave up." She flung herself into his arms and clung to him. "I need you, Fred. I need your strength. Your hope."

"Kathia?"

The sound of Bright Arrow's voice behind her drew Kathia quickly away from her brother.

She ran into his arms. Tears wetted his buckskin shirt as she held him tightly.

"Bright Arrow, it doesn't look at all good for Papa," she sobbed. "I only hope that White Moon can do something. If not, there isn't much else that can be done. The sea is too rough to go for Doc Raley. What if . . . ?"

"Do not say it," Bright Arrow said, placing a finger beneath her chin and bringing her eyes up to meet his. "My woman, do not give up hope so soon. Hope is what matters. When one loses hope, what else is left?"

"Yes, hope," Kathia murmured, nodding. She gazed into his dark eyes, seeing such wisdom there, such love.

For a brief moment she again thought of the huge bird with the strange eyes, then as quickly dismissed it from her mind.

"I am finished," White Moon said, stepping from the room and drawing everyone's eyes to him. He smiled gently at Kathia. "By morning your father will be much better."

"Can you tell us what is wrong with our father?" Fred asked as he came to stand beside Kathia.

White Moon's smile faded. He looked slowly from Kathia to Fred, then to Kathia again.

"From what I can tell, your father has poison in his body," he said tightly. Ignoring their gasps, he went on. "Yes, poison," he said. "But I have given him a remedy, a tea made of Oregon grape, ferns, herbs, and roots. Also I gave him medication made from crushed, dried thimbleberry leaves that will strengthen his blood."

He stepped back. He dropped his hands to his sides. He gazed from brother to sister. "Do you know how this could have happened?" he asked. "How your father might have poison in his body, so much that it made him almost die?"

"Almost . . . die . . . ?" Kathia gasped, glad when Bright Arrow placed an arm around her waist to steady her.

"I am horrified by the diagnosis," Fred said. "Poison? Our father has been poisoned?"

"Do you know what he might have eaten today?" White Moon asked. "Sometimes a particular fish can poison someone who is already in a weakened state."

"He has eaten well today, but offhand, I do not know what," Kathia said, still stunned by the diagnosis. "I will ask Mariah. She prepares all our meals."

"Did you have fish today?" White Moon persisted, gazing from Kathia to Fred.

"No, no fish," Fred said, frowning. "Damn. I'm so confused, I'm not certain. Maybe we did have fish. I . . . don't . . . know."

Something flashed into Kathia's mind, causing her to turn and stare at the spiral staircase that led up to the lighthouse.

Dusty Harper's face flashed before her eyes.

But surely not. Surely he would not do anything so insane as to poison her father.

No. Surely it was something her father had eaten, yet . . . ?

"We must leave now," White Moon said, looking over at Bright Arrow. "You have come to escort me back to the village, have you not?"

Bright Arrow gazed down at Kathia, then smiled at his uncle. "Yes, I have come not only to see how Kathia and Fred's father is, but also to see you safely home, White Moon," he said.

Bright Arrow turned to Kathia. He took one of her hands. "I will leave early tomorrow on another whale hunt," he said thickly. "I will see you again when I can." He looked toward her father's door, then into Kathia's eyes again. "Will you give your father my best?"

"Yes, and . . . and . . . Bright Arrow, please be careful while you are out at sea," she said, her voice breaking. "The weather. It seems the storms come upon us so quickly these days."

"That is because it is spring," Bright Arrow said, nodding. He placed a gentle hand on her cheek. "I know the sea well. I know the weather, too. I can read the clouds and what each one promises . . . stormy or fair weather. So do not worry."

"I will always worry while you are out at sea," Kathia said, gently hugging him. "I cannot help it."

"Yes, she is a worrier," Fred said, smiling at Bright Arrow as he stepped away from Kathia.

"It seems I suddenly have so much to worry about," Kathia said, her voice drawn.

"Your father will be well by morning," White

Moon quickly reassured her. "What I have given him will cause the poison to leave his body. You will see the change in the morning. But until then, you might want to sit vigil at his bedside. Watch all that is given to him. We do not want him to take any more poison into his body."

"Fred and I both will be with him," Kathia promised.

"Yes, we'll both sit vigil," Fred said, nodding. He smiled at Magdalena, reaching a hand out for her. "Also Magdalena, won't you, honey?"

Magdalena rushed to him, smiling. "Yes, I wish to help in whatever way I can," she murmured. "I have such fond feelings for your father."

Kathia walked Bright Arrow and White Moon out of the house, and to their horses. The air was fresh and sweet now, after the rain. The moon was bright overhead. She wished that she could be alone with Bright Arrow, if only for a moment. She longed to hug and kiss him.

But with White Moon there, she had to hold back her true feelings for Bright Arrow.

She watched until they rode out of sight, then stepped away from the house and gazed up at the beams as they slowly made their way across the tree-tops, and then far out to sea.

"Dusty," she whispered, sighing.

Could he have been giving something to her father to poison him? Had he put something in his tea?

She shuddered at the thought and hurried inside the house.

She would not allow herself to think that Dusty was such a monster that he could actually be slowly murdering her father!

Chapter Twenty-eight

You ask me what since we must part
You shall bring back to me.
Bring back a pure and faithful heart
As true as mine to thee.
—Juliana Horatia Ewing

"Papa, I'm so glad you are better today," Kathia said, leaning over to hug him. "Whatever White Moon gave you has worked a miracle."

"Miracle enough for me to get out of bed," Melvin said, sliding his legs from beneath the blanket. He patted them. "They feel stronger today, Kathia. I might try the stairs."

"Papa, *no*," Kathia softly argued as she watched

him place his bare feet on the floor. "You know that you were very ill yesterday. Your legs must be weak."

"Hogwash," Melvin argued. "Take a long look at me, Kathia, as I put my full weight on my legs. I feel so much stronger. I want to try my luck at the stairs. Arguing with me won't change my mind."

He gestured with a hand toward the door. "Go on, Kathia, scat while I dress," Melvin said, his eyes twinkling. "I might even take a ride on my horse to the Makah village and show that shaman just how well his magic worked on me."

"Papa, you wouldn't," Kathia gasped, placing a hand to her throat.

Melvin chuckled. "No, I'm not daft, Kathia," he said. "I wouldn't dare even try to saddle a horse, let alone ride one."

He gestured with his hand toward the door again. "Go on, Kathia," he urged. "And close the door behind you."

"Papa, please listen to reason," Kathia begged, then jumped with alarm when she heard a loud clap of thunder.

All morning she had heard the low rumbling of thunder in the distance, but thus far it had stayed far out at sea.

She wasn't sure just how far Bright Arrow was going to take his hunting canoe today, but he had said it would be farther than where he had hunted for his first whale of the season.

He had also told her that today only one canoe would be out at sea for the hunt, and that would be his.

After today, when more whales were sighted, other canoes would go to find them.

But for now, today, it was only his.

The very first thing Kathia had done when she awakened this morning was go to the window to look up into the sky.

She had sighed with relief when she saw a glorious, crystal blue sky, awesome in its intense color, with only a few fleecy cumulus clouds scudding along the horizon.

She frowned now, however, as she recalled White Moon's diagnosis last night. Poison, he had said.

But he had thought the poison was from food Melvin was eating, suggesting a fish might be the source.

The Makah people knew that particular fish well enough to throw them back in the sea if they were caught in nets, or on their fishing hooks.

But some white people were not as knowledgeable about the local fish. The poison one had no name. All she knew was that it was a rare fish, gray striped, and long and skinny. It had the ability to leap high from the water, as graceful as a ballerina, yet deadlier than a rattlesnake if someone ate enough of it.

But Kathia knew that Mariah had not prepared

that particular fish for their meals. Neither she nor Fred had grown ill, after all.

"Kathia, you seem suddenly lost in thought," Melvin said, interrupting her train of thought. "Are you missing Magdalena? The sweet thing, I didn't get to spend any time with her this time. But I see a future of many visits since she is going to be my daughter-in-law."

"Our time was cut short when you grew ill," Kathia said softly. "But, yes, we all will be able to see her more often when she marries Fred. Yet perhaps we will not see her as often as we'd like. She plans to continue her career even after they are married."

"That will last for only so long. When she becomes pregnant, she will most definitely become just a housewife and mother," Melvin said. "I wish Fred would live closer than Seattle. I hoped he would live here with me permanently. It has been nice having him here under the same roof, as it has been wonderful to have you, daughter, for longer than the blink of an eye."

Kathia giggled. "Yes, it did seem that my visits were that short, didn't it?" she said, going to crouch before him, the hem of her pale orchid silk dress settling on the floor around her. "But, Father, perhaps that will change. How would you like to have me around much more often than you are used to?"

"And how can that be?" he asked, raising a thick, shaggy eyebrow. "As soon as I get my full strength back, you'll hightail it outta here and I'll probably not see you except at your performances. I wish that could change, Kathia. I would love seeing you more often."

"Well, I'll work on that," Kathia said, her eyes gleaming.

She was dying to tell him now that soon she would give up her career for Bright Arrow.

But she still wanted to wait until Fred was with them, so that they could share the news together as a family. That was what a family was all about . . . sharing the most important news that one could have to tell.

Marriage to such a man as Bright Arrow was truly wonderful news, but seeing her father feeling better rivaled it at this moment.

"Yes, you work on that," Melvin said, chuckling. He reached up and drew her down closer, kissed her brow, then again waved her toward the door. "What do I have to do to convince you to leave so that I can get dressed and try my legs on those stairs?"

"All right, I'll leave, but, Papa, you must promise to wait until I can help you before you take one step from this room," Kathia said, rising. "Do you promise me?"

"Yep, I promise," Melvin said. "I cross my heart and hope to die."

"Oh, stop it," Kathia said, giggling again like a schoolgirl, for at this moment, she felt giddy and wonderful.

Her father was better, oh, so much better. Perhaps he just might be able to get up the stairs.

It would be a start, a start toward the goal of giving Dusty his walking papers.

Whenever she thought of Dusty now, she thought of that word *poison*. *He* was poison in her eyes, and she could not erase from her mind the possibility that he was responsible for her father's illness.

Today she would have the opportunity to talk with him. She would not stop until she got answers that . . . that . . .

"Kathia, *please*," Melvin said, again breaking through her thoughts. "Leave. Please leave. You are lost in thought again."

"Yes, I guess I was," Kathia said, laughing awkwardly, then flinching again when she heard another loud clap of thunder, this time closer than the last.

She gasped when she gazed out the window. The sky was dark and ominous. The storm was upon them.

Her heart skipped a beat at the thought that Bright Arrow might be out at sea this very moment.

Trying not to act as alarmed as she felt, so as not to concern her father, Kathia left the room with a smile, closing the door behind her. Then she ran to the parlor window and drew back the curtain. She was even more worried when she saw the heavy black clouds that were rolling in, like waves on an ocean.

She glanced at the sea, and the color drained

from her face when she saw the huge, white-capped waves crashing against the shore.

She flinched when she saw lightning flashing against the dark, scudding clouds, then racing zigzaggedly down into the water. A huge boom of thunder followed the horrible sight, causing the floor beneath Kathia to tremble.

"Stay calm," Kathia whispered.

Bright Arrow had told her that he had been whaling since he was old enough to hold a harpoon. She reminded herself that he knew the ocean and all its dangers.

The sky was now almost totally black with clouds, as though day had turned into night. Lightning continued to flash in crazed zigzags across the dark heavens, and then straight down again, into the water.

Kathia's breath caught in her throat when she saw something else.

She would know Bright Arrow's canoe anywhere. She would never forget the pride in his voice and eyes as he had shown it to her.

The canoe that had appeared out at sea *was* Bright Arrow's. As the ocean waves crashed, swelled, and crashed again in phosphorescent bursts, she saw the canoe's struggle.

The sky was getting even darker than it had been moments ago. Rain began to come down in torrents and visibility was terrible.

"The beams," Kathia gasped out, knowing that

Bright Arrow needed the guidance of the lights to get his bearings.

And . . . Lord!

As she searched the dark heavens, and the crashing waves of the ocean, she saw no lights!

Any lighthouse keeper knew to watch for storms such as this, so that the lamps could be lit for those who could so easily be lost at sea, or dashed against the huge boulders along the shore.

But . . . no! Not Dusty, not this lighthouse keeper!

Kathia was seized with a cold panic as she turned and gazed toward Dusty's room. Was he asleep? Wherever he was, he was being lax in his duty.

She ran to his bedroom and pounded on the door. When he didn't respond, she screamed his name. Still there was no response.

She opened the door. One glance inside proved that he wasn't there.

Surely he was upstairs and in the process even now of lighting the lamps.

Panting, eager, afraid for Bright Arrow, Kathia ran up the steep spiral staircase. She had to make sure Dusty was lighting the lamps!

If not, she would go for Fred. He knew how to operate the lights.

Finally, breathing hard, she reached the trapdoor that led into the control room.

She tried to push it open but couldn't. It seemed to be locked.

"Dusty!" she screamed. "Dusty, if you're in there, let me in!"

She grew cold inside when she heard laughter coming from the room overhead.

"What on earth?" she whispered, her eyes widening.

"Dusty, what do you think you're doing?" Kathia shouted at him. "Why is the door locked? What do you find funny about my calling your name? Lord, Dusty, there's a storm. Don't you know that the beams should be lit?"

When again the only response was laughter, she felt a knot forming in the pit of her stomach.

She closed her eyes as she pictured Bright Arrow's canoe battling the high, crashing waves. She could even feel the lighthouse trembling and swaying as its iron girders groaned.

Tears flooded her eyes. The chances that Bright Arrow would make it out of this storm alive were slim.

Her eyes jerked open. She doubled her hands into tight fists at her sides.

"Dusty, why have you locked me out?" she shouted. "Are the beams on now? Do you see Bright Arrow's canoe? Are the beams helping him in his time of trouble?"

Again, his only response was a menacing laugh.

"Lord, lord," Kathia whispered, turning and running down the steps.

When she got to a downstairs window, she looked

out and felt ill when she saw that the beams still weren't lit.

The storm was in its fullest fury now. Lightning flashed in jagged forks of white fire. Thunder rumbled and rolled, and rain poured down.

The waves crashed against the rocks, the sound as loud as the thunder. The dark water coiled over and over again, like a giant sea serpent writhing in foaming turmoil.

She felt a sinking feeling as a lightning flash revealed Bright Arrow's canoe to her. It was being sent landward by the waves, and surely Bright Arrow couldn't see where he was.

He needed the lights for guidance.

"Dusty, why are you doing this?" Kathia moaned to herself.

She was almost certain that she knew the answer. He was purposely not lighting the lights, so that Bright Arrow would perish at sea.

"Fred!" she whispered, breaking into a run toward his darkroom.

When she reached the darkroom and found that he wasn't there, she hurried on to his bedroom. She sighed heavily with despair when she saw that he wasn't there, either.

It seemed that she was in this thing alone. She had to find a way to deal with the murdering madman herself.

When she heard a strange sort of thumping sound

above her, echoing down the stairs, she realized that someone else knew about the lights. Someone else had climbed up to the trapdoor and was trying to get it open.

Her eyes widened and her heart skipped a beat. The voice she was hearing cursing Dusty, ordering him to open the door, was her father's!

He was telling Dusty that he'd better get the door open or her father would see that he was hanged by the neck till dead if anything happened to those at sea who needed the beams.

Kathia couldn't believe that her father had managed to get up the stairs. Surely willpower and sheer dedication to his job had given him strength. Or perhaps the medicine that White Moon had given him was creating a miracle.

Afraid of what Dusty might do to her father, Kathia raced back up the spiral stairs.

Just as she reached the step below where her father was standing, Dusty jerked open the trapdoor and stepped aside for her father to go on up into the control room.

She scurried in after him and stood with her father as he glared at Dusty. The insolent look was gone from the other man's face. Instead, he was cowering, looking like a frightened, cornered puppy that had had one too many accidents on its master's expensive rug.

"I couldn't get the lamps lit," Dusty stammered. "I

tried," he said, gulping. "Honest, I tried. But the more nervous and anxious I got about needing to do my duty, the clumsier I got. I'm sorry."

He gestured toward the controls as he stepped aside. "Go ahead," he said, his voice trembling. "Give it a try. Those at sea are in peril. I don't want to be at fault if anything happens to them."

As Kathia's father brushed past Dusty, leaning his weight on the cane he held in his left hand, he cursed beneath his breath.

Kathia glared at Dusty. "You're a liar and will be a cold-blooded murderer if Bright Arrow and his men die," she said flatly. "You purposely let it happen. You know that you did."

She went and stood directly before him, her eyes steady. "I shall never forget that maniacal laughter as I tried to get the trapdoor open," she said tightly. "You purposely wouldn't let me in, and you know why. You lied about the beams. You purposely didn't light them. You want Bright Arrow to die."

Sweating profusely, Dusty glared at Kathia. "Bright Arrow *should* die," he growled. "He isn't good enough for you."

He glanced over at her father, who was working hard to light the lamps, then smiled crookedly at Kathia. "Your father should be dead, too," he said.

"What . . . did . . . you say . . . about . . . my father?" Kathia gasped out, paling.

Realizing that he had blurted out something he

had never meant to say, Dusty pushed past Kathia and fled down the stairs.

"You're crazy!" Kathia yelled down at him from the top of the steps. "Run! But you won't get far. You will pay for what you did. You'll . . . pay . . . !"

"I've got it," Melvin shouted at Kathia over his shoulder. "They're finally lighting. The damn idiot did something to block the flow of the kerosene to the wicks. But I've got it straightened out. Watch, Kathia. The beams! Finally the beams are shining out to sea. One at a time, Kathia. Soon I'll have them all lighted."

Kathia rushed to a window and looked desperately out at sea, as her father steadfastly guided his powerful beacon over the troubled water, continually sounding the deafening foghorn to alert ships and canoes to the dangers of the rocky shore.

Kathia prayed as the lightning flashes revealed to her that Bright Arrow's canoe was still afloat. And then the beams fell upon him and his men, illuminating them more distinctly.

"Come on, Bright Arrow," she said, tears streaming from her eyes. "You'll make it now."

"Oh, no!" Kathia screamed when a large wave pushed the canoe toward the treacherous rocks.

"They'll be all right," Melvin said, coming to place an arm around Kathia's waist. "Bright Arrow is an expert with his canoe."

Kathia held her breath as the canoe was again

tossed toward huge boulders, then guided away by the muscled arms of the hunters.

"Just a little farther," Kathia said, as she watched the canoe moving closer to the shore. "Oh, God, please."

Finally the canoe was beached.

Kathia hugged her father, then, crying, ran down the stairs and rushed outside through the stinging rain. She didn't stop until she reached the canoe.

Just as Bright Arrow stepped from it, he spotted her. They rushed into each other's arms.

"I love you so much," she sobbed out. She clung to him.

Bright Arrow's eyes were filled with her, adoring her. He had not thought that he would ever see her again. Without the lights he had almost despaired of reaching the shore.

"Father is well enough to work the lights," Kathia said, smiling into Bright Arrow's eyes.

"Had he not been there . . ." Bright Arrow began.

"But he was, and I believe it was because of what White Moon did for him," Kathia said, glancing up at the bright beams. "Oh, Lord, had he not . . ."

Bright Arrow swept her up into his arms. He brought his lips down upon hers.

She clung as they kissed, silently thanking the heavens. Today could have turned out so terribly different.

But now? Everything was wonderful! She had her

man back, safe and sound, and she had her father back on his feet again, too.

There was only one thing still worrying her: Dusty's strange comment about her father, and the meaning behind it.

Chapter Twenty-nine

With thee conversing I forget
All seasons and their change,
All please alike.
—John Milton

Fred hurried up the stairs and into the control room. When he found his father slumped over in his chair, fear struck his heart.

Fred had returned from taking photographs of the electrical storm to find his father missing from his bedroom. After searching the whole house and finding no sign of his father, he had come up to the control room as a last resort.

It was a miracle that his father had been able to climb the steep stairs.

"Papa," Fred said, rushing over to him.

"I did it, Fred," Melvin said, smiling as he lifted his head, his eyes gleaming merrily. "Son, I saved the Makah hunters."

"You did it? Not Dusty?" Fred gasped out. "The beams were lit by you, not Dusty?"

"Yep, I did it," Melvin said. "I'm back at it again, and Dusty Harper had better never come near this place again."

Fred stepped back and took another, more lingering look at his father. "I don't quite understand any of this, but the important thing is how you feel," he said. "When I came into the room, your head was hanging. You were slumped down. I thought you might have had a heart attack, or worse. . . ."

"You thought I had exhausted myself right into my casket?" Melvin said, slowly rising from his chair. He took his cane from where he had leaned it against the chair and supported himself on it as he went back to the windows. "Nope, you won't be burying this ol' timer anytime soon, for I feel fit as a fiddle."

He smiled crookedly at Fred. "Yes, mighty exhausted, but truly just fine, Fred, just fine," he said.

He grabbed up his binoculars and with his free hand held them to his eyes so he could scan the ocean. He was glad to see that the white caps were gone, and that the ocean was much calmer than even moments before.

In the sky, the clouds were breaking apart, revealing patches of blue between them.

He squinted his eyes when the sun came out, flooding the waters below with its golden light.

"It's over," he said, feeling a keen relief. "Yep, this storm is over, but there will surely be another one sometime soon. Spring has the reputation, you know, of scaring up storms at the blink of one's eye."

"This one was a doozy," Fred said, settling down on a chair as his father continued to gaze through his binoculars.

"Yep, but the lights are no longer needed, not until tonight," Melvin said. He moved his binoculars slowly from the ocean, then scanned the beach below.

He refocused the binoculars when he saw Kathia in Bright Arrow's arms. He smiled to himself.

It gave him a feeling of pride to know that the man he had saved with his beams was the one his daughter loved . . . and a man Melvin had always admired.

Yep, he knew without her saying a word what Kathia's future held for her. Until she had met Bright Arrow, her career had been her life, her future, her everything.

But now?

He could tell by the way they gazed into one another's eyes that she was going to place her childhood dreams behind her and enter into a vastly different world from the one she'd always imagined.

He expected her to come to him soon and tell him of these changes, that she was going to marry Bright Arrow, for she was not the type to toy with a man's emotions by kissing him and showing such love for him if she did not intend to marry him.

A part of him was sad about this change. Yet another part of him that had always secretly longed for grandchildren was jubilant.

All that he had truly ever wanted for his children was their happiness. If Bright Arrow was the answer to Kathia's, so be it.

And wouldn't this marriage keep her closer, so that he could see her more often, instead of only a few times a year? Yes, her choice was his choice!

"Papa, I was outside taking photographs of lightning when all hell broke loose," Fred said. "I rigged up protection from the rain. I know that I got some fascinating footage."

He paused, then said, "I even got occasional shots of the canoe in peril as the lightning lit up the sky."

"Of course, at that time you didn't know it was Bright Arrow's, did you?" Melvin said, lowering his binoculars. He turned to Fred. "He almost lost his life at sea this time. Had I not made it up the stairs, he would have. That damn sonofabitch Dusty Harper had me locked out of my own control room."

"What?" Fred gasped, rising quickly from the chair. He stood there, rigid, stunned that so much had happened while he had been away from the lighthouse.

"The sonofabitch was going to let Bright Arrow and his crew die," Melvin said, nodding. "Had I not gotten here in time to light my beams, they'd have been lost at sea."

Fred suddenly looked around him, toward the stairs, and then frowned at his father. "Where was Kathia during all this?" he asked. "Where is she now?"

Melvin handed Fred the binoculars. "Look down at the beach," he said, chuckling. "I think you'll get your answer. But as for Dusty, he hightailed it outta here. I have no idea where he went to hide. One thing for certain, though, he'll pay for what he did today. He'll pay."

Fred took the binoculars and gazed down at the shore with them. He saw Bright Arrow and Kathia walking hand in hand toward the beached canoe where the other Makah hunters were looking it over, checking for damage.

"They're walking hand in hand," Fred said. "My sister and Bright Arrow. Doesn't that beat all? Looks like they're in love."

"Seems that way, don't it?" Melvin said, walking slowly around the room, extinguishing the flames in the lamps.

"And how do you feel about it?" Fred said, still watching.

"Well, now, how do *you* feel about it?" Melvin asked, stopping to lean his full weight on his cane.

"I really like the guy," Fred said, lowering the binoculars, then setting them on the counter.

"Well, I think she more than likes the guy," Melvin said, nodding. "I believe she has fallen madly in love. I expect she'll soon tell us a bit of news about her relationship with the handsome chief."

"You think she'll put everything she always dreamed of behind her for Bright Arrow?" Fred asked, cocking an eyebrow.

"Yep, sure do," Melvin said. Then he frowned. "But I expect there's somebody that's going to challenge that."

"Who?"

"Dusty Harper, that's who."

"As if he has anything to say about anything, especially after what he did today," Fred growled out.

"It's more like what he didn't do, son," Melvin said thickly. "Because of his negligence, Bright Arrow could have perished at sea."

Fred's jaw tightened. "Papa, I think I'm going to find that man and teach him a thing or two," he said, walking toward the trapdoor that led to the stairs. "When I get through with him, he'll not try anything else as far as our family is concerned."

"Be careful, son," Melvin said, coming to watch

Fred hurry down the stairs. "That man is the devil and he knows the trouble he's in. He might resort to anything now to protect himself."

"I know," Fred said over his shoulder as he continued down the stairs. "But I must do what I must."

Fred hurried to his bedroom and got his holstered pistol from where he kept it hidden in his bottom dresser drawer. He slapped the holster around his waist, fastened it, then strode to Dusty's room. As he expected, the coward had fled.

Something caught Fred's eye. A drawer stood open beside Dusty's bed.

He could see a small jar with something white in it poking out from beneath a pile of folded white handkerchiefs.

"Is that sugar?" Fred whispered to himself.

Surely not.

Why would Dusty have sugar hidden in a drawer, for it was obvious that the jar had been hidden. Probably the handkerchiefs had slid away from it when the drawer was shoved shut. In Dusty's haste, he had probably not noticed that the drawer was still partly open.

And surely that was not sugar inside the jar. He had never seen Dusty use sugar in either his coffee or tea.

He had not even offered Fred's father sugar when Dusty had taken him the many cups of tea Fred had always wondered about. He had always thought that bit of kindness was out of place. Dusty was anything but kindly and loving toward any of the members of their family.

Oh, he had made overtures toward Kathia, but after she had put him in his place, that had stopped. Since then, he had been harassing her, not being friendly.

"Who cares about whether the man uses sugar or not?" Fred said, turning to leave.

But something stopped him. He turned and stared at the small bottle again.

Hadn't White Moon said that Fred's father had been poisoned by something? In Dusty's twisted mind, was poisoning Fred's father the way he planned to keep the lighthouse to himself? Or was it all done out of spite because Kathia had rebuked him?

Angrily, Fred went to the drawer and grabbed the bottle from it. He grew icy cold inside when he saw the words RAT POISON in tiny print on the label of the bottle.

Lord, Dusty had been feeding his father small doses of rat poison in his tea!

Feeling sick to his stomach over his discovery, Fred hurried outside with the bottle in hand. He ran down the steps and toward the beach.

Not wanting his father to see the bottle through his binoculars, Fred slid it inside his front breeches' pocket. He was afraid the shock of knowing what Dusty had been doing to him might give his father a setback.

When he reached his sister and Bright Arrow, they realized right away that something was terribly wrong. No doubt it was in Fred's eyes.

"Fred, what's happened?" Kathia asked, hurrying to him. "Why are you wearing that pistol? Why do you look so . . . so . . ."

"So disturbed?" Fred said. He glanced up at the windows of the lighthouse control room, glad when he didn't see his father there.

But just in case, Fred took Kathia by the hand, then nodded at Bright Arrow. "Come with me," he said. "You won't believe what I discovered in Dusty's room."

"What?" Kathia asked, stumbling clumsily over a rock when Fred continued to walk hastily toward the shadows of the forest.

When they finally reached the trees, where they could not be seen from above, Fred hurriedly explained what he had discovered in Dusty's room.

"No," Kathia gasped, horrified that her suspicions were all too well founded.

She turned away from Fred and Bright Arrow, struggling to get control of herself, and when she finally felt as though she could stand whatever else her brother had to tell her, she turned back toward him.

"Sis, Dusty is guilty of many things," Fred said angrily. "He's got to be found. He should be jailed and made to pay for his crimes."

"But, Fred, it will be so dangerous for you to

search for him," Kathia said. She reached a hand to his arm and gripped it. "Let's send word to Port Angeles. The authorities will take care of this."

"In the meantime, what else might this crazed man decide to try?" Fred grumbled. "No, Sis. We can't wait until the authorities at Port Angeles get involved."

"I will find him," Bright Arrow said, his voice flat and stern. "I will see that he is punished for not only attempting to kill your father with poison, but also for attempting to kill me and my warriors."

"I want to go with you," Fred said, his hand resting on his pistol. "I want a role in that lunatic's comeuppance."

"I want to go, too," Kathia blurted out.

"I know how badly you both want to be a part of stopping this man, but it can be done better and much more quickly if only I search for him," Bright Arrow said thickly. "I know every inch of this land. There is no place for Dusty to hide."

"Maybe it *is* best that you do this alone," Fred said, sighing heavily. "But remember how crazed he is. He still wants *you* dead, Bright Arrow. He won't stop at anything now to succeed. He knows that his time is almost up. If he can, he'll take you down with him."

"He will not get the chance," Bright Arrow said flatly. "He is inexperienced against such a man as a Makah chief. *Ah-ha*, he had me and my men at the mercy of the sea, but I am now on dry land. He will be at my mercy."

Kathia flung herself in his arms. "Please, oh, please be careful," she sobbed. "If I should lose you, I . . ."

"Do not fear what I am about to do," Bright Arrow said, stroking her back. "Just go back to your home. Be with your father and brother. I will come and let you know when the deed is done."

Kathia stepped away from him, her eyes searching his. "What are you planning to do?" she asked anxiously.

"Just do not worry," Bright Arrow said. He framed her face between his hands. "All right? You will not worry?"

"If you promise not to do anything that will place you in danger," Kathia said, swallowing back a sob. "If I were to lose you . . ."

"The only man who has anything to lose is Dusty Harper," Bright Arrow said reassuringly. "I will go now. Go to your father. Give him my thanks. Tell him I will always remember this day and how he saved me and my crew."

"I will tell him," Kathia said, then flung herself into his arms again and clung to him for a moment longer before he returned to his canoe.

She watched him shove the huge canoe back into the water, then board it with his men. They were soon traveling back in the direction of their village.

"I wonder what he has planned for Dusty," Fred said, turning to question Kathia with his eyes.

"I only hope that he stays safe," Kathia said, moving into her brother's arms. "Fred, we almost lost Father to Dusty's poison. And . . . and . . . Dusty almost took the life of another wonderful man . . . Bright Arrow. Bright Arrow *has* to find him and stop his madness!"

Chapter Thirty

> It lies not in our power to love or hate,
> For will in us is overruled by fate.
> When two are stripped, long ere the course
> begin,
> We wish that one should lose, the other win.
> —Christopher Marlowe

Realizing that he had finally shown his true self to Melvin and Kathia, and not sure where to hide until they gave up the search for him, Dusty was running frantically along the beach. Every now and then he dodged in and out of the forest, then ran along the beach again, sweating and panting.

He no longer looked over his shoulder to see if anyone was following. He had gotten away from the lighthouse; he could no longer be seen from the high circle of windows.

He planned to find a place to hide until the next ferry boat was due at Ozette from Port Angeles. He'd sneak aboard. He knew that he had just ruined any chances of ever being able to manage a lighthouse again, or be with Kathia.

He was afraid that he couldn't even go to any more of her performances, for surely she would tell the authorities about him and they would keep an eye out for him.

The only thing the Parrishes hadn't figured out was how he had been slowly poisoning Melvin. He had implied to Kathia that her father should be dead, but she would never guess what he meant by that.

He stopped in midstep, paling, his eyes wide when he recalled what he had stupidly left in the top drawer of the bedside table.

He had kept the bottle of rat poison there. When the Parrishes went to clean out his personal belongings, they would find it.

They would surely put two and two together and finally realize what had been making Melvin Parrish so ill.

"I'm a goner," Dusty groaned to himself.

Now he knew for certain that he had to find a way to escape. He might have to lie low in the forest until he found a way to get as far as Seattle. Once he reached Seattle, he could get lost in the crowd, far from where anyone would know him, or even look for him.

Breathing hard, his shirt wet with perspiration and clinging to his back, Dusty found himself running along the shore again, wincing when the sharp rocks managed to thrust through the soles of his shoes, hurting his feet.

He searched until he found a straight stretch of sand. He ran to it and started running even harder. He had to find a hiding place.

If Bright Arrow or his warriors were out in their hunting canoes, they could spy him from this vantage point. If they saw him running and saw the guilt on his face, they would realize that he was running from something.

He gazed to his left and saw a thick forest of trees not far from the beach.

He started to leave the sand to seek shelter there, but suddenly his feet wouldn't move. The sand was sucking them downward, into it.

His eyes wide, his heart pounding with fear, Dusty gazed down and saw what was happening.

He was in quicksand!

He had heard there was quicksand in this area, but until now he had forgotten all about it.

"Help me!" he screamed as his efforts to get out of the sand only caused him to sink more deeply into it.

He was in it now, up to his ankles. As he tried to raise a foot, he felt icy cold with fear. Nothing he did was helping.

He was afraid that he was going to be sucked all the way into the sand. He would disappear from the Parrish's lives, all right. He would be totally gone from this earth!

"Oh, someone, please, can't you hear me?" he screamed, looking wild-eyed around him.

He was no longer afraid of being caught and blamed for what he had done to the Parrish family. All he cared about was surviving. He would rather survive in a cell than die choking on sand!

Suddenly he saw a flash of lightning. But no. It couldn't be. There were no storm clouds anywhere to be seen.

He blinked his eyes and saw it again, and this time he heard the clap of thunder. But still he saw no clouds.

Then his heart skipped a beat and he sucked in a wild breath of fear when he saw the flash of light again. But instead of lightning, it was the angry flash of the eyes of a monstrously large bird flying down from the heavens, toward him.

The thunder that he had thought he had heard was the loud flapping of the bird's huge wings.

He had heard of the great spirit bird, the Thunderbird, that the Makah Indians spoke of, yet he had always thought it was a legend, that the bird only lived in the minds of the people.

Yet hadn't he seen the huge bird flying in the lights of the beams only recently? He had thought he was seeing things, that the bird had not been real.

But this bird was certainly real enough. The creature was sweeping down from the heavens, its huge talons open.

"No!" Dusty screamed.

He held his arms over his head to protect himself as the bird began flying around him, its eyes like rivers of fire glaring at him.

The wind made by the huge wings lifted Dusty's hair and blew it. His body shuddered, sending him more deeply into the sand.

He did not know which was worse . . . the bird killing him with its great golden talons and sharp beak, or sinking beneath the sand, choking to death on it.

He flailed his arms in an effort to keep the bird away from him. But no matter what he did, the bird was not to be frightened away. It was seemingly there for a purpose, and Dusty soon found out what that purpose was when the bird's large talons grabbed him by the back of his shirt and yanked him free of the quicksand.

Was it possible that the bird had come to save him from dying a slow, terrifying death in the quicksand?

Mythical or real, it didn't matter. All he knew

was that he was no longer being sucked farther into the sand. He was free.

And the bird wasn't making any attempt to eat him. It seemed peaceful enough as it carried him farther and farther away from the quicksand.

"I don't know why you did this for me, but thank you," Dusty cried.

He knew that if he ever tried to tell anyone about this, they would lock him away in a loony bin, for even he still could not believe it was happening.

But he soon realized that he was not yet out of danger. The bird was now carrying him up into the sky, farther and farther away from land.

"What are you doing?" Dusty cried, unable to get free, the bird's talons still holding him tightly by his shirt. "Oh, Lord, no! Please, oh, please take me back to the land and let me go. Where are you taking me?"

Dusty's eyes grew wider by the minute as the bird swept higher and higher into the sky. He could see ocean below him now, not land.

He inhaled deeply, his fear paralyzing him. It seemed the bird had only rescued him from the quicksand to drop him far out at sea.

"Why are you doing this?" Dusty screamed. "Where are you taking me?"

The wind was harsh against his face as the bird flew at unbelievable speed upward into the sky, then made a wide turn to his left and flew toward a high butte that looked out over the ocean.

As the bird carried Dusty closer to the butte, he saw that it was dangerously narrow, high, and rocky. If the bird released him there, which now seemed to be its intent, Dusty would be stranded, for he was not skilled at climbing, and it was too high for him to dive into the ocean and swim back to shore.

When the bird did release Dusty and he fell hard onto the narrow butte, he rolled over once and found himself on the very edge, his eyes looking far down below him, where on one side of him was a sandy beach and on the other . . . the sea.

He shuddered with fear as he clung desperately to the sides of the bluff when the bird's heavy wings made a draft as it flew away, high up into the sky, until it was no longer visible.

"Help! Help!" Dusty screamed, still clinging as he lay on his stomach, gazing downward. "Someone please hear me! I'm stranded!"

Then he went quiet, for he knew that he was wasting his breath, crying for something that would never happen.

He was far from humanity. He was not even certain how far he had been taken.

All that he knew was that something incredible had happened to him today, and if he were to be rescued and tell how he happened to be on that bluff, no one would believe him.

Even he found it hard to believe, yet he knew it was real, for here he was, stranded far from humanity, the thrashing waves of the ocean pounding over and over again against the rocks below him.

He dared not move. He clung with all his might. He stared at the waves. He listened to them.

He was doomed to die alone on this godforsaken cliff.

"Either I am already dead and in hell, or I am about to die!" he sobbed out.

He closed his eyes and saw Kathia in his mind's eye. He smiled, as in his illusion he saw her pirouetting on stage.

Then his smile faded. He frowned darkly. He hated Kathia with a passion now!

Everything that was happening to him was because of her!

He gritted his teeth. "I wish I had never seen you that first time," he muttered beneath his breath, for after that first evening at the ballet, he had been lost to her.

He was going to die alone because of her.

"If ever I get out of this mess, I'm coming for you," he hissed.

Chapter Thirty-one

Sweet is the breath of morn,
her rising sweet,
With charm of earliest birds;
pleasant the sun.
—John Milton

The sun poured its glorious light into the parlor, all remnants of the almost fateful storm swept away. "Father, I am so happy for you . . . and for Bright Arrow," Kathia said, giving her father a big hug. "You were actually able to climb the stairs and take control of your beams. You . . . you . . . saved Bright Arrow's life, and those who were in the canoe with him."

Fred stood back, quiet as he circled his hand around the small bottle in his right pocket. He wasn't quite sure how to tell his father about having found the poison.

He gazed at the pride in his father's eyes, and his warm smile as he stepped away from Kathia to go and light his pipe. At this moment, things were as they were supposed to be. Their family was together.

His father was truly on the road to full recovery. And Bright Arrow had said that he would take care of Dusty and make certain he did not harm anyone else.

How Bright Arrow was going to do that did not concern Fred. The fact that it would be done was all that mattered.

But what should he do with this bottle of poison? Keep his knowledge of it hidden until it was needed at Dusty's trial, if there was a trial?

Yes, Fred decided that was best.

He did not want his father to know just yet, if ever, that he was walking around with traces of rat poison in his body. Fred only hoped that in time it would all vanish, and that his father would be as good as new.

Only if the proof of Dusty's guilt was needed would he reveal the horrible truth.

"Fred, you are so quiet," Kathia said, as he slowly slid his hand from inside his pocket. "Come here, big brother. Let's hug. And then I have something to share with you and Father."

Fred smiled and went to her. He not only hugged

her, he lifted her up and laughingly swung her around in playful circles.

"Quit that," Kathia squealed as she had when she was a child. "Let me down, Fred."

He chuckled as he set her back on her feet.

He lifted his hand to her golden hair and drew his fingers through it. "All right, Sis, what is it you want to tell us?" he said, then lowered his hand to his side. He smiled at his father as he sat down in a rocker, his pipe between his lips, the smoke spiraling slowly from the bowl.

"Come and sit with me on the floor before Father," Kathia said, motioning with a hand for Fred. "You know, the way we always talked things over when we were children."

"So what you have to say is that serious, eh?" Fred said, going and sitting down beside her, facing their father.

"Very serious," Kathia said, smiling mischievously. "Well, not all that serious. I'm just so happy to have something wonderful to share with my father and brother."

Melvin took his pipe from his mouth. He rested it on an ashtray on the table beside him.

He placed a gentle hand on Kathia's shoulder. "I get the feeling this might be about Bright Arrow," he said.

"Papa, Fred, you know my plans have always been to be known worldwide for my dancing," Kathia murmured. "You know that my life became dancing. It has been my one dearest love."

"Yes, and has that changed?" Melvin asked, his eyes twinkling into hers, for he knew that it had.

"Papa . . . Fred . . . I'm madly in love with Bright Arrow," Kathia said, looking from one to the other. "I . . . I . . . have accepted his proposal of marriage. I am going to give up my dancing for a life with him."

She did not see all that much surprise in her father's eyes, but she did in Fred's. She knew that Fred had known she felt something special for Bright Arrow, but she understood why he would be surprised to know just how much she was willing to give up in order to have him for herself.

"Fred?" she said. She reached over and took his hands in hers. "You and Magdalena have made plans for your future. So have Bright Arrow and I. I am going to marry him."

"But . . . what about your dancing?" Fred asked. "How can you give it up? I didn't ask that of Magdalena. We reached a compromise. She will be much happier for it. But you? Are you truly certain you are ready to give it all up for marriage?"

"I love Bright Arrow with all my heart," Kathia said softly. "I know it seems strange that I am ready to change my life so much in order to have this man for my husband. But loving him so much, it will not be that hard for me."

"But Kathia, you have a ballet performance

soon," Fred argued. "Are you going to honor your contract?"

"I would enjoy seeing you perform one last time," Melvin said. "So would those who have bought tickets for the performance. I am certain they are sold out at the opera house. You just can't disappoint everyone."

"Nor shall I," Kathia murmured. "Bright Arrow will understand that I have made this commitment. He knows that I am a woman of my word. He would not expect me to cancel my last performance. I shall dance. I shall dance my heart out."

She placed her hands together and closed her eyes. "I can hear the applause even now," she said, her voice lilting. "I have so cherished that applause. I shall savor it one more time."

Then she drew her hands apart and rested them on her lap. "But I cherish even more the knowledge that I have a man such as Bright Arrow who loves me so much," she said. "I will make him a good wife. Even though I do not know the first thing about cooking or housekeeping, I shall learn. I will be the best of students."

She gazed from her father to Fred. "I do hunger for the applause, and I also hunger to see the pride in both of your eyes this one last time," she murmured.

"Kathia, don't you know that I am proud of you whether or not you perform on the stage?" Melvin said, reaching down to take one of her hands. He held it tenderly. "But yes, I will enjoy it very, very much."

"And so will I," Fred said, taking her other hand, then releasing it as a knock came on the front door. "I'll go and see who that is."

He rose to his feet, slowly slid a hand inside his breeches pocket again, his fingers circling around the bottle of poison, then went to the door.

When he opened it, he saw a slow smile lift Bright Arrow's lips.

"It is done," Bright Arrow said. "Dusty is taken care of. He will not be bothering your family again."

"What did you do with him?" Fred asked, sliding his hand free of his pocket again. "Where is he?"

"I would like to tell your father and Kathia as I tell you," Bright Arrow said, smiling at Kathia as she hurried toward him.

She squeezed past Fred in the doorway and gave Bright Arrow a hug. "I heard," she murmured, then stepped away and gazed into his eyes. "Come into the parlor. Father will want to hear all about it, too."

They all went to the parlor.

Melvin smiled up at Bright Arrow, but remained in the chair. He had not told Kathia or Fred that what he had done today had exhausted him.

But he would fight this exhaustion. He would climb those stairs again tonight and be there with his beams, guiding them across the sea. No one would be in danger while he was in control of his lighthouse.

"Dusty will not be bothering any of you again," Bright Arrow said, all eyes on him.

In unison, they asked, "Where is he?"

"This man needs to feel the wrath of his God before he feels the wrath of the white man's law," Bright Arrow said thickly. "Where he is, is the best place for him to be. He is face to face with his God."

"But Bright Arrow, where?" Kathia persisted. "How is he face to face with God?"

"I would rather not say," Bright Arrow replied, placing a gentle hand on her cheek. "Just know that at this moment, he is more afraid than anyone could ever be."

Kathia's eyes widened. She wished to question him further, but she saw that he did not want to reveal any more about what he had done.

His reticence made her even more curious, but she would not press him for answers. She trusted his decisions in all things.

All that mattered was that Dusty was finally getting his comeuppance.

"Soon I will go for him and hand him over to the white authorities," Bright Arrow said. "It is for them to say what his final fate will be, not a Makah chief."

Kathia threw herself into his arms. "Thank you," she murmured. "This man has been a thorn in my family's side since he arrived. Who is to say what would have happened if he had stayed for much longer?"

Yes, who is to say, Fred thought to himself, again sliding his hand into his pocket and touching the bottle. He would keep this proof of Dusty's guilt for his trial. This would bury him.

"Thank you for everything," Melvin said, slowly rising from the chair.

His knees were wobbly, but he forced himself to walk steadily so that his children would not know the extent of his weakness. He gave Bright Arrow a warm hug.

"Bright Arrow . . ." Kathia said as her father stepped away from him and returned to his rocker. "I told Father and Fred about our planned nuptials. They are happy for us."

"I will make her a good husband," Bright Arrow said, sliding an arm around her waist. "I love her with all my heart. I will never allow any misfortune to come her way."

"Both Fred and I know that," Melvin said, nodding.

She looked up into Bright Arrow's eyes. "But there is one thing I must do before we get married," she murmured.

"What is that?" Bright Arrow asked, searching her eyes.

"Perform one last time on the stage," Kathia said guardedly. "Bright Arrow, this ballet performance has been scheduled for a long time. Many tickets have been sold. I can't back down on my commitment to my fans. I must perform. Do you understand? Will you attend?"

Bright Arrow's eyes wavered. "I understand about your commitment, but please understand when I tell you that I cannot be there," he said thickly. "My woman, it is not a place for a red man, but my heart will be with you as you make your last appearance on the stage as a proud ballerina."

Kathia's smile wavered. She was deeply disappointed that he would not be able to watch her last performance, but she did understand. She had never seen any Indian in the audience and knew that Bright Arrow would feel awkward were he to be there. She did not want that.

"I understand," she murmured. "It is only one evening, and then the rest are ours!"

"I must go back to sea tomorrow," Bright Arrow said. "It is time for another hunt. But I will first see to Dusty Harper. I will hand him over to the authorities. You will never have to worry about him interfering in your lives again."

He smiled at Melvin and Fred, then took Kathia by the hand and led her out onto the porch. The day was turning slowly and softly to night. The sunset was brilliant along the water's horizon.

"I have many days at sea ahead of me," he said. "I shall probably not see you until after your performance. My heart will be there for you. Please know that."

"Yes, I know that it will," Kathia murmured. "Please be careful while you hunt."

"As long as storms stay far away, and as long as your father's lamps are lit, all will be well with this man who loves you with his entire heart," Bright Arrow said. He drew her into his embrace. "Until we are together again, just know that I am always with you. Our hearts are always together."

He brought his lips down upon hers in a gentle kiss.

She clung and fought back tears, for she knew that she had several days ahead of her when she would not see him. She also had her last performance ahead of her.

She hoped that she could dance without sadness.

Chapter Thirty-two

My passion shall kill me before I show it,
And yet I would give all the world he did
know it.
—Sir George Etherege

His warriors were in his village, preparing their large canoes for another day at sea, but Bright Arrow had something else he had promised to do before he joined them. He was in a small canoe, one that would only hold two travelers. He was rowing toward a high bluff, its shadow already falling over him. A voice familiar, but hated, shouted down at him.

Smiling smugly, Bright Arrow did not give Dusty Harper the satisfaction of knowing that he was keenly aware of his presence on the bluff. Nor would he ever tell how he knew of Dusty's whereabouts.

The important thing for Bright Arrow to do was to carry through on his promise to Kathia and her family that he, personally, would see to the criminal. He had sent word to the sheriff at Port Angeles that Dusty Harper needed to be incarcerated, and why.

Sheriff James was to meet Bright Arrow on a small island a few miles out from Ozette. He had not wanted to make his people nervous by bringing the sheriff to their village. Too many people resented white lawmen.

Sheriff James had, for the most part, worked against the Makah, not with them. But Dusty Harper was the responsibility of the white lawman, not the Makah.

"Bright Arrow! Help me!" Dusty shouted, still trying to draw Bright Arrow's attention. "Surely you hear me. How can you not hear me?"

Bright Arrow still ignored Dusty's ranting and raving. He beached his canoe, then with the skills he had learned long ago, when he was a young brave, he began climbing the rocky wall.

As a boy, he had slipped and fallen into the sea more than once as he tried to learn what he was so expertly doing now. But always he'd climbed on the sea's side, not the beach, so that should he fall, he would land in the softer cradle of water.

Ignoring how his fingers burned as he clung first to one cluster of rock and then another, Bright Arrow continued to climb. Higher and higher he went, until he finally reached the tiny ledge, where there was scarcely room for one man to stand, much less two.

He stood now, eye to eye, with Dusty Harper, who looked even more disreputable than ever with an overnight growth of whiskers on his face.

Bright Arrow realized that Dusty was staring at him with confusion in his pale gray eyes. Bright Arrow smiled knowingly at the man, making Dusty's eyes waver.

"You *knew* I was here. How *could* you?" Dusty gasped out, starting to take a step away from Bright Arrow. He stopped, however, when he realized that one step backward would send him plummeting downward. A fall from this height, either on the sand or the water, would be a fatal one.

"And what makes you think I knew?" Bright Arrow taunted.

"Because after I saw you coming in this direction, it seemed to me that you had a destination in mind," Dusty said uncertainly. "Yet how would you know I was here? Unless you saw me from a distance, which seems unlikely. Still, there is no reason for you to be this far from Ozette alone."

"You can wonder all you want about how or why, but you will get no answers from me," Bright Arrow said, frowning at Dusty. "I *will*, however, tell you the reason I am here. It is to take you to the authorities. Your days of harming innocent people, white or red-skinned, are over. You will never be at the controls of Melvin Parrish's lighthouse again."

"Why doesn't anyone understand that that damn lighthouse isn't Melvin's!" Dusty screamed, his eyes wild.

Then he sobered up again, and his eyes filled with questions. "This is frightening," he said, swallowing hard. "A huge bird brought me here, and now you have come. Is there truly a connection between you and . . . and . . ."

Bright Arrow interrupted him. He grabbed him by an arm. "You are to leave this rock with me," he said flatly.

"How?" Dusty gasped, turning pale. "I can't scale the wall the way you obviously did. I'll fall to my death."

Dusty gulped hard. "Unless the bird is to appear again?" he asked, searching Bright Arrow's midnight dark eyes.

"No, there is no bird," Bright Arrow said. "There is only Bright Arrow. Come. I shall help you. Nothing will happen to you. Just do as I do. Soon you will be on solid ground."

"I'm too afraid to try," Dusty cried, tears shining in his eyes. "I can't."

"You, who would pretend to be such a giant of a man, are afraid?" Bright Arrow taunted. "Look at you: a big man who is ready to cry like a child."

"I am . . . too afraid to go down the sides of the bluff, and to hell with what you think of me," Dusty said, wiping the tears from his eyes with his free hand. He clenched his jaw. "I'm staying. And why should I even want to leave? What you probably have planned for me will be worse than dying alone on this slab of rock."

"I am going to hand you over to the sheriff, nothing more," Bright Arrow said flatly. "Either you come with me, or I shall shove you into the water. You might live. You might die. You will make that choice, not I."

Dusty turned his head sideways and gazed down at the ocean. The waves were gentle today, yet dangerous should anyone dive—or jump—into them from this height.

His gaze slid over to the rocky shore.

He swallowed hard, thinking about the pain that would come with landing on the rocks. And he might not die.

He might end up being a twisted, crippled old man, who lived out the rest of his life in a wheelchair behind bars.

"You are thinking through your choices?" Bright Arrow said, slowly taking his hand away from Dusty.

"I truly believe you do not have any. You must do as I do, or die one way or the other."

"No, I have no choice," Dusty said, his voice trembling.

"Then come with me," Bright Arrow said, already going down the side of the slab of rock. "Follow me. I will not let you fall."

"Why should you care?" Dusty cried as he followed Bright Arrow's lead, his fingers already burning as he desperately grasped the outcropping of rock. "Wouldn't it be easier for you and Kathia's family if I did die?"

"It is not our intention that you die, at least not until you live through the punishment for what you are guilty of," Bright Arrow said, his eyes watching Dusty as he followed Bright Arrow's every move.

"I am not guilty of all that much," Dusty said, his eyes wide as he continued downward. "I didn't turn on the lighthouse lights. That isn't a serious crime."

"You intentionally did not turn them on, hoping that your not doing so would cause deaths," Bright Arrow said tightly. "My death. My warriors' deaths. And anyone else far out at sea who needed the beams during the storm."

Dusty chuckled. "Yes, I am guilty of that, and you would be surprised to know what *else*," he said, again speaking before thinking, then growing pale when he realized just how close he had come to admitting the worst truth of all . . . that he had been slowly poisoning Melvin Parrish.

"No, I doubt that anything you did would surprise me," Bright Arrow said, finally on the rocky shore. He reached out and helped Dusty down beside him, then clasped his hands tightly on Dusty's shoulders and turned him hard, to face him. "But since you seem proud of what you did, I want you to tell me what it is."

"No, I can't," Dusty said, cowering beneath Bright Arrow's dark, accusing eyes. "I'd . . . I'd . . . get a much stiffer sentence."

"Do you want to return to the butte?" Bright Arrow said, his eyes gleaming. "That can be arranged easily enough."

Seeing the look in Bright Arrow's eyes, Dusty was reminded of other eyes. He pictured the huge bird's talons, reaching down for him, then grabbing him by the back of his shirt and carrying him to the frightening slab of rock.

"You wouldn't . . ." Dusty gasped out.

"Would you want to chance it?" Bright Arrow said, smiling smugly at Dusty. "I want you to tell me what you were referring to. What else did you do?"

"I . . . I . . . hate Melvin Parrish," Dusty hissed, his eyes narrowing. Then his eyes softened. "But I adore Kathia Parrish. I . . . I . . . have watched her perform as a ballerina for at least three years now. I have followed wherever she was going to be. I never failed to see her. I fell in love. I wanted her for my wife. When I saw the opportunity to be at the very lighthouse where she would probably be, since her father had fallen ill, I jumped at the chance."

"And then what did you do?" Bright Arrow asked, his jaw tightening as he thought about this evil man gazing at Kathia, lusting after her as she performed on the stage.

It caused a sick feeling in the pit of his stomach to think of what this dirty-minded man might have imagined while thinking of Kathia in the darkness of his bedroom.

That Dusty had actually placed himself in her father's home, so he could be close to Kathia, made Bright Arrow want to strangle him.

"What did I do?" Dusty said, at first looking frightened. Then that fright turned to a twisted sort of smugness as his lips moved into a crooked smile. "I made certain Melvin Parrish stayed sick longer than he would have had I not fed him . . . rat poison."

Bright Arrow felt a rush of cold fury surge through him. He visibly shuddered.

Then he sank his fingers more deeply into Dusty's shoulders. "You fed that wonderful, kind man . . . poison?" he said between clenched teeth.

"I'd do it again, if it meant that I could stay longer at the lighthouse and be around Kathia," Dusty snarled. "But *no*. You had to interfere. Damn you to hell, Bright Arrow. I hope the next time you are at sea a storm comes again, and you are not able to make it to shore. I hope your men are dashed against the rocks!"

"I have heard enough," Bright Arrow said. He released his hands from Dusty's shoulders and gave him a shove toward the beached canoe. "Get in the canoe. I am anxious to rid myself and the Parrish family of the likes of you. I have never met such a deranged, evil man as you. I hope I never do again."

"I'll haunt you into your grave," Dusty said, cackling throatily as he climbed into the canoe. "I won't give you a minute's rest."

"You have no power to do any of that," Bright Arrow said, walking knee-high into the water as he took his canoe out where he could board it himself. "You have no powers at all. Your God would never bless you with such a thing. Someone as evil as you? No. Never."

"You tell what I confessed about the poison and no one will believe you," Dusty said, clutching hard at the sides of the small canoe as Bright Arrow paddled out farther to sea, then headed toward the island where the ferry should even now be waiting. "You are nothing but a low-down, stinking savage. No whites with any kind of a mind would ever believe you. You are looked down upon. You are nothing. Do you hear? Nothing."

"I am more than you want to know," Bright

Arrow said, turning and smiling mischievously at Dusty.

Remembering the huge bird that had grabbed him and carried him away, Dusty's gaze wavered. Feeling the heat of Bright Arrow's eyes, Dusty lowered his. He held them down until he heard the sound of the ferry's engines, then looked up and saw it moored at an island that Dusty had seen often from the lighthouse. It was not the same island where Doc Raley made his residence. It was an uninhabited one.

He then looked at those who were on board.

He stiffened when he recognized Sheriff James and his tall-crowned ten-gallon hat. He was known to be from Texas. He sported ugly, big, holstered pistols on either hip, and he wore high-heeled boots.

He had a bright red beard and mustache, and never had Dusty seen the sonofagun smile. He was all business, and loved putting a noose around a guilty man's neck.

Dusty swallowed hard as the canoe crept closer to the island, then was beached when Bright Arrow rammed it hard onto the sandy shore.

"And so here's the culprit, eh?" Sheriff James said as he walked down the gangplank toward Bright Arrow and Dusty. "Dusty Harper. I believe we've been acquainted before, haven't we?"

Dusty said nothing, only glared back at the bearded man.

"Well, makes no difference to me if you've lost the ability to talk," Sheriff James said, shrugging. He grabbed handcuffs from a pocket. He glared at Dusty. "Well, what's keeping you? Hold out those wrists to me, or by God, you'll be sorry."

Dusty grumbled beneath his breath as he held out his wrists and watched as the handcuffs were secured. Then he glared at the sheriff. "That you would take the word of a savage over any white man is beyond me," he said flatly.

"Just shut up, fool," Sheriff James growled. He gave Dusty a shove toward the gangplank, then turned to Bright Arrow. "We've had our differences, but I'm glad as hell to take this man off your hands. I think the world of Melvin Parrish. If you did this for him, I won't forget it."

Nodding at the sheriff, Bright Arrow turned and went back to his canoe. He was paddling away from the island when the ferry whistle resounded, loud and squawking, and then he heard the large splash of water that came as the ferry got underway.

"You'll be sorry!" Dusty shouted at Bright Arrow from the boat. "Nothing'll keep me behind bars. Nothing! I'll still have Kathia. She belongs to me, not a damn heathen!"

Bright Arrow's spine stiffened, but he went on his way. He had to get this man off his mind. He had a day of hunting ahead of him, and then soon, ah, soon, he was going to take Kathia as his wife!

"You'll be sorry!" Dusty screamed at Bright Arrow, and then went suddenly quiet.

Bright Arrow smiled, for he was almost certain that the sheriff had silenced Dusty.

He rowed onward until he saw the waiting canoes, the warriors beside them, ready for the day's hunt. He beached the small canoe and walked toward his huge hunting vessel, his shoulders squared, his spirit cleansed of the filth of spending the morning with a man that he would always deplore with every fiber of his being.

He soon found himself far out at sea, the sea breeze in his face, the sound of a whale blowing out air somewhere close.

"Let us go and make our people proud!" Bright Arrow shouted, then spoke softly to himself as he prayed to the spirit of the whale, a thank you that these huge water mammals would provide for his people again.

Chapter Thirty-three

Oh, how I am pleased
when I think on this man,
That I find I must love,
Let me do what I can.
How long I shall love him
I can no more tell,
Than, had I a fever,
When I should be well.
—Sir George Etherege

The opera house where Kathia performed in Port Angeles was packed from the lower floor to the balcony. The Seattle Symphony Orchestra was visiting, playing for Kathia's performance.

She wore a beautiful tutu, its short skirt revealing

her long, slender, shapely legs. Her golden hair was pulled up on her head, showing off her graceful neck and shoulders as she pirouetted to the haunting strains of violins.

Her satin ballet slippers kept her steady and poised, as she spun around on her toes, then did a breathtaking leap that made her look as if she were flying.

As she danced, she became something else, a swan, perhaps, its sleek elegance something she had always thought of as she performed before audiences, both small and large.

Tonight the audience was everything she had wished it to be. She could feel the total absorption of the people as they gazed in admiration at her dancing, thrilled by the music wafting to the rooftop.

Tonight Kathia could not help being torn by conflicting emotions. She adored the stage. She adored the audience. She adored everything about dancing.

Yet this would be the last time she would perform before an audience. She had chosen Bright Arrow over everything and everyone else.

She loved him so intensely, she was performing her last time with a smile on her face and a song in her heart. The battle within her had been won, the man she would love forever the cause. She was the true victor!

And tonight, as she felt so many eyes on her, she

felt blessed that her father was among those who were witness to her last performance.

He was well! The poison Dusty had been slowly feeding him was finally gone from his bloodstream.

The thought of Dusty made Kathia's smile falter for a moment. She was eager to testify against him. She wanted him to rot in prison.

She didn't like where her thoughts had wandered. She wanted her last performance to be her best ever. She wanted the reviews written about it to be glowing.

But there was one thing lacking. Bright Arrow was not there.

She had told him that she understood why he wouldn't come, yet inside her heart she yearned for him to change his mind.

As she danced across the stage, her gaze caught a movement at the back of the opera house. Her eyes widened and her heart skipped a beat when she saw someone there, in the shadows, his gleaming copper skin contrasting with the red velvet curtains that hung from the walls behind him.

It was Bright Arrow!

He had come to witness her final moments on the stage.

He had put aside all his doubts about mingling with such a crowd as this, and come to prove his undying love for her.

Her heart now thumping wildly, Kathia looked

into the audience and saw a sheepish grin on her father and brother's faces. They were responsible for Bright Arrow being here. They had talked him into it. They had convinced him that his presence would make Kathia's last time on stage truly memorable.

She gave them a grateful look, tossed Bright Arrow a big, knowing smile, then continued with her performance, more content than she had thought anyone could ever be.

When the last chord was played by the orchestra and Kathia spun around one last time, she was smiling so widely, her jaws ached.

She sank into a slow, graceful bow. She remained in that position as the applause thundered over her. She did not want her audience to see her grateful tears. She wanted them only to witness her smiles.

When Kathia finally straightened and smiled out at the audience, the applause was deafening. The shouts of "Bravo, bravo," confirmed her ardent fans' love for her.

Then she saw Bright Arrow approaching the stage, a huge bouquet of bright spring flowers in his hands. They were just like the flowers where the two of them had made love for the first time.

She wanted him now as never before. She wanted his arms. She wanted his kiss. She wanted all of him!

When he reached the stage to hand her the lovely bouquet, Kathia bent low again and kissed him on the lips. This was the happiest moment of her life.

She was quickly aware of a sudden hushed silence in the opera house. She drew her lips from Bright Arrow's and looked up at the audience. Everyone was gaping openly at her with incredulous stares.

She realized for the first time in her life the treatment Indians must get when they mingled among whites, the sharp pangs that came with being the object of prejudice.

Her heart racing, Kathia gazed at her father, and then Fred, and saw the anger in their eyes as they looked around at those whose silence and disapproving glares said so much about the ugliness inside them.

Kathia knew that her father and brother felt the same as she. She also knew that even if she did want to dance again, it would not be a wise thing to do.

This audience tonight had turned on her. Word would spread.

She imagined there would be much written about tonight's events in newspapers all across the country, not her successful final performance, but what would be labeled as her "shameful behavior" afterward.

She held her chin high and smiled boldly at the crowd, then gazed down at Bright Arrow. "Let's meet in at my dressing room," she murmured, and ran from the stage, clutching her beautiful flowers.

"The crowd," Bright Arrow said as he rejoined Kathia in front of her dressing room moments later.

"I am sorry the people here no longer look at you with favor, but instead as though you are suddenly foreign to them."

"Bright Arrow, I don't care what they are thinking," Kathia murmured. She twined her arms around his neck as he swept her up into his arms and laid her cheek on the soft buckskin shirt that covered his muscled chest. "I am radiantly happy."

He carried her into her dressing room, then turned to close the door. Bright Arrow had just placed Kathia on her feet when she heard a noise behind a folding screen at the far end of the room.

She grabbed at her throat, her eyes wide with fear, when Dusty stepped from behind the screen, blood on his brow, evil in his eyes, a pistol aimed directly at her.

"Yeah, you didn't expect me to come to your final performance, didja?" he said, glowering at Kathia. "You didn't expect me to escape, didja? You thought I was locked up in a cell here at Port Angeles, didn't you? Well, seems the sheriff's deputy got a bit careless."

With his free hand, Dusty wiped at the blood on his brow. "I got injured in the escape, but my injury is nothing like the one I inflicted on the deputy," he said, laughing. "He was the only one in charge. He was easy to trick. When he came into the cell to see what my complaint was, I grabbed the pistol from his holster. I made him unlock the cell. Then

I took good care of him. He won't be talking to no one about my escape for some time. His skull took quite a blow from his very own pistol."

Bright Arrow glared at Dusty, but just as he decided to try something to distract him so that he could grab the gun, the door suddenly opened and Kathia's father stepped into view.

This was all the distraction Bright Arrow needed. He lunged at Dusty, grabbing for the pistol.

Dusty dropped it. But as the weapon hit the floor, it discharged.

Kathia screamed, for she thought that Bright Arrow or her father might have been shot.

She sighed with relief when she saw Dusty grab at his chest, blood streaming between his fingers, the victim of his own evil.

He fell to his knees. "Bravo, Kathia," he said in a strange sort of gurgle. "Your last performance was . . . your . . . best."

He gave Kathia a pitiful look, then fell over, face forward, dead.

Kathia turned to Bright Arrow and flung herself into his arms. "It's over," she sobbed. "Finally, this man's evil days are over."

"Kathia!" Fred screamed as he rushed into the room, then stopped abruptly as he caught sight of the dead man's body.

He looked at Kathia, then at Bright Arrow. "Thank God you are all right," he said thickly. He gazed again at Dusty. He scratched his brow. "But what I'd like to know is how this man got in here? I thought he was . . ."

"In jail?"

A booming voice caused everyone's eyes to move to the door as a large, burly man pushed his way past Fred. He had a huge, bloody, purple knot on his forehead.

Kathia surmised this was the man Dusty had injured in order to escape.

He turned to Kathia. "I'm Deputy Cline," the man said. He extended a hand of friendship that Kathia quickly accepted. "I'm new in Port Angeles. I've been a lawman in Seattle until a few days ago. I was the one who was assigned to stay at the jail today while the sheriff and the two other deputies were in the audience, watching your last performance. I'm sorry something like this had to happen to ruin your special night."

He slowly slid his gaze to Bright Arrow, then broke into a wide smile. "Hello, cousin," he said, now offering his hand to Bright Arrow. "Long time no see."

Bright Arrow chuckled as he took his cousin's hand and shook it. "*Ah-ha*, our lives have taken different roads," he said, nodding. "It is good to see you again, Alan."

"Our grandmothers were sisters," Alan explained to Kathia. "Of course, no one but our family knows that I am part Makah. I don't much announce it. You know about prejudice. Had anyone known about my relationship with the Makah, I'd not have been able to be a lawman, especially here in Port Angeles, and you know that was my dream since I was a little boy."

"*Ah-ha*, as mine was to follow my *ahte* into chieftainship," Bright Arrow said, nodding.

Alan slid his gaze over to Kathia, noting the way Bright Arrow held his arm around her waist.

"My woman," Bright Arrow said, smiling at Alan and then at Kathia. "She performed beautifully tonight. I was proud."

"Word is already spreading through town of your relationship with Kathia," Alan said. "Of course, you know that whites do not approve. If my skin was not white like my father's, everything would be different for me."

"It matters not to me or Kathia whether whites approve of us as a couple," Bright Arrow said tightly.

"You see why I protect my own identity so well?" Alan said thickly. "It is not that I am not proud of my Makah heritage. It is just that I enjoy my job as a lawman."

"All our people understand," Bright Arrow said, nodding. "So do not feel you need to explain or apologize about it. I enjoy being *tyee*. You enjoy being a lawman. That we both are able to do as we desire is good."

"Kathia, honey, I'm so sorry that Dusty Harper had to ruin everything for you today," Melvin said, holding himself steady with his cane as he stepped up to her. "Come on, daughter. Let's get you out of here."

"I would like for Bright Arrow to visit the house where I live, to see the side of me that he has not yet known," Kathia said, smiling up at Bright Arrow. "But remember when you see my fancy things that I leave them without sadness, for when I leave them behind, I enter into another world, *your* world. That is my desire, my love. Only that."

"Then let's get out of here," Fred said. He stepped around Dusty and took Kathia by the elbow. He ushered her toward the door as Bright Arrow lingered to give his cousin a hug.

Then all but the deputy and the sheriff, who had just arrived after having heard the gunfire, left the gruesome scene behind.

When they were outside, Kathia stopped and took one long, last look at the opera house. In it she had found such happiness, such completeness.

But when she went to her new life, as wife to Bright Arrow, she would find her true happiness, for only he could complete her.

"Come on, Kathia, it's time to say good-bye to that life," Bright Arrow said, seeing her taking her last look at the place she had performed so often.

"Yes, and hello to all my tomorrows," she said,

smiling brightly as she gazed up at Bright Arrow. "I am ready, Bright Arrow. I am, oh, so very ready."

His smile was all that she needed to know she had made the right decision.

Chapter Thirty-four

Thou art my life—if though but turn away,
My life's a thousand deaths.
Thou art my way.
Without thee, Love, I travel not but stray.
—John Wilmot, Earl of Rochester

Kathia was standing at the window of her bedroom in her father's house. She drew back the sheer curtain and sighed as she gazed heavenward.

"What a beautiful evening," she murmured as she continued to gaze at the sky.

Day was waning. The clouds were fringed with flaming pinks that softened to paler tones as the light illuminated their billowy surfaces.

Streaks of magenta, orange, and yellow swept out

from the western horizon, reflecting off the sea and coloring the distant hills in purples and blues.

Mesmerized, Kathia kept watching as fingers of darkness edged over the land. Gradually, the colors paled, then faded into the shadows of oncoming night.

This was to be a special night, the first that she would spend with Bright Arrow. She had already spent her last night in her father's house. The evening before, her family had gathered around a fire in the parlor, laughing and talking and sharing popcorn.

Although she was the happiest she had been in her entire life, last night had been bittersweet. She had seen sadness in both her father and brother's eyes, even when they laughed and joked with her.

But their sadness was born of her happiness. She must leave their world to join Bright Arrow's. And even though they were sad to see her go, they were also happy . . . happy for her.

She laughed to herself as she recalled the occasional piece of fluffy white popcorn that Fred would playfully toss at her. One had even landed in her hair.

Yes, it had been a wonderful, playful evening, one that she would remember for the rest of her life. She hoped it would help ease the sadness her father would feel tonight when he gave her a final kiss before she left to live with Bright Arrow forever.

She had only been told today that there would

not be any marriage ceremony that her family could witness.

After a certain ritual had been performed that he had not yet explained to her, they would privately speak their vows to one another. From thereon she would be his. He would be hers.

She hoped that before a full year had passed, she would give birth to her and Bright Arrow's first child.

"Perhaps a boy," she whispered.

Yes, a boy born in the image of his father. He would be wondrous to behold!

Then a daughter. She would be delighted if her daughter had a big brother just as she had. It was wonderful for a girl to have a big brother who would always be there to defend her until she found the right man to take over that responsibility.

"Big brother, if you only knew how I always placed you on a pedestal," Kathia whispered as she went back to packing her clothes.

Yes, she *had* placed her brother on a pedestal. She had always looked up to him, admiring his knowledge in so many areas of life, and the kindness with which he treated all those whose lives he touched.

And his love of photography.

No one could ever be as dedicated to his craft as Fred.

Well, no, she knew that was not altogether true. Her father was devoted totally to his lighthouse.

Bright Arrow was devoted, heart and soul, to his people, and now, also to her.

Recalling her mind to the task at hand, Kathia hurriedly finished packing. She had brought only one suitcase of clothes from Port Angeles.

She would go to her house soon and get the rest and put her beautiful home up for sale. All the money she received would be devoted to the welfare of the Makah. Everything she had would be theirs, for she felt a keen loyalty to them now. Being their chief's wife, she wanted to prove that she was worthy of such a title.

After closing the suitcase, Kathia turned and looked slowly around the room. Except for those years when she had lived alone in Port Angeles, this room had been hers since she was ten, when her father had moved here from his lighthouse post just outside of Seattle.

He had loved it there, but had grown to love this area even more. He loved its remoteness and its natural beauty.

Kathia's thoughts were brought back to the present when she heard the arrival of a horse outside. Her heart pounded with excitement, for she knew who had come.

Her husband to be. He had come to escort her to his village.

She would soon know what the secret ritual was that was required of her before she became Bright

Arrow's wife. He had not yet told her. He said that he wanted to wait until it was time for the ritual to be performed.

When Kathia had questioned him once about it, she had seen a mischievous glint in his eye. She knew then that whatever it was the ritual was innocent enough, and not worth worrying about.

"I hope," she whispered as she left her room, struggling with the weight of her suitcase.

"Kathia, you're going to break your back carrying that heavy thing," her father said as he found her lugging it down the stairs.

"Yes, let me help you," Fred said as he came from the parlor and quickly took the suitcase from her.

Fred chuckled as he felt how heavy it was. "Do you truly believe you can carry this on your horse?" he asked.

"Well, yes, I had planned to," Kathia said.

"I'll bring it in the carriage the next time I come with my photography equipment to take more photos," Fred said. "Is there anything in here that you'll need tonight? If so, you'd best take it out now."

"I think I can survive the night without what I have packed," Kathia said, feeling the seriousness of the moment as the time to say good-bye approached. The next time she saw her father and brother, she would be a wife.

She had seen the puzzlement in their eyes when she had told them they could not attend her wedding. But when she explained the privacy that was required, that it would only be Bright Arrow and herself at the ceremony, speaking vows to one another, they had seemed to accept it.

Melvin came to her and gave her a tender hug. Then Fred set the suitcase aside and hugged her, too.

"You both act as though you aren't going to ever see me again," she said, laughing softly. "I won't be far, you know. You can come and visit me anytime you please. And I'll return home often, Papa."

She turned to Fred. "But I doubt that I can make it to Seattle very often," she murmured. "I *will* go with Bright Arrow when he travels there for supplies, though."

"Before Fred or I come to call, we'll give you several days with your husband," Melvin said thickly. He steadied himself with his cane as he walked Kathia to the door, while Fred stepped ahead of them to open it. "But you'd best know that when I'm well enough, I will come for some of your home cooking and hospitality as a wife."

"Please don't even mention cooking," Kathia groaned. "What if I can't learn how? That will be a major disappointment to my husband."

"Nothing you do, or cannot do, could ever disappoint Bright Arrow," Melvin said, chuckling. "I know. I've been there before, too."

"What?" Kathia asked, her eyes wide.

"Your mother knew nothing about cooking when

we got married," Melvin said, his eyes twinkling. "I taught her. Now what do you think of that?"

"You . . . ?" Fred and Kathia said at almost the same moment.

But their lighthearted banter was over when Bright Arrow stepped up to the opened door, his eyes smiling at Kathia as she walked toward him.

"I'm ready," she murmured, her pulse racing at the thought of what this evening meant to both of them.

It was the true beginning of the rest of their lives as man and wife. She still couldn't believe it was happening when only a short few weeks ago she had not even known he existed.

But there they were. They were everything to each other, and after tonight they would be bonded together forever.

"I will take good care of her," Bright Arrow said as he looked past Kathia and gave Melvin a nod, then Fred. "You do not have to worry about a thing. And you are welcome at our lodge any time you get lonesome for Kathia. Our home is your home. Our food is your food. Everything that is ours is yours, for you were her family first."

"That is mighty generous of you," Melvin said, clasping a hand on his shoulder as Bright Arrow placed an arm around Kathia's waist and drew her close to him. "And believe me when I say we're both going to take you up on it."

"Kathia and I look forward to your first visit,"

Bright Arrow said. He smiled down at Kathia, then at Melvin and Fred. "We really must go now."

He glanced down at Kathia again. Their eyes met when she returned his smile. "We have a lot planned for this evening," he said thickly.

"Be happy," Fred said, suddenly embracing Kathia, then giving Bright Arrow a hug.

"Yes, be happy," Melvin said, doing the same.

Melvin and Fred walked out onto the porch and watched Bright Arrow ride away with Kathia on his lap, although Melvin had told Kathia that the strawberry roan could go into the marriage with her and Bright Arrow. Bright Arrow had quickly reassured him that he owned many horses, one of which had been chosen for Kathia.

But tonight, in everything, they were as one, even while riding from one life to enter another.

As Kathia rode away with Bright Arrow, she laid her cheek on his chest. She could feel the thumping of his heart. It matched the rhythm of her own. Even in that, tonight, they were one.

"I'm anxious to see what this secret ritual is," Kathia murmured.

"Soon you will not have to wonder any longer," Bright Arrow said, riding alongside the sea, where the moon was reflected in the sparkling waters.

"You still won't tell me?" Kathia murmured. "I still have to wait? We are alone. No one else will hear if you tell me."

"The stars will hear, the moon will hear, as will the ocean," Bright Arrow said, now in a teasing fashion.

"They won't tell anyone," Kathia teased back.

"Well, all right, if you insist," Bright Arrow said, catching Kathia off guard, for she truly did not expect him to tell her until they reached the village.

She leaned away and gazed up at him. His sculpted features gleamed beneath the bright shine of the moon. "I didn't really expect you to," she murmured. "Are you truly going to tell me? I don't have to wait?"

"I will truly tell you," Bright Arrow said, smiling. "My woman, my uncle awaits our arrival. He awaits with pulverized charcoal for us."

"Pulverized charcoal?" Kathia said, her eyebrows lifting. "Why? What is he going to use pulverized charcoal on?"

"You," Bright Arrow said, his eyes twinkling.

"Me?" Kathia said, her eyes widening even more. "What on earth for?"

"You must become tattooed to be my bride," Bright Arrow said, her horrified gasp causing him to stop his roan.

"I . . . must . . . be tattooed?" Kathia asked, her eyes wavering. "I have not seen tattoos on any of the women. Is it a new ritual? Will I be . . . the . . . first? Or is it only required of a chief's wife?"

"All women are tattooed, and they make their

own choice where the tattoo is to be placed," Bright Arrow said, putting a gentle hand on her cheek. "You have not seen the tattoos because their clothes cover them."

"Where are they tattooed?" Kathia asked softly.

"Some are on arms, others are on legs, and some are very privately hidden," Bright Arrow said, his eyes searching hers, for he had not yet seen any sign that she approved of such a ritual.

If she did not, it would prove that she would not be willing to accept change in her life. That would mean she might not even marry him if she stopped and thought about what else would be required of her as his wife.

"Well?" Bright Arrow said guardedly. "Should we proceed to my uncle's lodge for the tattooing? Or should we not?"

"It is something I must do to become your wife?" Kathia asked, her eyes searching his. "Truly? I have no other choice?"

Bright Arrow had not been altogether truthful with her about this. Tattooing was not required of all women who would become wives. But it was a fact that most Makah women did have a tattoo.

Bright Arrow had wanted to think of something that would test Kathia, for he knew how different her life was going to be now. Perhaps this new existence would be too hard for her to adjust to.

He had thought that if she could pass this one

test, it would prove to him that she could accept everything else that would be required of her as a Makah wife.

He had the reputation of being an honest man, who never lied or cheated, so his behavior tonight made him uneasy. But he did feel that he had to test her. He would not want Kathia to change her mind later.

If she did agree to the tattoo, something which obviously made her uneasy, then he would give her the choice of whether or not she wanted to be tattooed.

He hoped that even then she would agree to the tattoo, for if she did, he would know that she was committed to fitting into his world, a world that was vastly different from the one she had always known.

"You have not answered me," Bright Arrow said, beginning to worry that she would not accept the tattoo.

"Kathia, still you are quiet," Bright Arrow said after another moment.

His heart skipped a beat when she suddenly slid from his lap to the ground and ran toward the sea, then dropped down on her knees beside it where the waves lapped against the shore.

He stayed in the saddle, his eyes wavering as he saw her bow her head. A part of him died at that moment, for he feared that everything had changed between them.

When she lifted her head and turned her eyes toward him, and he saw the shine of tears in them, he felt his heart slowly tearing apart.

"Yes," she blurted out, a slow smile curving her lips upward. "*Ah-ha*, I will be tattooed."

A rush of relief swept through Bright Arrow, so keen it momentarily dizzied him. He smiled broadly, leapt from his horse, then ran to her and lifted her up into his arms. As her laughter mingled with his, he swung her around and around, then laid her down on the soft sand, kneeling over her.

"It is not necessary," he said huskily, his one hand sliding up inside her dress. His fingers stopped when she slapped his hand away.

She sat up and folded her arms across her heaving chest. In her eyes he saw a gleam he could not interpret.

"It is not necessary?" she said, her eyes narrowing angrily. "I went through all that worry and dread about getting a tattoo, and you tell me it's not necessary? Why did you do this, Bright Arrow? I don't think this is a time for games. This is our wedding night!"

"It is not my way of doing things, to purposely lie, but, my woman, you do have so many changes ahead of you. I was afraid you might have trouble with them," he said. He took her arms down from her chest, then held her hands as he searched her eyes. "My woman, your life has been so easy, so trouble-free. The life of a Makah wife is so different from anything you have ever known. I thought if you could pass such a test as being tattooed, then you would be able to pass all tests beyond that. Can you understand why I felt the need to do this? Can you forgive me?"

"Thank goodness I passed the test," Kathia said, suddenly giggling. "Lord, did you have me going! And I even envisioned myself with a tattoo. Thank you for not truly requiring it of me."

"Then you forgive my lie?" Bright Arrow asked, drawing her up against him as her arms slowly twined around his neck.

"I would forgive you anything," Kathia said, her voice soft and loving. "I love you so much, Bright Arrow. And . . . and . . . I was serious. I would accept a tattoo on my body."

She drew away from him and slowly lifted the skirt of her dress. She took one of his hands and placed it on her inner right thigh. "I want it right there," she said, taking him by surprise.

"You want *what* right there?" he asked, his eyes widening in wonder.

"I want a small tattooed rose blossom on my inner thigh," she said, her eyes shining. "There. Does that prove to you that I can withstand anything?"

"You truly want it?" Bright Arrow said, his voice filled with the wonder he was feeling.

"*Ah-ha*," Kathia said, giving a final nod. "Is your uncle truly waiting for us? Will he have his pulverized charcoal ready?"

"No, but he can get it ready if you are serious," Bright Arrow said, then drew quickly away from her when she began laughing so hard that tears rolled from her eyes.

"Touché," she said, wiping the tears from her cheeks. "Now we are even."

"What do you mean . . . *even?*" Bright Arrow said, confused by her attitude.

"I truly don't want the tattoo, so do you see?" Kathia said, framing his face between her hands. "I lied to you about wanting the tattoo as you lied to me about me needing to have one in order to be your wife."

"And so, *ah-ha*, we are, as you say, even," Bright Arrow said, chuckling.

He swept her down onto her back. His hands brought the skirt of her dress to rest around her waist. He bent low over her and gently opened her legs with his hands, then rose over her and slowly undressed as she watched.

Soon he was inside her, his strokes rhythmic and gentle. Their lips came together in a passionately hot kiss, as their bodies rocked and swayed together in their dance of love.

Clinging around his neck, her heart pounding, Kathia gave herself over to the wild ecstasy.

Bright Arrow wrapped his arms around her and brought her closer to his heat as he sculpted himself to her moist body. He pressed himself endlessly deeper as the rapture grew almost to the bursting point.

"I love you so," he whispered against her lips. "Tonight, my woman. We will be as one tonight, and then forever and ever."

"*Ah-ha*, forever and ever," Kathia whispered back against his lips.

Their bodies were lost in each other, flesh against flesh. The sound of the sea whispered around them, but so overwhelmed were they by their passion for one another, they did not hear it.

They were both consumed by the desire that washed over them. Bright Arrow kissed her again, his mouth urgent and eager this time, his thrusts just as urgent.

She clung to him. She wrapped her legs around his waist. She strained her hips up, crying out at her fulfillment when they both reached that special place only known by those who truly, fully loved.

Breathing hard as they came down from that cloud of rapture, Bright Arrow rolled away from her and lay on his back on the sand.

Kathia moved onto her side next to him. She traced his sculpted features with a finger.

"Never was there a man as handsome as you," she murmured. "Nor could any man fulfill a woman as you fulfill me."

"My woman, my woman . . ." Bright Arrow said, reaching over and drawing her atop him.

Again they made love, this time slowly and sweetly, with the moon's glow soft on them and the ocean's waves lapping at their feet as the tide began to rise.

Soon they were laughing and rushing from a wave that had come upon them, its effervescence tickling their toes.

"The tide will be high tonight," Bright Arrow said, grabbing his clothes just in time, before the waves took them out to sea with them.

"A perfect time for tattooing, wouldn't you say?" Kathia asked, shoving the skirt of her dress back down in place as Bright Arrow hurried into his clothes.

"Tattooing?" Bright Arrow said, giving her a quizzical stare.

"*Ah-ha*, tattooing," Kathia said, giggling. "You know, the more I think about it, the more I want a tiny rose tattoo on my inner thigh. Am I shameful to want it?"

"Not shameful at all," Bright Arrow said. He framed her face between his hands. He brushed a soft kiss across her lips, then smiled into her eyes. "Almost every woman of my village has a tattoo one place or another. But as I said before, they are hidden."

"But I thought that was a part of your lie," Kathia said, searching his eyes.

"No, not that," Bright Arrow said. He took her hand and led her to his horse. "Most do have tattoos, but they have them by choice, not necessity. If you want a tattoo, we will go to my uncle tonight and see that you have one."

Kathia felt a sweep of uneasiness pass through her, for she did not truly want a tattoo. Still, if Bright Arrow had devised this test, it must be important to him that she prove her ability to accept new customs.

"Then I want one, too," Kathia said. When she saw how happy her declaration made him, she felt as though her heart was melting. She knew that she would be able to do anything required of her if it was something that would make this wonderful man happy.

"A tattoo it will be," Bright Arrow said. He swept her into his arms again before getting on the horse. "My love for you is as vast as the waters of the ocean."

Chapter Thirty-five

Without thy light, what light remains in me?
Thou art my life; my way, my lights in thee;
I love, I move, and by thy beams, I see.
—John Wilmot, Earl of Rochester

Kathia could hardly believe that she and Bright Arrow had already been married for six years. They had gone fast. They had been good years. The Makah village was thriving. Kathia's father was still alive, but not all that strong. Fred had moved in with him so that he could assist him in the lighthouse. Otherwise, Melvin would have had to either hire someone else to help him or retire.

Although Fred and his wife lived with his father, he still pursued his photography career. He was even more enthusiastic about it because of the invention of gelatin-coated dry plates, which reduced exposure times, making documentary photography more feasible. People no longer had to stand still for minutes at a time to have their image preserved for posterity.

But carrying the fragile glass plates and heavy cameras from one spot to another was still a cumbersome business. It took special dedication on the part of the photographer.

No one could be more dedicated than Fred. He had finally gotten enough photographs of the Makah to complete his book and it had been a great success.

For his part, Kathia knew that her father was completely happy teaching his grandsons, five-year-old twins, how to work his beams.

The boys were Fred and Magdalena's children. Magdalena had retired from performing. She was now a full-time wife and mother.

Fred and Magdalena had been thrice blessed. They also had sweet, adorable Sasha, a lovely daughter with flowing red hair.

Kathia was utterly content to be a wife and mother. At this moment she was in her six-room longhouse, showing her three-year-old daughter Snow Feather how to pirouette in the new ballet slippers she had received for Christmas. Berry cakes, from Bright Arrow's mother's recipe, were cooling on the kitchen table.

Kathia could not help smiling when she recalled the time when Bright Arrow's mother had refused to give her the recipe, saying that she guarded it well and shared it with no one. The fact that Whispering Wind had shared the recipe with Kathia demonstrated the closeness they now felt for one another.

Kathia had promised not to give the secret recipe to anyone else, except for one person. Whispering Wind had told Kathia that Snow Feather should learn the recipe when she was old enough to cook.

Bright Arrow gazed over at his wife and daughter from where he sat on the floor, carving the last of four beautiful chairs for his wife's new kitchen table. He had made the table for her during the long, idle winter months that were almost behind them.

This last chair would be finished just in time to begin his preparations for the first whale hunt of this season.

As Bright Arrow continued carving, he became lost in thought. It had been a wonderful six years for himself and his wife, and his people.

Although it had taken a while for Kathia to become with child, their sweet Snow Feather had been worth the wait.

And now Kathia was with child again. She was so largely pregnant and clumsy, she could barely make it around inside the house without bumping into something.

She called herself "Mrs. Waddle." He found that

amusing, but made certain that he, himself, never called her that.

No matter how large she got—her ankles were swollen twice their normal size today—she would never be any less beautiful to Bright Arrow. There was a radiance about her all the time, especially during her pregnancies.

"Mother, have I practiced enough?" Snow Feather asked as she stopped and gazed questioningly at her mother. "May I go and skate with my friends? The ice won't be strong enough much longer. And Sun Feather is always anxious to use the skates that I gave her for Christmas."

"Bright Arrow, what do you think?" Kathia asked, easing down onto the soft cushion of her favorite chair.

She recalled the day she had thought the ice was strong enough, and what had happened. Even now it gave her a feeling of horror to recall being trapped beneath that solid slab of ice.

"I checked the ice on the pond by the village this morning," Bright Arrow said, setting his carving aside. "It is still strong and thick. *Ah-ha*, you can go and skate with your friend."

"Oh, thank you," Snow Feather said, plopping down on the floor and untying her ballet slippers. "Sasha is going to skate with us, too. And Aunt Magdalena might even be there. She loves to skate, too."

Snow Feather's smile faded as she gazed at her

mother. "I wish you could skate with us, too," she murmured.

"Well now, wouldn't I make a lovely picture out there on the ice with my belly this big?" Kathia said, laughing softly. "No. This Mrs. Waddle doesn't think so. I won't be able to skate with you until next winter."

"Oh, Mama, that name you gave yourself is horrible," Snow Feather fussed. "Please, please stop calling yourself that."

Kathia giggled. "Well, okay, I guess it isn't very flattering, is it?" she said. She nodded toward the door that led to the bedrooms. "You go and change into something warm, and as you skate, your father and I will watch you from the window."

Kathia groaned and put a hand to the small of her back as she pushed herself up from the chair.

"When I get on the ice, I shall do an expert figure eight for you, Mama," Snow Feather said, rushing from the room.

"She is such a delight," Kathia said, bending to pick up the ballet slippers. "I love having a daughter, but . . ."

"But you want the next child to be a son," Bright Arrow said, going to help her.

"It did not happen the way I planned. I had wanted first a son and then a daughter, so the daughter could have a big brother," Kathia said. "But I am sure our daughter will look out for her little brother as much as a big brother would look out for a little sister."

"Either a girl or a boy will be happily welcomed," Bright Arrow said, waving at Snow Feather as she rushed past in her coat, fur hat, and gloves, her skates in hand.

Kathia placed the ballet slippers on a chair, then went with Bright Arrow to a window and waited for their daughter to perform on the ice. There was a small pond close to the spot where Bright Arrow had made his bride a larger, more spacious longhouse.

"Life is so wonderful," Kathia murmured, then gazed quickly up into the sky as a dark shadow suddenly fell over the longhouse. When she saw only an eagle flying low, she was reminded of another bird, another time.

"Bright Arrow, I am still mystified over the thunderbird I thought I saw six years ago," she murmured. She turned to him. "Can you tell me again about the thunderbird?"

She would never forget her father telling her that some people believed Bright Arrow had the power to turn into the Thunderbird to work for the good of his people.

She would never forget that one night, when she had thought the thunderbird had come to her when she was so ill, or the night when she had seen it while dancing in the beams with Magdalena.

She had only briefly questioned him once about

the thunderbird. His guarded response had made her vow never to ask him again. But now curiosity had gotten the better of her.

"Sometimes life is not as good as it has been recently for our people. Sometimes famine strikes in the Makah world," Bright Arrow said. "There is one story that recalls a hard winter when it was impossible to fish, there was no game to be found, and the food storage baskets became empty. One man went up on the mountain to pray. Hearing a noise, he looked up. There was the Thunderbird, so huge it darkened the sky. He made the thunder sound with the beat of its wings. Its eyes were flashing lightning. Then it flew straight down. Just as it was about to hit the water, it swooped back up carrying a whale in its talons. It flew toward the village. It flew close to the beach, and there it dropped the whale. Then it flew away. The man who saw all of this said to the people, 'We're saved, we're saved!' And so they were. And the Thunderbird became a thing of legend, wondrous to behold."

"I truly believe that I have seen the Thunderbird myself," Kathia said, watching his reaction.

"I, too," Bright Arrow said, but that was all he would say about it.

He turned to the window. His eyes lit up as he pointed. "Look at our daughter," he said. "She promised a figure eight. She is doing a figure eight."

Kathia was distracted from asking anything else about the Thunderbird.

She smiled and waved as Snow Feather stopped and turned to them, pride in her eyes.

"Do you know, I have heard about competition in skating now, and that awards are won by those who are the best at it," Kathia murmured, recalling the time when she had been a proud ballet performer.

She saw the same skills in her daughter, the same desires. Perhaps Snow Feather would not only excell in ballet, but also in skating.

"Bright Arrow!" Kathia said, suddenly grabbing her abdomen. She looked quickly up at him. "I think it's time!"

Everything happened quickly after that. In less than an hour, Kathia was holding her tiny bundle of joy in her arms.

As Bright Arrow sat on the bed beside her, he reached down and drew aside a corner of the soft blanket.

"A son," he said, beaming. "We now have a son!"

There was a squeal of excitement as Snow Feather rushed into the room. Whispering Wind had just gone out and told her the wondrous news.

"I have a baby brother!" she squealed again, her cheeks rosy from the cold outside.

"Yes, a baby brother," Kathia murmured. "When you are warmer, you can hold him."

"I shall hurry along the warmth," Snow Feather

said, going toward the door. "I shall stand before the fire!"

"You have chosen a name?" Whispering Wind asked, looking pleadingly into her son's eyes.

"Kathia has agreed to my wish to name our son after my father," Bright Arrow said, seeing the radiant smile his words brought to his mother's face. "Moon Thunder. And like my father, he will one day be a powerful Makah chief."

"Do you wish to hold him?" Kathia said, offering the child to Whispering Wind.

As Whispering Wind held him and slowly rocked him in her arms, Bright Arrow bent low over Kathia and gave her a sweet kiss. "You will no longer waddle," he whispered to her, bringing a giggle to her lips.

She felt a deep, deep contentment, and all because of that one chance meeting on the day she had chosen to skate rather than practice her dancing.

Yes, destiny had taken her there that day, as it had brought her to this wonderful point in her life.

She was filled with hope for a wonderful, secure future, not only for herself, but for all the Makah. And it was all because of Bright Arrow.

Kathia thought back to what they had been talking about earlier . . . the Thunderbird. Could it be true that Bright Arrow was . . . ?

No. Surely not!

It was intriguing, though, to think that just perhaps he did have such powers!

Dear Reader:

I hope you enjoyed *Savage Hope*. The next book in the Savage Series, which I am writing exclusively for Leisure Books, will be *Savage Courage*, about the great and noble Chiricahua Apache. This book is filled with much excitement, romance, and adventure. *Savage Courage* will be in stores in February 2005.

Many of you say that you are collecting my Indian romances. For an autographed bookmark, my entire backlist of books, information about how to acquire the books that you cannot find, and for my latest newsletter and news about my fan club, please send a self-addressed, stamped, legal-sized envelope to:

Cassie Edwards
6709 North Country Club Road
Mattoon, IL 61938

You can also visit my website: www.cassieedwards.com.

Thank you for your support of my Indian series. I love researching and writing about our country's beloved Native Americans, the very first, true people of our great, proud land.

Always,
Cassie Edwards